THE DESERTER

Also by Jane Langton

THE DESERTER

MURDER AT GETTYSBURG

JANE LANGTON

THOMAS DUNNE BOOKS
ST. MARTIN'S MINOTAUR   NEW YORK

THOMAS DUNNE BOOKS.
An imprint of St. Martin's Press.

www.minotaurbooks.com

Photographs courtesy of: Harvard University Archives, Historic Northampton, U.S. Army Military History Institute, Adams County Historical Society, Wisconsin State Historical Society, the Patent Office Historical Collections of Judy, Diane and Jim Davis, the Burns Archive, the National Archives and Records Administration, Radcliffe's Schlesinger Library, the Boston Athenaeum, the Rockaway Borough Library in Rockaway, New Jersey, and the Meserve Collection in the National Portrait Gallery.

Design by Phil Mazzone

Library of Congress Cataloging-in-Publication Data

Langton, Jane.
　　The deserter : murder at Gettysburg / Jane Langton.—1st ed.
　　　　p. cm.
　　ISBN 0-312-30186-3
　　1. Kelly, Homer (Fictitious character)—Fiction. 2. Gettysburg, Battle of, Gettysburg, Pa., 1863—Fiction. 3. Military deserters—Fiction. 4. Gettysburg (Pa.)—Fiction. 5. College teachers—Fiction. 6. Concord (Mass.)—Fiction. I. Title.

PS3562.A515D476 2003
813'.54—dc21

　　　　　　　　　　　　　　　　　　　　　　　　　　　　2002191961

First Edition: June 2003

10　9　8　7　6　5　4　3　2　1

For Anna Caskey

G. K. Chesterton's fictional detective,
Father Brown, posed two riddles.

Where would a wise man hide a leaf?
In the forest.

Where would a wise man hide a body?
On a battlefield.

THE DESERTER

IDA

Through the entire course of her expectation, Cornelia had been sickly. As her time grew short, she sent a whining letter from Philadelphia to her cousin in Concord, way up north in Massachusetts. Cousin Ida was also in a family way.

> *Dear Ida,*
>
> *Why dont you come? You still have two or three months to go and you are strong as a cow and if I should die Ida wont you be ashamed.*
>
> *Yr affectnt Cousin Cornelia*

Ida was willing. She told her mother, "I'll just stay a little while and then I'll come straight home."

"Well, I don't know what your husband will think," said her

mother, helping her up the high step into the car at the depot. "If anything happens, Seth will blame me."

Ida smiled as the cars picked up speed and rattled past the pond on the way to Boston. She had felt well from the beginning, so her mother had no call to be worried. And perhaps somehow she might see Seth, because his regiment was somewhere down there in Pennsylvania.

In Philadelphia Cornelia's frantic husband met Ida at the station, "You're only just in time," he said, and indeed she was. At the door of the house they were greeted by Cornelia's shrieks and the strong loud voice of the midwife.

At once Ida tore off her bonnet and pulled on an apron. She knew what to do, having helped to care for her mother when little Alice was born.

But no sooner did Cornelia stop screaming and her infant daughter utter her first cry than a strange noise began somewhere outside.

It was a sultry afternoon in early July. Coming from Massachusetts, Ida had never heard the sound before. It was soft and far away but it went on and on, a faint booming like the rumble of thunder in another county.

"What is that noise?" said Ida.

Holding her baby close to her breast, Cornelia turned her face away. The midwife looked disapprovingly at Ida and said, "My dear girl, you should be at home. What are you, six or maybe seven months gone?"

Cornelia's husband sank into a chair. "They'll telegraph the list," he said. "The Boston paper will have a list."

A list of the dead and missing, that was what he meant. Ida remembered the terrifying list after the Battle of Antietam. Colonel Dwight of the Second Massachusetts Volunteer Infantry had been among the dead, but, thank God, not First Lieutenant Seth Morgan. And after Chancellorsville there had been another list, but once again Seth's name was not there.

The distant noise was now incessant. It trembled the crimson water in the basin and shook the limp curtains at the window. Cornelia's baby whimpered and waved its little fists.

"I'll stay," said Ida.

PART I

THE TABLETS

The Memorial Hall of Harvard consists of three main divisions: one of them a theatre, for academic ceremonies; another a vast refectory covered with a timbered roof, hung about with portraits and lighted by stained windows . . . and the third, the most interesting, a chamber high, dim, and severe, consecrated to the sons of the university who fell in the long Civil War.

—Henry James, *The Bostonians*

THE SHAME

Your great-great-grandfather did something shameful?" Homer couldn't believe it. "But all you Morgans are so stalwart with Yankee integrity. Your ancestor couldn't have done anything very bad." Homer stared up at the names on the marble tablet. "He was in the class of 1860? Then he must have known all these men."

"Well, I suppose so," said Mary. "But then in the Civil War there was some sort of scandal. Nobody wanted to talk about it. I can remember my father shaking his head and keeping his mouth shut about Seth Morgan."

"Gettysburg," murmured Homer, still gazing at the tablet. "They all died in the Battle of Gettysburg."

The pale inscribed stone was enshrined within a wooden frame. The pointed gothic arch was only one of many, each with its solemn tablet, lining the central corridor of the monumental building that towered above the city of Cambridge next to the firehouse. Above the tablets rose the wooden vaults, gleaming with new varnish, and the upper reaches of the walls glittered with heroic Latin remarks in gold.

But nobody any longer understood the quotations and hardly anyone paused to read the names of the 135 men who had walked so long ago in Harvard Yard and read the *Iliad* with Cornelius Felton and modern literature with James Russell Lowell and mathematics with Benjamin Peirce before going out to die for the Union cause in the bloody battles of the Civil War.

All those young men had lived and died so long ago. Widows no longer wept for their husbands, mothers no longer sorrowed for their sons. The Civil War was several wars back in time.

But Memorial Hall was still a familiar landmark in Cambridge, celebrated for its medieval immensity and for the polygonal tower that loomed above the university. It was especially famous for Sanders Theatre, the wooden chamber that rounded out one end of the building like the apse of a cathedral.

Otherwise, Mem Hall was useful for the enormous dining hall that projected like the nave of a church from the transept of the memorial corridor. Here the first-year students ate their meals in the colored light of stained-glass windows, never glancing at the marble busts of long-forgotten professors that lined the walls, never looking up at the painted portraits of Union soldiers. But the soldiers looked blandly down at them year after year, and the busts gazed out at them with their white stone eyes.

Until today, Homer and Mary Kelly had been as oblivious as everyone else to the tablets, the portraits and the marble busts. They had taught classes in the building for years, they had lectured in Sanders Theatre. Homer had even climbed the tower, where he had looked down on the wooden vaults from above, teetered along swaying catwalks, climbed shaky ladders and hurled himself across perilous chasms to witness something amazing. Gaping upward, he had seen a president of the university fall from the topmost rung of the topmost ladder and break his neck in one of the upside-down vaults.

Well, all of that had happened long ago. But Memorial Hall was still one of the spindles around which their lives were wound. Therefore it was odd that in all these years they had paid so little attention to the marble tablets in the memorial corridor.

But today a yellow ray from the colored window over the south door had fallen on one of the tablets like a pointing hand, and they had stopped, transfixed.

"Maybe you could find out what your great-great-grandfather did that was so shameful," said Homer, glancing sideways at his wife.

"I'm not sure I want to know."

"I'll bet there are records somewhere. If you looked up these men from his class you might learn something about—what was his name?"

"Seth. Seth Morgan."

The yellow beam from the stained-glass window drifted away, and now the tablet was flushed with red.

"Good," said Mary. She whipped out a notebook and wrote the names down. "I'll ask about Seth, and then I'll get to work on Mudge, Fox, Robeson and—who's the other one?"

"Pike, Otis Mathias Pike."

PART II

THE SECOND MASSACHUSETTS

THE SECOND MASSACHUSETTS VOLUNTEER INFANTRY

The sons of the first gentlemen of New England generously vied with each other in seeking commissions therein. . . . From the first it was often spoken of as the model regiment in the army for its admirable drill; and so tenaciously has it preserved its early distinction, that in its last battle, when half its number of privates and eleven of its officers had fallen, it manoeuvred still under the severest fire with "every man in his place;"—a proud deed!

—*BOSTON HERALD, JULY 1863*

PRIVATE OTIS PIKE

*OTIS MATHIAS PIKE
Class of 1860

Pvt. 2d Massachusetts Vols. (Infantry) 12 July,
1862. Killed at Gettysburg, Penn., 3 July,
1863.

—Harvard Memorial Biographies

Otis was sensible enough to recognize the error of his ways on
several occasions in the past.

For one thing, he should never have loaned five dollars to a penniless classmate.

In the second place, he should never have accepted a bowie
knife as collateral for the loan. What use did Otis have for a bowie
knife? Nevertheless he had stuck it in his belt because it gave him a
certain air.

In the third place, he should certainly have avoided the low tav-
ern on the Boston waterfront where his pocket had been picked,
last year in the summer of '62.

In the fourth place, he should never have attacked the pick-
pocket with the bowie knife.

The fact was that if Otis Pike, the witty darling of his class, had
not been kind enough in the first place to help out a friend, he

would not have had to choose between a prison term and recruit-ment into the Second Massachusetts Volunteer Infantry.

What kind of choice was that? The prison was an infamous black hole.

"You are fortunate, young man," the judge had said, "that your classmates in a distinguished regiment have spoken up for you."

Oh, that was all very well and good, but his dear old college classmates had entered the service as officers, whereas poor old Otis was only a private.

"But, Your Honor," he had pleaded, "when I confronted that man, he attacked me. I could have been killed."

"Whereas," the judge had said sourly, "it was he who had the misfortune to be killed."

"But it was self-defense, Your Honor, that's all. Pure self-defense."

Self-defense! For over a year now, *self-defense* had been Otis Pike's watchword in all the battles in which the regiment had been called upon to fight.

In self-defense he had run from the carnage in Miller's cornfield at Antietam. In self-defense he had fled the slaughter of Chancel-lorsville. Where now were some of his old comrades in the Second Massachusetts? Where were Wilder Dwight and Tom Spurr and George Batchelder? And Stephen Emerson and William Temple?

Dead at Antietam, dead at Chancellorsville.

"Watch your step, Otis," his captain had warned him. "One more desertion and you're a dead man." The captain of Company E was Tom Robeson, fellow reveler and funny fellow.

"I warn you, Otis," his colonel had said, "if you run again, we'll have no choice." The colonel of the entire Second Massachusetts Volunteer Infantry was good old Charley Mudge, another comrade from the Hasty Pudding Club, comic gymnast and consummate artist of the banjo.

Otis had snapped a salute. "Yes, sir, Colonel, sir. But, hark! do I hear a mockingbird?" It was a passage from the Minstrels of the class of 1860, every line and note of which had been composed by Otis Pike.

But Charley Mudge had looked at him solemnly and said, "I mean it, Otis. It's no joke."

LIEUTENANT COLONEL MUDGE

★CHARLES REDINGTON MUDGE
Class of 1860

First Lt., 2d Mass. Vols., 28 May, 1861; Capt., 8 July, 1861; Major, 9 Nov., 1862; Lieut. Colonel, 6 June, 1863; killed at Gettysburg, Penn., 3 July, 1863.

. . . *Straightway he gave the brief order, "Rise up,—over the breastworks,—forward, double-quick!" And up rose the men at the word of their dauntless commander. . . . He led them boldly and rapidly over the marsh straight into . . . thick, fast volleys of hostile bullets . . . in the middle of the marshy field a fatal ball struck him just below the throat.*

—*HARVARD MEMORIAL BIOGRAPHIES*

They were resting at last in the small Pennsylvania crossroads of Two Taverns. The whole Twelfth Corps had marched all night. When the halt was called at last, eight thousand men lay down on their rubber blankets and went to sleep beside the Baltimore Pike, their heads pillowed on their haversacks. They were deaf to the creaking of the wagons moving past them, deaf to the thudding hooves of the six-mule teams hauling ammunition trains toward something that was about to happen up there farther to the north.

Or maybe it was already happening. They could all feel it, a sense of the gathering of forces, the massing of opposing armies.

There was a rumor—thousands and thousands of men were flowing together from a dozen different directions. As the men of the Twelfth Corps lay down, they murmured to each other, "The ball's about to open."

Colonel Mudge was asleep with the rest of them when he was prodded awake at dawn.

It was a sergeant from the Tenth Maine, the regiment of provost guards. "Sorry, sir," said the sergeant, "but the goddamn fool's done it again."

"Done what again?" Mudge pushed himself up on one elbow. When he saw what the sergeant was dumping on the ground, he said, "Oh no. Oh God, Otis, it's not you again."

Otis had fallen with his left arm twisted under him. "You're in for it now," said the sergeant, jerking him roughly to his feet.

Rubbing his shoulder, Otis looked at Mudge piteously and whimpered, "I was drunk, Charley, that's all. I couldn't help myself."

"He's Colonel Mudge to you," said the sergeant, giving him a shove. The sergeant nodded at the colonel. "He wasn't just drunk, the dumb fool. He was skedaddling again, hightailing it for Baltimore."

The morning of July first was already hot. Mudge had not slept well. He picked up his coat and stood up, trying to absorb the fact that this old friend had done something so fatally stupid as to desert for the third time.

Otis pulled out his best card. It had saved his neck twice before. "Come on, Charley," he said, his voice shaking, "you wouldn't shoot an old classmate? Not a fellow thespian from the good old days in Hasty Pudding, would you now, Charley? My God, Charley, who was it wrote that farce with the Female Smuggler? And all the songs? And all those hilarious playbills? Remember the whistling, Charley? Remember the stamping feet?"

"You promised me, Otis," said Mudge in a low voice. "You swore you'd never do it again."

"Oh, Charley, everybody was drunk, back there in Frederick." Otis scrambled up from his knees with a winning smile. "I couldn't help myself. God's truth, Charley, I didn't know where in the hell I was going. I was just trying to catch up, coming after you double-quick." Otis made a comical pretense of trotting at high speed. "I

wasn't going to let my colonel down, not good old Charley
Mudge, nor my captain neither, not good old Tom Robeson."

Mudge looked wretched. He muttered something to the provost
guard, who grunted and turned on his heel. Mudge walked away
from Otis and stood in the shade of a tree.

Thoroughly frightened, Otis fumbled at the cork of his canteen. His throat was parched. Swallowing the warm water, he kept
anxious eyes on Mudge's back. Was Charley calling for a firing
squad? Were they going to put an end to him here and now? They
wouldn't do it on the march, would they? Not without a court-
martial?

But Otis had seen it happen in another regiment, and that boy
had only skedaddled twice. He had screamed for mercy, but they
had shot him anyway.

Then Otis took a shaky breath of relief. It was only Tom
Robeson. And, thank God, good old Tom Fox was strolling up with
his sack coat slung over his shoulder, eating cherries from his
hand.

And Seth Morgan was right behind Fox. *Oh, Seth, Seth, you
won't hurt me, will you, Seth? Not sweet-natured dear old Seth?*

Otis watched as the four of them stood murmuring with their
backs to him. Fear always made him sick to his stomach.

He couldn't keep quiet. "Tom," he called out to Robeson,
"remember that piece I wrote for you? It was my piece, Tom,
remember? Oh, those were good times, weren't they, Seth?" Then
Otis's sentimental pathos gave way to a cry from the heart, "Oh
God, Charley, oh Jesus, Seth, how did we get into this mess?"

They were deciding his fate. Otis couldn't stand it. He hurried
forward into the pool of shade and fell on his knees. He could only
jabber, "A classmate, boys, you wouldn't shoot an old classmate."

Somehow, against all hope, it worked again. Mudge glanced at
the others, then looked down at Otis and said severely, "Listen,
Otis, I don't know exactly what's coming, but there's going to be a
fight. And every man in this regiment will be told to shoot you
dead if you're caught skulking one more time."

Otis got up from his knees, sobbing and gushing his thanks.
Mudge strode away. Fox and Robeson hurried off and didn't look
back. Seth hurried away too, but he looked back and smiled.

. . . *a mighty work was before them. Onward they moved, night and day were blended, over many a weary mile, through dust and through mud, in the broiling sunshine, the flooding rain . . . weary, without sleep for days . . . yet these men could still be relied upon, I believed, when the day of conflict should come.*

—*Lt. Frank Haskell, 16 July, 1863*

PART III

THE ARCHIVES

THE BLANK PAGE

Your great-great-grandfather?" said the woman at the reference desk in the Archives department of the Pusey Library. "What was his name?"

"Morgan, Seth Morgan." Mary found it oddly uncomfortable to say the name aloud.

The Pusey Library was a small jewel tucked away underground. Its highly visible neighbor in Harvard Yard was Widener, a monumental building with a vast stone staircase and towering granite columns, one of the great libraries of the Western world. Tourists understood its importance at once, and they clustered on the steps to be photographed before gathering around the bronze figure of John Harvard to be photographed again.

No pictures were taken on the steps of Pusey. It was too self-effacing. The broad stone stairs descended from ground level to a glass wall of doors that led to a pair of specialized libraries, the Harvard Archives and the Theatre Collection.

The Archives library was a cheerful well-lighted space. The librarian was cheerful too. "What class did he belong to?"

"That's the only thing I'm sure of," said Mary. "He was in the class of 1860. And I'm pretty sure he served in the Civil War."

"We'll find him in a jiffy." The librarian whisked away, returned with a thick book, smacked it down on the counter, and flipped briskly through the pages. "The Quinquennial Catalogue. Everybody's in here, absolutely everybody."

"Everybody?"

"Everybody from the dawn of time, 1636 to 1930." She ran a finger down a page. "Lots and lots of Morgans. Look, here he is, *Morgan, Seth*. You're right, he was class of 1860." She swirled the book around and tapped the name with her finger.

"Oh, thank you." Mary stared at the long column of people named Morgan, grateful that her ancestor's name had not been crossed out. There he was, one of dozens of Morgans who had attended the university at one time or another—

Morgan, Seth, 1860.

She looked up at the librarian gratefully. "My name's Mary Kelly. I teach around here, but I've never been in this library before. I'm so glad to see what it's like."

"Oh, yes, Professor Kelly, and I'm glad to meet you in person. You and your husband are famous." The librarian reached her hand across the counter. "Angelica Doyle."

Mary doted on librarians. She took Angelica Doyle's hand and shook it heartily. "I'm delighted to meet you. I should explain that my maiden name was Morgan, but I confess I don't know much about my great-great-grandfather. Do you have records about individual students, even that far back?"

"I'll see what I can find. Meanwhile you can see if his photograph is in our picture collection." Angelica Doyle nodded at a set of file cabinets against the wall. "The drawers with the blue labels."

Mary was charmed by the old-fashioned wooden drawers, but

when she pulled out the *M–N* drawer and flicked through the index cards, she found no *Seth* among the Morgans.

"Well, there's an album for the class of 1860," said librarian Doyle. "Make yourself comfortable and I'll bring it out."

Mary looked around the room, chose a table and sat down. Nearby an elderly man was crouched over a gray box of files—was he looking up an ancestor? In one corner a young woman tapped away softly at a computer keyboard.

"Here we are," said Angelica Doyle, approaching with a large box. She set it down with a thump and removed the cover. Inside lay a big book, its gold-stamped binding crumbling at the edges. Angelica dropped a pair of white cotton gloves on the table and went away.

Mary took the hint and pulled on the gloves before lifting the cover of the album and turning the pages. They were of heavy stock with gold edges. Only a single photograph was mounted on each page.

Young men's faces, solemn and unsmiling. Mary guessed that the reason for their quiet dignity was not merely that the exposures were too long to capture a fleeting expression. Perhaps in those days people didn't have to pretend eternal happiness.

There were old Yankee names among the faces. Some of the men were in uniform. Occasionally their ranks in particular regiments in the Union army were listed beside their signatures.

She worked her way through Edward Gardiner Abbott and Henry Livermore Abbott and Nathaniel Saltonstall Barstow and Henry Austin Clapp and Noah Gobright.

When she came to the *M*'s, she looked intently at each one. The first was Charles James Mills.

He was followed by an empty page.

The next was Charles Redington Mudge. Mary stopped, with a small cry of recognition. The elderly man at the next table looked up in surprise. She smiled at him apologetically and looked back at Mudge. He was one of the men in Memorial Hall. His name was on the tablet, the one she had chosen to begin with. "Mudge," whispered Mary to herself. "Charles Redington Mudge." He had been killed, she remembered, in the Battle of Gettysburg.

Mudge was a thoughtful-looking, slightly bewhiskered young

man in uniform. He sat behind a cloth-covered table, his chin resting on his hand. Mary could imagine the voice of the photographer—*Now, sir, stay quiet, if you please.*

Hungrily she stared at Mudge's face. He seemed to be looking back at her, but of course he had really been staring into the dark glassy lens of the camera. She wanted to ask him if he had known her great-great-grandfather, but she had an even stronger urge to say something else, something crude and impulsive. *Oh, I'm dreadfully sorry, Charles Redington Mudge, but you have only a few more years to live. You're going to be killed in battle. I'm terribly sorry.*

The next picture was of a classmate named Newcomb. Somehow she had missed Morgan.

She flipped the page back to Mudge. No, it would be before Mudge. There was a page between Mudge and Mills, but it was the blank one.

She stared at it, and her face grew hot. Her great-great-grandfather's name was written at the bottom of the page—*Seth Morgan, 2d Mass. Vol. Infantry.*

But there was no photograph, only a few streaks of dried paste.

The shame had been too great. His classmates had rejected him. They had torn out his picture in disgust.

When she could collect herself, Mary took the heavy book back to the librarian at the counter. "Is it possible to get photocopies?"

"Yes, of course," said Angelica Doyle. "Here, you just make out one of these yellow slips."

"Good. I'd like copies of two of the men in this book, Mills and Mudge. No, three. Would they photocopy this page too?"

"That one? But it's blank."

"Yes, but it once had my great-great-grandfather's picture on it. You see? His name is there at the bottom."

"Well, of course it can be photocopied, but all you'll get will be a few smudges."

"Yes," said Mary unhappily, beginning to scribble her request, "I know."

PART IV

OTIS SKEDADDLES

The swift thought came to him that the generals did not know what they were about. It was all a trap.

—STEPHEN CRANE, *THE RED BADGE OF COURAGE*

SEEING THE ELEPHANT

★**Thomas Rodman Robeson**
Class of 1861

Second Lieutenant 2d Mass. Vols. (Infantry),
May 28, 1861; First Lieutenant, November 30,
1861; Captain, August 10, 1862; died July 6,
1863, at Gettysburg, Pa.

*The Second became engaged on July 3d. . . .
At about six o'clock the regiment was ordered
to advance . . . when he was hit by a conical ball. . . . His wound was found
to be so serious that his life could not be saved. . . . "Well, I suppose I must
go. It is hard to die, with so many bright prospects before me. I feel the cause has
been just, and I have tried to know and do my duty."*
—HARVARD MEMORIAL BIOGRAPHIES

Otis could barely see Tom Robeson far ahead, marching at the
head of the company. It was the second day of slogging northward,
although, thank God, they hadn't yet been called upon to charge
the enemy and have their guts ripped out or their heads blown off.
Both days it had just been dragging one foot after the other, hay
foot, straw foot, weighed down by fifty-seven pounds of knapsack,
rifle, ammunition, cartridge box, shelter tent, blanket, rations and
canteen. The corporal in front of Otis had a skillet dangling from
his rifle. Behind them a wagon train stretched for miles.

Yesterday, Otis had still been suffering from the aftereffects of his
carousing in Frederick. This morning, after the life-and-death con-

frontation with his dear old classmates, his headache was worse, throbbing with every step. But as the thirty-three regiments of the Twelfth Crops, all eight thousand marching men, dragged themselves wearily through Taneytown, they were serenaded by a cluster of pretty girls along the roadside, and Otis cheered up.

He waved his cap and cried, "Fair damsels, we salute you," and the girls laughed. One of them piped up with a song everybody knew, "When This Cruel War Is Over," and the regimental band struck up with the same tune.

But the cruel war was far from over. They could all see the smoke drifting high in the sky from somewhere up ahead, and there was an ominous thunder of guns. Something tremendous was happening not far away. The man with the skillet muttered again that the ball was about to open, and somebody else said they were going to see the elephant this time for sure.

"I've seen enough of that goddamn elephant already," said Otis, and there were grunts of assent. Grimly they dragged themselves forward under the hot sun until there was a sudden halt up ahead, and a wave of laughter came down the line.

It was geese, a small flock of geese, scattering in all directions. A boy with a stick was running after them, and one of Otis's mates was pretending to help, flapping the skirts of his coat and calling, "Here, goosey, goosey," but all he got for his trouble was a savage nip on the arm.

The booming of the guns was louder now, but the countryside was still green and fair, the corn tall in the fields, the farmhouses neat with white fences and flowering gardens. And then there was another halt. What was the matter now?

Otis's friend Rufus soon found out. "It's them generals," he said. "It's them stuck-up generals."

Otis climbed a tree and stared toward the head of the line. Sure enough, a mounted courier was dashing up and shouting something at General Slocum, and whatever it was, the general didn't like it. From his vantage point in the tree, Otis could see Slocum's red and furious face. More couriers came and went. Orderlies and officers gathered urgently around.

Otis climbed down and reported, "It's some kind of puffed-up standoff." Rufus said that the general must have a boil on his backside, and the men all grinned and filed off into a field and sat down. The crash of artillery was very loud now, and half the sky was filled with smoke. Something very bad was going on over there, just out of sight to the west.

Whatever it was, they were in no hurry to find out. Some of Otis's messmates stretched out and went to sleep. Others filled their canteens from the creek that ran through the field. Rufus took off one shoe and mended his sock. His brother Lem removed his shirt to look for critters.

But before long Tom ordered everybody up, because the corps was finally on the march again. One way or another, the dispute had been settled. The men plodded on for a while, then turned off the pike onto a narrow country road, their sweltering coats and sweating faces covered with dust. Soon all three brigades of the First Division surged into a wooded grove and came to a halt. At last Tom Robeson told his company they could settle down.

Otis watched as Tom spread a map on the ground and dropped to his knees. Seth Morgan and Charley Mudge were also kneeling. They were all staring intently at the map.

Otis envied them their comradeship in important matters, their friendly decision making, their power to send underlings like himself into battle. As officers they were a breed apart.

The years at school had been so different. Of course the others had never been in danger of expulsion—oh, no, not they, not Mudge and Robeson and Morgan, not Tom Fox. Poor old Otis had been perpetually in the bad graces of tutors, professors, the President and Fellows and all the other lords of the universe, but among his friends it had not mattered at all.

Why should their army rank make such a difference? Otis himself had not changed. He was as ready as ever to amuse, to dash off a comic song, to rally the campfire with "Hardtack, Come Again No More," to conduct a mock burial for an ancient piece of salt beef, to spread a little cheer. But now the pall of war had cast a grim shadow over the faces of Tom Robeson and Charley Mudge. Even with Seth the old camaraderie was not the same. It was painfully clear that on the field of glory, comic songs were not what was wanted.

He watched Tom Robeson look up and point at a rise of

ground, over there beyond the trees. He heard him say, "Culp's Hill" before staring down at the map again with Charley Mudge.

Otis felt an impulse to shout at them, "Mrs. Jarley's Waxwork, remember, Tom? Hey, Charley, will you ever forget Au*nt Charlotte's Maid?*"

But it was no use. Privates did not jest and pass the time of day with lordly colonels and captains, no matter how chummy they had been in the past.

Fortunately Otis had fostered a friendship with two younger men in his company. Rufus and Lemuel Scopes were a pair of nineteen-year-old twins from some one-horse town in western Massachusetts. Keeping Rufe and Lem in stitches was child's play.

But now, Christ, their respite was over. An orderly appeared, Tom and Charley stood up, and before anybody knew what was happening, the whole regiment was on its feet and obeying an order to march up a hill to attack a bunch of rebel cavalry. But it didn't amount to much. By the time Otis and Lem and Rufe were halfway to the top, everybody turned around and marched down again.

"Like Jack and Jill," said Otis, grinning at Rufus and Lem, but they'd never heard of Jack and Jill. Thankfully, the men of Company E settled down again, bivouacking beside a little creek. Otis owned a piece of soap, so he stripped down, sudsed out his underwear in the creek, and put it on again wet, so it would cool him when he lay down.

But in the morning the drawers were cold and clammy next to his skin. He had been awake half the night listening to the rumbling wheels of gun carriages on the Baltimore Pike and the clash of picks and shovels. The regiment's band of Pioneers was hard at work the whole night, wielding axes to fell trees and spades to dig trenches. They shouted at each other as they dragged the branches into line to make breastworks. It sounded like hundreds of them yelling at once and rattling their picks against rocks and crashing heavy boulders down against the trees.

Their noises were bad enough, but there was another noise that was worse, a tinny whine around his ears. Otis guessed there was a swale nearby because the mosquitoes were so thick. He pulled his blanket over his head and slept at last, but it was only a few minutes before he woke up to the sound of rebel caterwauling over there on the hill across the ravine, and a spattering of rifle fire. Sitting up, he was aware of a familiar knot of fear in his chest.

Oh Lord, now they were all getting up again. Tom Robeson was urging them onto their feet. The whole damn regiment was shifting position, in fact it was everybody, the whole goddamn division. Otis did his part of the shifting with his eyes half-closed as the regiment climbed an entirely different hill and spread out in a thick new line.

Unfortunately the new position was on the side facing the enemy. Otis chose his place with care, crouching down behind Corbett, the fattest man in the company. If any stray bullets found Corbett, they'd lose themselves in his spongy flesh and never come out the other side. Otis beckoned Lem and Rufe to huddle beside him. Corbett was so fat, there was plenty of room for three.

But the day passed, and nothing much happened. They relaxed and rummaged in their haversacks for pieces of hardtack, and Rufe shared out his cold beans. Not until late afternoon did the artillery on both sides begin to make a racket. And not until dusk did the enemy start fighting in earnest, but luckily it was no concern of Company E.

"Well, if that don't beat the devil," said Lem. "They've changed their minds again."

Sure enough, Tom Robeson was making huge "Come on, boys" gestures and first sergeants were running around giving orders. The entire First Division was supposed to hightail it someplace else, and in a tearing hurry, that was clear.

Where, for Christ's sake?

Otis caught sight of the commander of the division, Alpheus Williams. He knew the general from afar by his big black slouch hat and the long mustachios that drooped on either side of his pudgy face. The general was right there in plain sight, looking anxious.

Otis fell in with Rufe and Lem. As the sun sank lower and lower, they headed south. At first the three of them were somewhere near the front of Company E, but before long they edged to the rear in a clever way they'd worked out in other battles in other places.

You just let the boys behind you turn into the boys in front.

SOMETHING MAGNIFICENT

Things had been quiet enough where they came from, but all day they had heard the raging storm of battle to the south. Obviously, the men of the First Division were being called on to shore up something or other down that way, whether they felt like it or not. Otis was not particularly interested in shoring anything up, but there was no help for it. He trudged along with the others in the gathering dusk, and when everybody jogged to the right, he jogged that way too.

Otis was captivated by the sight of a small stone building along this road. It was obviously a schoolhouse. A man stood in the doorway looking out at them. The schoolmaster, thought Otis. At once he was distracted by the memory of a class in the postulates of Euclid under Professor Eustis, and he wanted to fall out of line and offer his services to the schoolmaster. *"Now, class, this morning we will study the axiom that halves of equals are equal."* How delightful, the cheery faces of the little boys and girls!

But as they drew away from the schoolhouse Otis looked back and saw a couple of medical stewards with a litter. The school was now a hospital.

"Column left." They were turning into another road, and the boom of artillery and the crash of rifle fire was louder, and now the marching regiments began encountering the side effects of a bloody battle. A train of white-topped ambulance wagons pulled out of the way to let them go by, and every one of the marching men—all walking upright on two legs—looked in at the litters and winced at the sight of bleeding heads and smashed limbs. Crowds of the walking wounded were on the road too, and so was a band of jolly skulkers, cheering at them, shouting, "Go in and give them Jerrie."

But nobody up front seemed to know where they were going. Behind them Culp's Hill was in the thick of a battle at last, because you could hear the crashing and thundering from back there, and over the brow of the ridge in this neighborhood something huge was going on because you couldn't hear yourself think for the artillery.

Were they lost? Stepping out of line and staring forward, Otis could make out some kind of excited conference up in front, and now Lockwood's brigade was taking off at a trot toward the fighting on the other side of the ridge.

Would they be next? Otis could feel his heart pounding, but then it settled down because it looked like they weren't about to follow the unlucky Second Brigade. And then Tom Robeson walked along the line and told them to move back into the trees.

Oh, yes, sir, gladly, Your Honor, sir. By this time Otis was dead tired, so he was grateful to drop to the ground and lean against a tree and close his eyes. When he opened them again it was nearly dark, and the battle noises were dying away. Otis didn't give a damn which side had won the day, as long as Private Otis Mathias Pike had not been called into gallant action in the line of fire.

It was absurd, he knew it was, and philosophically unsupportable, and yet it seemed to Otis a fact that his own death in battle would be more tragic than the deaths of other men, sadder than Lem's or Rufe's, for instance, or even of those noble souls, his classmates Mudge and Robeson, Morgan and Fox. Those high-class people would no doubt be useful members of society if they lived, highly respectable statesmen and pillars of the church. But if his own life were ruthlessly cut short, something more important would be lost.

Dreamily Otis imagined the world going on without him. In the theaters where he had been welcomed in the old carefree days before he had been dragged into this war—in Boston and Baltimore, in Washington and Philadelphia, even in Richmond and Lynchburg, Virginia—would they miss him, the actors, the managers, the musicians, the pretty singers, the buxom dancers?

Would Rosalie miss him, the rose of Philadelphia? Or that adorable sweetheart of Washington, darling Flora, the nymph of the Grove? Unfortunately the lovely Lily LeBeau would not miss him, because they had never met. Bitterly Otis imagined the lighted carriages sweeping up to the doors of the famous theaters after he was gone. He envisioned all the fine ladies and gentlemen descending for yet another brilliant performance, none of them aware of the demise of Otis Pike. His name would be no more to them than the horse droppings on the street. Other men would write the witty pieces they came to see and the comic songs.

But what a waste if the fanciful cleverness of Otis Pike should be smashed by a minié ball or blotted out in a shower of grapeshot. Of course it was too bad about all the others, it was criminal that the lives of so many thousands of boys from North and South should be snuffed out in this savage war, but the truth of the matter was that most of them would be missed only by mothers and wives and sweethearts, whereas his own death would be a loss to the world, even if the world didn't know it yet.

Oh, yes, the idiot birds would go on singing when he was no longer there. The horsecars would jingle along Massachusetts Avenue, the curtains would rise in the Howard Atheneum and Arch Street and McVicker's and Ben Debar's, and no one would remember the quick inventiveness of Otis Pike behind the scenes, his transformation of crude comedies like *Sweethearts and Wives* into witty confections, and *Toodles,* and *The Way to Get Married* and *A Kiss in the Dark.*

All he needed was time—time for his budding gift to flower at last into something truly magnificent.

A LONG NIGHT
FOR OTIS PIKE

They were back. Oh God, they were back.

Sullenly, half-dead with exhaustion, the whole goddamned division had shambled back in the moonlight over the rough ground, only to find out there'd been a god-awful bungle. They never should have left Culp's Hill, because while they were someplace else, the enemy had taken over their works, all the trenches for which sweating men had shoveled dirt and felled trees and dragged boulders into rocky barricades the night before.

Otis could see the disgust on the faces of Charley Mudge and Tom Robeson. He watched in alarm as Seth Morgan and Tom Fox found out what had happened and looked disgusted too. There'd been hell to pay while the First Division was elsewhere, and hell was still smoldering and belching up and down the hill and over there beyond their rocky knoll. From high overhead the full moon shone down on Colonel Silas Colgrove's five regiments as calmly as if two thousand footsore men were gathered there for a Sunday school picnic. *I'll thank you to pass me another of them chicken legs, teacher, and I won't say no to a piece of pie.*

Otis threw down his pack in almost the same place as before except it was a little way up a wooded slope. From there he could look across a patch of open ground toward the same infernal hill, the one that belonged to some poor unlucky farmer named Culp, where the two armies had been slugging it out for the last two days.

Now the bullyboys were chopping down trees again and digging more trenches. Otis could see them levering up stones and piling them against boulders as big as streetcars.

It would be another wretched night. Otis sprawled with his head on his haversack. Lem and Rufe were soon snoring on the ground a little way to his right, nestled together like boys in one bed, but Otis was too scared to doze off, even though he'd slept so badly the night before.

Over there across the swale lay the rebel army. They were out of sight, but he could feel them, he could even imagine he heard them breathing, because it wasn't like a woods inhabited by a few snakes and rabbits or woodchucks, it was tens of thousands of men inhaling and softly exhaling, and every one of them had it in for Otis Pike.

Fearfully he rolled over on his other side. From here he could see the red lights of an ambulance moving through the trees and hear the crack of a whip and a shout, and then a whimpering cry. In what part of the battle had that boy dropped down, half-killed by a rifle shot or a twelve-pound ball? Would Otis himself be screaming in an ambulance tomorrow? Or lying dead right here at Culp's Hill?

In a fit of terror he sat up. Looking around wildly, he saw a friend only a few feet away, writing a letter in a patch of moonlight. Earlier that day Otis had found Captain Adams companionable enough, even though he commanded another company.

Desperately he struck up a conversation. "A letter to your sweetheart, I'll bet."

He could see the flash of Adams's grin. "I'm just wondering if she's looking at the same stars, way up there in Maine."

"Well, I guess they've got the same stars pretty much everyplace." Otis moved uneasily and lifted his head from his knapsack. "What do you think that noise is?"

It was a steady low moaning, coming from somewhere behind them, rising and falling, fading away and then beginning again.

Adams stopped writing and listened, but then, instead of answering, he hunched down again to his letter.

The moon was bright enough to read by. Otis was not surprised to see one of his messmates holding a page up to the light. Beyond the curled shapes of Lem and Rufus, Sergeant Luther Willow was racing through another of his police detective stories. Lucky Sergeant Willow, to be able to distract himself with the adventures of some stouthearted policeman.

Otis crawled over beside him. "What is it this time, Sergeant?"

Willow kept his eyes on the page. "Case of switched identity. The duke, he don't know he's got a twin brother, but then the brother kills him and hides his body and takes over his castle, but then Police Detective Bone, he finds a clue, a bloody coat, and when the duchess sees the coat, she screams, and then Detective Bone . . ." Willow flipped a page. His voice trailed away.

Otis crawled back to his knapsack, wishing he had a dime novel to read, or better yet a sweetheart to write to. Rosalie and Flora were sweethearts of a sort, but they weren't the kind you wrote a letter to. He had no kin to write to either, not since the blessed day when his uncle had expired. No, there was no family whatever to miss Otis Pike if he never came back from this fight.

Well, great God on high, it had never been his fight in the first place. The whole damn war, it was no business of his. What did these fools think they were fighting for? The Union? What the hell difference did it make if North America was four countries instead of three? And he sure wasn't fighting for the darkies. This white soldier wasn't going to die for any colored man.

The whole thing was insane. Otis had been thrown into the army because he'd stuck a knife into a thief in a saloon. Murder, they called it. Now it was his duty as a soldier to murder as many rebs as he possibly could. He was supposed to stick his bayonet in the belly of some Alabama farm boy or blow the head off some poor Johnny Reb from Mississippi before they did the same to him, and maybe he'd end up in a field hospital in the hands of some butcher with a saw, so he'd spend the rest of his life explaining his cork leg.

"Gettysburg," he'd say, and the pretty ladies would all say, "Oo," and call him a hero.

Before long the whole country would be full of heroes with only one arm or leg, or no arms or legs, or half their faces blown away, courtesy of Chancellorsville or Fredericksburg or First or Second Bull Run.

They weren't heroes, they were cattle to the slaughter, choice cuts of human flesh chucked in a meat grinder. They were thousands and thousands of healthy young men forced to march forward double-quick, straight into the guns of a firing squad, as though condemned to death for committing some awful crime, when they were innocent as newborn babes.

After all, why should brother be killing brother? Why should one day's bloody work leave eight thousand corpses rotting in an orchard where the cherries were ripe, or dead in a field where the corn had been growing tall only yesterday? Why should barefoot boys be slaughtered in a country lane where folks had been driving the buckboard into town only yesterday and clucking at the mule?

Last year after skedaddling from Antietam, Otis had found himself picking blackberries with a fifteen-year-old boy from Georgia who had talked about his pig. Otis had nothing against the boy, nor against his pig either. He had nothing against any of those mothers' sons from Georgia or Louisiana or Arkansas. In his opinion, they had as much right to live as he did.

Glancing to his left, Otis saw that Captain Adams had finished his letter. He was sound asleep under his blanket. At three in the morning, Otis wrenched paper and pencil out of his haversack and began writing a letter of his own.

THE WORD OF GOD

The generals were at it again. Otis had at last fallen asleep, but in less than an hour he was jerked awake by the boom of artillery from the hills to the rear. He had seen the guns yesterday as the teams hauled them wallowing along the road, the ten-pound Parrotts and the smoothbore Napoleons. Now the low arc of their shot and shell was invisible in the dark, but he could see the blazing mouths of the guns.

The bombardment lasted only a few minutes. When it was over, Otis sat up slowly, feeling the old dread in his stomach. An artillery barrage usually meant action: *Smash 'em first, then send in the boys.*

He took out his watch, the gold repeater he had won in a game with a bunch of like-minded gentlemen at Chancellorsville—the four of them had politely refrained from engaging in anything so vulgar as a battle. Now he held it up to the light. The moon was setting behind the hills to the west, but the moonlike face of the watch was clear enough. The spidery hands said five o'clock.

Below him the officers were beginning to stir, whispering to one another and moving among the sleeping men. What kind of god-awful decisions were they making now, his dear old friends and Harvard classmates? Otis felt fear rise again in his chest, making his breathing shallow and his limbs flimsy and weak. But mixed with his fear was his usual unhappy feeling of resentment.

The officers of the regiment were like members of a private club, from which he was excluded. Otis hungered to put his arm around Seth Morgan and grin at Charley Mudge and laugh with Tom Robeson and share a joke with Tom Fox—even now, even right now on the edge of some murderous action. If only he were one of them, a genuine brother in arms, they would see how brave he could be, how eagerly in their company he would defy the enemy.

But Otis was at the bottom, not the top. Heroism had no meaning for a humble private, only blind obedience to whatever insane orders came down the line from the lords of creation.

Then to his astonishment he saw Seth Morgan look up at him, straight up at him, across the slumped bodies of a hundred sleeping men. Even in the shadowy light of dawn Seth's face was recognizable, and the direction of his gaze was as plain as if he were only a few feet away. Perhaps he was about to beckon, to call him forward to join them, to become one again in the band of old friends.

But then as Otis watched, his heart beating high, he saw Seth's eyes drop. He was looking down, writing something, tearing off a slip of paper, handing it to a corporal, or maybe it was a sergeant, Otis couldn't see the stripes on the man's sleeve. Now Seth was pointing at him, and the other man was looking up at him and beginning to pick his way among the sleeping men, heading for Otis.

"Well, what have you got there?" murmured Otis. The corporal—he had only two stripes—handed him the folded piece of paper and turned away without a word.

With trembling fingers Otis opened the paper and read it, then looked down the hill to smile at Seth, wanting to talk to him, to tell him that he loved him, that he had always loved him, but Seth had melted away. Otis could no longer make him out among the rest.

Rufus and Lem were sitting up now, wide-awake. The three of them sat silently side by side, dreading they didn't know what.

The order wasn't given until full light of day. Finally Captain

Tom Robeson was shaking the men up, talking cheerfully, encouraging them to be ready to go right out and take back the lost entrenchments from the rebs across the swale. It was painful to think that such an order could come from an old comrade who had once brought down the house as a girlish charmer in a masterpiece that was entirely the work of Otis Pike. *For God's sake, Tom, what are you asking us to do?*

Below them there was another hurried conference. It was all colonels this time—Charley Mudge and Colonel Colgrove and Colonel whatsit of the Twenty-seventh Indiana, plus a stranger from somewhere else. This time the confabulation was only a few yards away. Otis saw the four of them turn together and stare across the swale.

The conference was over. Otis watched Charley move quickly along the line to talk to his captains. When he reached Tom Robeson, Otis failed to hear the order but he heard Tom say, "But, Charley, it's madness."

Distinctly then, Otis heard Charley's reply: "It's murder, but it's an order." He saw Tom shake his head, turn smartly and repeat the order to his men.

Rufus had heard the word *murder.* Lem had heard it too. Their faces were ashen, but Rufe winked at Otis. The entire regiment was standing now. Looking left and right, his panic rising, Otis saw the pale faces of three hundred men waiting for the command, and then his knees gave way. He wanted to move his bowels and his stomach was in convulsion. Rufe caught him and helped him shamble to his feet.

But now he saw Charley mount to the top of the heaped-up dirt and branches and rocks that were the only bulwark from enemy fire for the men of the Second Massachusetts. "Up, men," shouted Lieutenant Colonel Charles Redington Mudge. "Over the breastworks. Forward, double-quick."

And now, good God, they were all up and over, they were stumbling and running after Colonel Mudge and Captains Fox and Robeson, running straight over the swampy open ground of the swale, and so were the boys from Indiana, while the rebs in the trenches uttered their shrill turkey gobble and opened up with a hail of rifle fire.

Seth Morgan vaulted over the breastworks with the rest of them, but as he ran into the storm of rebel bullets he looked back at Otis and shouted to him gaily, "Come on, Otis." He was beckoning, waving his arm and shouting, "Otis, come on."

At times like these. Otis forgot that he was not a believer and said a prayer. He had often said the same prayer before, "Dear God, what shall I do now?" And God had always looked down from heaven and given the same kindly answer, "Otis, skedaddle."

In the middle of the open field, Charley Mudge was down, and so was Tom Fox. Otis saw Tom Robeson reel and fall.

"Come on, Otis," Seth had said, calling to him, encouraging him, inviting him to join their little circle, to be one of them at last. But Otis had a higher call. Obeying the word of God, he backed away from the breastworks, away from Company E, away from the whole entire regiment as it sacrificed itself in a desperate attempt to take back its lost entrenchments from the thousands of country boys from Virginia and Maryland and North Carolina who were basking in the trenches now, all of them raking the swale with Enfield rifles that were accurate to a thousand yards. Not me, dear friends, not me.

So good-bye, dear classmates, farewell and good-bye. Me, I'm taking off down the Baltimore Pike.

PART V

THE HONOR OF
THE FAMILY

The bright sunshine gleams from their bayonets; above them wave their standards, tattered by the winds, torn by cannon-ball and rifle-shot,—stained with the blood of dying heroes. . . . Ask them what is most dear of all earthly things, there will be but one answer,—"The flag! the dear old flag!"

—CHARLES CARLETON COFFIN

A STUDY OF
WHISKERS

Beginning with his wife's embarrassing ancestor, Homer was being drawn into the whole progress of the Civil War.

"You see," he said grandly, "I have an earthshaking new theory of history."

"Oh, Homer, what is it this time?"

"First you have to back away and look at the nineteenth century as a whole."

"Well, all right, I'm backing away. So what?"

"If you look at everything, absolutely everything, you see that there was a general crescendo. Everything got louder and crazier and more and more exaggerated as the decades went by, until at last the war broke out in a general smashup and the boil of the antagonism between North and South burst at last."

"To mix a metaphor or two."

Homer swept all the papers off his desk. "I'll show you. Look what happened to women's skirts. Wait a sec—I've got a book here somewhere."

"There was a crescendo in women's skirts? That's your theory? Oh, I know, you mean the way they got wider and wider."

"Exactly. At precisely the moment the war began at Fort Sumter, after the feelings on both sides had been firing up for decades, women's skirts reached their hugest circumference. Look at this." Homer slapped open a book of old photographs. "See? It's Mary Todd Lincoln in full regalia. That skirt of hers must be seven yards around."

"Hmm, I see what you mean. And everything else was swelling too, in some kind of frenzy. Think of the furniture, all carved within an inch of its life and upholstered and doileyed and antimacassared. Even the mantels had petticoats. How strange."

"And what about genius? The boiling up of poets and writers? All that stuff we teach, Whitman and Melville, Thoreau and Dickinson. My God, masterpieces were busting out all over."

"You're right, Homer, it's amazing. I never thought of that."

"Wait a sec, there's more." Homer snatched up a paper from his desk. "What about the fashion in facial hair? I've been making a study. Take a look."

It was a page of caricatures—

Mary laughed. "Oh, Homer, you should write a scholarly paper."

"Of course. I've already got the title—*Victory and Defeat in the Civil War with Reference to the Growth of Facial Hair.*"

"Great. It would enhance your reputation no end."

Homer tossed his sketch aside. "How're you doing with that old skeleton in the closet?"

"What? Oh, that. You mean my great-great-grandfather." Mary bit her lip. "It's funny, but it bothers me. It shouldn't, I suppose, but it does. Oh, Homer, there's a nice woman in the Archives department. She found a book for me, the album for the class of 1860. It was so sad. There was a page for Seth Morgan's picture, with his name at the bottom and his regiment, but the picture itself was missing. They must have removed it."

"They? Who do you mean by 'they'?"

"Oh, I don't know. His classmates, probably. Poor old Seth, I'd just like to know what he did that was so bad."

"My dear, why should you care? After all, your great-great-grandfather was four generations back."

"I know." Mary looked stubborn. "But I do care, I really do."

"Well, there must be records. What was the regiment he belonged to?"

"The Second Massachusetts. It was one of the classier ones, I know that."

"And what about your family? There must be old trunks in your sister's attic. My God, your family's lived in that house since the dawn of time. Have you tried Gwen's attic?"

"No, but I will. That's the next thing. Gwen and Tom are back from Australia. Why don't we drop in on them with a meal? You know, a casserole or something. Do people still make casseroles? And then we can go up-attic." Mary frowned. "Because I've just got to find out about Seth Morgan. Honestly, Homer, I really do."

"For the honor of the family?"

"No, nothing like that. I want to resurrect him, dust him off, take a good look at him."

"Even though he was a scoundrel?"

"How do we know that for sure? I want to weigh all the evidence in court. That's it, Homer. I just want to give him a hearing."

UP-ATTIC

Mary Kelly's sister Gwen was the wife of Thomas Hand. Gwen and Tom lived in the old Morgan house on Barrett's Mill Road in Concord. The place was still a working farm, but lately much reduced to a few acres of orchard behind the house.

Gwen was nearly as tall as Mary, but chunkier. "The house is a mess," she said, opening the door.

In truth, it was a mess. Mary laughed. Her sister and brother-in-law were just back from an instructional tour of the world. This time Tom had been bringing his professional know-how to orchardists in Australia. Their unpacking was spread all over the downstairs. The only bare spot was the kitchen table.

"It doesn't matter," said Mary, setting down her pan of macaroni and cheese. "All we need is the attic."

Tom snorted. "The attic? Well, the attic's neat enough, all right."

He led the way. Homer looked left and right as they climbed the stairs. Mary had been living in this house when they had first met. In fact, she had grown up here. Indeed, her Concord ancestors had lived here as far back as the Civil War, which was why it was important to see the attic.

Homer caught a glimpse of the antique second-floor bathroom as Gwen opened the door to the attic stairs, and he wondered if the bathtub drain was still reluctant. But of course the care of this ancient house was none of his business, thank God.

"You'll be disappointed, I'm afraid," said Gwen, pushing back the trapdoor.

They stepped out on the wide old boards of the attic floor, four tall people ducking under the slanting roof beams.

"But there's nothing here," said Mary, gazing around.

"Right," said Tom.

"Well, he left a few things behind," said Gwen. "A portfolio of Annie's drawings, John's mineral collection, that kind of thing. He wasn't interested in those."

"He? What do you mean, 'he'?" Mary was appalled. "You mean you sold everything to somebody else?"

"Oh, no." Tom glanced at Gwen. His smile was grim. "She loaned it to somebody. That is, she thinks it was only a loan."

"Cousin Ebenezer Flint," said Gwen. "He's only a third cousin twice removed, or something like that, and his name isn't really Ebenezer, it's Howard. He's decided to call himself Ebenezer after his great-great-grandfather. Don't you remember when his part of the family came for Thanksgiving? He was Howie then, a real pain. None of us could stand him. Oh, I suppose you don't remember. You were only two."

Homer was bewildered. "You mean your third cousin twice removed walked off with everything in the attic?"

Tom took Homer's arm. "Come back downstairs and we'll explain the whole damn thing."

Tom's office was furnished with mementos from their travels. On the wall hung a grass skirt from the South Seas, along with a Japanese print of apple blossoms, a Balinese shadow puppet, and a brass tray from Benares. Twelve ebony elephants paraded across the mantelpiece.

But the office was less cluttered than the front room across the hall, where all the furniture was buried under clothing and books and Christmas presents for the grandchildren—plastic boomerangs, stuffed emus and a hand-carved platypus.

"I'd forgotten all about Howard Flint—Ebenezer, I mean," said Gwen, waving Homer and Mary toward the sofa.

"He's this big genealogist and architectural historian," said Tom. "Or so he claims."

"He went crazy over the house," said Gwen. "We had to show him around. We kept saying we didn't have time because we were packing up to go to Australia, but he just charged up the stairs on his own, so we had to follow him. And then he made up the most ridiculous theories."

"You know the kind of thing," said Tom. "The crack in the ceiling meant it was once a stairwell. The fireplace in the kitchen must have been a lot bigger and it probably had a beehive oven. The house was once a saltbox. Well, it was all just baloney."

"You should have seen him," said Gwen. "He had a wild bushy beard and little glittering eyes and the craziest way of talking. Well, he was just bonkers. I had to take him to the attic to study the beams up there, because he was so positive he'd find proof about the salt-box idea, but when he got up there and saw all the trunks and cardboard boxes he forgot about the roof beams and began clawing through the boxes. In two seconds there was stuff all over the floor."

"Didn't you stop him?" said Homer, fascinated by another example of human folly.

"Well, naturally," said Tom, "I hollered at him, but the guy was just insane. He kept babbling that genealogy was his field of expertise, and since *his* great-great-grandfather was the brother of *Gwen's* great-great-grandmother, it was perfectly all right because all this stuff belonged to him too."

"But surely—" said Mary.

Gwen laughed bitterly. "Well, it was pretty dramatic. You should have seen your dignified brother-in-law take Ebenezer by the scruff of the neck and haul him downstairs, still babbling and flapping his hands. I was afraid he'd charge Tom with assault and battery."

"He didn't?" said Homer. "Too bad. I'd have galloped to the rescue with expert legal advice."

"Oh, no," said Tom, shaking his head gloomily. "It was worse than that."

Gwen reared up from her chair, strode to the fireplace, and stared fiercely at the elephants on the mantelpiece. "All of a sudden, he stopped arguing and complaining and went very quiet. He just bowed and smiled his way out the door, and we thought we'd heard the last of him."

"So," said Tom, "we went happily off to Australia, leaving the house in the care of one of the kids."

"Uh-oh," said Mary. "Which one?"

"Well, it was Benny."

"Oh no, not Benny."

"I'm afraid it was Benny." Gwen began turning the elephants around, heading them back the other way.

"I can guess what happened," said Homer. "I suppose Ebenezer showed up and Benny let him in."

"Exactly," grumbled Tom. "He came back and sweet-talked old Benny into letting him look through a few things in the attic because he was this big important scholar."

"Oh, poor Benny." Mary laughed. "For the genius of the family he can sometimes be pretty stupid."

" 'Righto,' says Benny." Gwen plumped herself down in her chair. "And then what does he do, our Benny? He goes traipsing off on a camping trip with his friend Stuart Grebe, and does he lock the door? He does not."

"Oh God," groaned Mary.

"Well, that empty attic is what happened," said Tom. "When we got home on Tuesday, we knew something had happened, because Benny was gone again and there were bits and pieces of stuff trailing down the attic stairs."

"One of Mother's old dresser scarves, for instance," said Gwen angrily.

"You mean Benny didn't notice?" said Homer.

"Oh, he came back and he was all apology. He'd trusted this guy, he said."

"Our Benny," said Homer sourly, "the little friend of all the world."

"And I must say," said Gwen, "he pitched in and helped us clean up. But you saw what's left."

"Nothing," said Mary.

"Ebenezer took it all. He must have rented a pickup truck." Tom slapped his knees and stood up. "Who's for a drink?"

They trooped into the kitchen. But as he accepted his glass, Homer struck a lecturing pose and proclaimed, "History can be defined—"

"Uh-oh," said Mary again.

"History, as I was saying, can be defined as that which is left in the attic after everything of interest has been discarded by the children."

"Or the third cousin twice removed," said Gwen.

"Surely you can get everything back," said Mary. "Do you have his address?"

"I've got an old letter somewhere," said Gwen. "I think he lives in Washington, D.C."

"We'll call on Ebenezer on the way home from Gettysburg," said Homer.

"You're going to Gettysburg?" said Gwen. "That's nice."

"So I guess we'll also tour the nation's capital," said Mary.

"Be sure and go to the Smithsonian," said Tom.

"Right," said Homer. "We'll see the Smithsonian and the National Gallery and we'll also pay a call on one Howard Ebenezer Flint."

PART VI

SKEDADDLING AGAIN

*It was 1 pm by my watch when the signal guns were fired . . .
and as suddenly as an organ strikes up in a church, the grand roar
followed from all the guns of both armies.*

> —Lt. Col. Edward Porter Alexander,
> Artillery Reserve,
> First Army Corps,
> Army of Northern Virgina

PURE HAPPINESS

At first glance they looked like an entire company, but they weren't marching down the pike in any kind of order.

It took Otis only a second glance to see that they weren't a company, they were sensible boys like himself on their way elsewhere, but they were all muddled together with a bunch of wounded men who were limping to the rear.

He didn't want to fall in with that outfit, because any minute now a company of provost guards would come along, shouting and flailing with the flats of their swords, driving the skulkers back where they came from.

So as soon as he could, he dodged into a lane that led across lots in the direction of the Taneytown Road. The noise of the battle around Culp's Hill was louder here, the rapid fire of musketry from both sides and the shrieks and screams of thousands of men dutifully trying to kill each other.

Poor old Lem and Rufus, they were still in the thick of it. Right now they'd be out there in the open swale, scrabbling in their car-tridge boxes and ramming the cartridges down in the scorching muzzles of their guns—an operation that took six seconds—while the rebels behind the barricades fired at their helpless heads and hearts and lungs and livers and everything else of vital importance that was packed inside them someplace.

Otis hoped the two boys would come out all right, but there was nothing he could do about it. The fight for possession of the scorched and blasted hill that belonged to some old Dutch farmer was no longer any concern of his.

He slogged along easily, meandering up and down with the lay of the land. There were a few other skulkers on this road too, but by mutual agreement they avoided looking at one another.

Then Otis slowed down and stopped. Beside the road stood the stone schoolhouse, the one they had passed last night. He remem-bered his keen desire to walk away from the column and enter the classroom and teach the pink-cheeked boys and girls the axioms of Professor Eustis, only it had turned out to be a hospital.

But the stone building still looked attractive to a gentleman on the loose. Otis walked up and tried the door. It was locked. Look-ing in a window, he could see the desks, the dusty slate blackboard and a map of the world with pale blue oceans and a patchwork of pink-and-yellow countries. The desks were screwed to the floor, and therefore the hospital cots had been jammed between them, but all the beds were empty of shot-up men. Behind the building stood a pair of privies, but Otis chose to relieve his bladder in a stand of trees. Then he went back to the schoolhouse and flopped down in its shade, sitting up comfortably with his back against the cool stone wall.

The sound of the battle on the other side of the trees was dying down. Soon he could no longer hear the rattle of the guns that had been so busily engaged in killing miscellaneous human beings var-iously dressed in blue or butternut or gray.

It occurred to Otis that his haversack still contained a few scraps of food more or less fit for human consumption. He groped in the sack, found his slice of salt pork and laid it between two pieces of hardtack, remembering the joke about somebody who found some-thing soft in his hardtack, only it wasn't a worm, it was a tenpenny nail. For a while he wrenched at the sandwich with his teeth, washing it down at last with the tepid water in his canteen. Finally, stretching out luxuriously on the sun-dappled ground, he took a small book from an inner pocket of his coat and a pipe from an outer pocket, struck a match against a rock and settled down for a moment of midmorning repose.

The book was his own copy a popular play called *The Marble Heart, or the Sculptor's Dream*. Otis had underscored the lines for the part of Phidias, and in the margins he had scribbled a few changes in the high-flown dialogue.

Now, as the sun rose over the embattled hill and climbed higher in the sky, pouring midsummer light and heat down on the 160,000 men of the two armies that faced each other across the broad and flowering meadow, Otis studied his book and poised his pencil over the page.

The next line was another absurdity—

No, no, Diogenes! Gold cannot buy genius!

Swiftly Otis scribbled another version in the margin—

Naturally, Diogenes, gold cannot buy genius, at least not that much gold. How about coughing up a little more?

Then he began inventing speaking parts for the living statues.

It was pure happiness. It was what Otis was good at. What a waste if this gift were to be destroyed in the carnage of the battlefield!

The day was growing hotter still. Before long, Otis put away the little prompt book and stretched out full-length beside the schoolhouse wall. He could see no harm in taking a noonday nap. After all, there was no need to hurry. Walking away from the war would be easier come nightfall. And anyway, maybe the entire battle was over, the whole monkey show.

OLD HARVARD CHUMS

*HENRY ROPES
Class of 1862

Second Lieutenant, 20th Mass. Vols., 25 Nov.,
1861: First Lieutenant, 2 Oct., 1862: killed, at
Gettysburg, Penn., 3 July, 1863.
—*Harvard Memorial Biographies*

. . . a painful accident happened to us this
morning: First Lieutenant Henry Ropes (20th
Massachusetts in General Gibbon's division), a most estimable gentleman and
officer—intelligent, educated, refined . . . while lying at his post with his regi-
ment in front of one of the batteries . . . was instantly killed by a badly made
shell, which . . . fell but a few yards in front of the muzzle of the gun. . . .
—LIEUTENANT FRANK HASKELL

But the monkey show was not over. While Otis slept behind the
schoolhouse, the coming afternoon loomed in the heavy air. Across
the valley, 170 pieces of artillery were shifting and moving, hauled
into place in a line two miles long between a Lutheran seminary to
the north and a peach orchard to the south. Yesterday morning the
trees of the orchard had been laden with green fruit. Now the
peaches lay trampled in the ground.

Two hundred Federal guns were moving too, drawn by their
laboring horses, rattling with their caissons into a line that stretched
from the tombstones of a cemetery on the north to a pair of
round-topped hills to the south.

The enlisted men of 633 regiments waited for whatever was fixing to happen, while their generals pondered and stared across the
field.

In blissful ignorance Otis slept through the rest of the morning in the pleasant shade of the schoolhouse. He slept past the hour of noon. He would have dreamed through the rest of the day if a thunderclap of artillery had not jerked him awake.

It was the first signal shots of the rebel guns. The order for the cannonade had been given at last by Colonel E. Porter Alexander, who was undoubtedly enjoying it, because it was the way he always felt—*The very shouts of the gunners ordering . . . Fire! . . . in rapid succession thrill one's very soul.*

The noise was ten times the volume of sound that had exploded from the guns on Power's and McAllister's hills last night. Over Otis's head a tree shattered. Splintered branches crashed down amid a shower of deadly shrapnel. To his horror Otis saw a dark object whirl into the air and come down a mangled mass of flesh and bone, another skulker torn from his hiding place.

Otis sprang to his feet, snatched up his haversack and took to the road again, running away from the thundering guns, back toward the Baltimore Pike.

His comfortable skedaddling was over. For the next two hours, Otis encountered one crisis after another, while the guns roared at each other across the valley. The first crisis was a dazzle of sunlight on a hundred bayonets, Yankees in blue coats charging on the run in the direction of the Baltimore Pike. They weren't charging the enemy, they were charging poor old Otis Pike and his fellow skedaddlers. By order of the high command, no poor private or drummer boy or digger of latrines was to absent himself this day from the field of slaughter.

But Otis's high command was not Colonel Silas Colgrove, chief officer of the Third Brigade, nor was it Brigadier General Alpheus Williams, commander of the First Division. It was not even Major General Henry Slocum, in whose charge were both divisions of the Twelfth Corps. And it was certainly not Major General George Gordon Meade, the topmost commander of the entire Army of the Potomac. It was—well, who was it? After God, of course, that amiable major general in the sky.

Otis struggled to explain to himself the sense of purpose that stiffened his malingering spine. How could it be put into words? Well, it was art, of course, it was high art, no matter how melodramatic the words sounded, nor how foolish. All he needed was the rest of his life.

But today, as he discovered to his dismay, it was not the lofty commanders who were trying to deprive him of the precious years he needed, nor was it the bayonets of the provost guards. It was his own classmates.

Instead of fighting the battle, some of the men at Gettysburg could have rented a tent and held a jolly old college reunion, because Harvard men were all over the place, among the rebels as well as the Yankees.

Most of them, Otis knew, had come into the service as second lieutenants and risen rapidly to a higher rank. At Gettysburg they commanded companies, regiments, brigades, even divisions. Tens of thousands of foot soldiers who had never had the good fortune of strolling across Harvard Yard were obliged to obey their orders.

Or not obey them, like Otis Pike.

Otis encountered the first of them on the Taneytown Road. Although it was nearer to the tremendous noise of the bombardment, he reversed course in a hurry and loped that way because the rebel shells were falling thick and fast in his neighborhood. The twelve-pound shells had been aimed so high, they were sailing right over the heads of the fighting regiments along the ridge and smashing down in the rear, and the rear was where Otis just happened to be.

But on the Taneytown Road he was horrified to find himself just behind the battle line. Far into the distance the regiments lay cowering behind a stone wall while the shells from across the valley hurtled and burst over them, and in thunderous reply the Federal gun crews sponged and loaded and rammed their shot home and leveled and sighted their pieces and shouted in threadlike voices, and then the guns went off in blast after blast of fire and smoke and violently recoiled.

Otis ran crazily toward the first men he saw, a company ranged along the stone wall, all of them lying flat. Scared out of his wits, ducking and dodging while the air over his head exploded with enemy shells, he told himself wildly that he wasn't a skulker, he was an orderly carrying an extremely important message, racing from one high-up general to another on a matter of life and death

"Get down, you fool," shouted someone, "get down. Oh my God, Pike, is that you?"

Otis gave a frightened glance at the man who had recognized him, and then instead of shouting in reply he kept on running, flinging one arm forward in the direction of an eminent brigadier general who was impatient for his report.

But then there was a louder crash, and in spite of himself Otis looked back. He saw something appalling. That popular athlete Henry Ropes—Henry Ropes of the Harvard boat club and the victorious university crew—lay dead, with his blood gushing into the ground.

Panic-stricken, Otis dodged away, ducking and running past a couple of batteries whose gun crews were sponging and loading and shouting and firing, too busy to notice a pitiful skedaddler. Still pretending to be the bearer of an important dispatch, Otis began to feel safe.

That is, until he encountered three more of his dear old class-mates.

EUSTIS AND FARRAR

PROFESSOR HENRY LAWRENCE EUSTIS
Class of 1838

Colonel, 10th Massachusetts Volunteer Infantry.

Beyond Doubleday's left, [Major General John Newton] found the ground to be "almost denuded of troops. . . ." Meade suggested that he ask Major General John Sedgwick, Sixth Corps commander, for units to fill the gap. . . . Eventually, the Sixth Corps brigades of Brigadier General A. T. A. Torbert and Colonel Henry L. Eustis extended the line. . . .
—JEFFRY D. WERT

HENRY WELD FARRAR
Class of 1861

Vol. A.D.C., staff of General Sedgwick, March, 1863; Second Lieutenant, 7th Maine Vols., 10 April, 1863.

As for the Sixth Corps, it had become the manpower pool of the army from which infantry units and artillery batteries were drawn and used to plug gaps or bolster weak places in the main Union line.
—EDWIN B. CODDINGTON

Good God, it was Professor Eustis. It couldn't be Professor Eustis, but it was.

Otis halted his urgent scramble down the Taneytown Road, unsure what to pretend he was doing.

Professor Eustis was running directly toward him at the head of a great mass of men, three or four regiments, it looked like a whole brigade. The professor had always had a fierce and accusing eye. Otis blanched and shuddered and stopped breathing as it fell upon him now with a look that pierced him through, just as it had pierced him in the old days when a horribly distinguished trio of professors—James Russell Lowell, Evangelinus Apostolides Sophocles and Henry Lawrence Eustis—had officially "admonished" poor Otis and nearly thrown him out of school.

Luckily this was not the moment for another admonishing. Professor Eustis swept past Otis at the head of a column of eight or nine hundred men who were churning up the dust on the road and keeping their heads down, heading for another part of the line.

Breathing again, Otis kept going, but he was severely shaken. No longer could he persuade himself that he might just possibly have been entrusted with a vitally important dispatch from one commander to another. He was just another cowardly skulker heading south on the Taneytown Road.

And there was no cover, no handy little woodland to duck into when Henry Farrar appeared out of the smoke.

Otis had not seen Farrar since the Grand Opening Night of Hasty Pudding in March of 1860, when Otis's playbill had promised "*Talented Company! Gorgeous Scenery!! Magnificent Costumes!!! Utter Recklessness as to Pecuniary Considerations!!!!*" and Henry Farrar had appeared in a frolicsome farce as Mr. Snoozle.

Now the hilarious Mr. Snoozle was in uniform, shouting at a battery commander who was trying to move his pieces from one part of the ridge to another. While Otis stood frozen and staring, a shell struck one of the horses. It staggered and fell, spilling its guts on the road. The other horse reared in its traces and the whole caboodle tipped over and fell in a smash of flailing legs and spinning wheels.

The captain of the battery seemed dazed. He stood sweating and staring while Farrar threw himself at the dead horse and grasped the harness. The men of the gun crew gaped at Farrar as his fingers struggled with the buckles, then came to their senses and began pulling at the other horse, heaving it up on its legs. At once a crowd of men from another battery massed around the gun and set it upright.

If Farrar had seen Otis, he was too busy to do anything about him, and now a heavy layer of sulfurous smoke drifted over the road, hiding the guns and the panting men and Second Lieutenant Henry Weld Farrar.

The blanket of smoke smelled of brimstone, but in the welcome cover Otis scrambled away from the Taneytown Road and dove into the woods. He had no idea where in the hell he was going, and even among the trees there was no safety from the hideous random fall of the rebel shell, but he wouldn't run into anybody he knew. If he could make his way across lots and find a cozy shebang among the trees until nightfall, then maybe he could get away from this place entirely, without running into a provost guard eager to nab and put to death a habitual deserter like Otis Pike.

All would have been well—in fact he had just found a handy path through the wilderness—if another familiar face had not suddenly loomed at him out of the wreathing smoke.

Otis would have laughed if he hadn't been nearly out of his wits with fright, because it was some kind of joke, the way this battle seemed to be the exclusive property of a bunch of Harvard men.

This one was staring straight at him only a few feet away. It was his idolized old friend and champion, First Lieutenant Seth Morgan. Seth had wandered away from the costly victory at Culp's Hill into the solitude of the woods, careless of the fall of shot and shell. He was overcome by grief.

Otis carried in the pocket of his coat the scrap of paper that had been Seth's kindly warning, written only a moment before the entire regiment had plunged over the breastworks into the deadly swale below Culp's Hill—the entire regiment, that is, with the exception of Private Otis Pike.

Both Seth and Otis knew the penalty for a fourth desertion. He was to be shot on sight.

OTIS, WHERE WERE YOU?

Corps and other commanders are authorized to order the instant death of any soldier who fails in his duty at this hour.
—Major General George Gordon Meade

The battle of Gettysburg has become one of those legendary nodes of history like Salamis, Waterloo and Trafalgar. Rightly or wrongly it is remembered as the greatest battle of the Civil War.

In Otis Pike's blundering circuit of the battlefield during the aftermath of the immense bombardment, he'd failed to see what every Union soldier waiting behind the stone wall on Cemetery Ridge was never able to forget, the magnificent advance of forty-two regiments of the Army of Northern Virginia, eleven thousand troops of rebel infantry approaching in parade formation across the shallow valley. He was not there to see them falter, cut down like stands of ripened grain by long-range fire from the hills to north and south and double-shotted canister from batteries closer at hand. He did not witness the murderous rifle fire of Hancock's Second Corps nor the flank attacks of Hays to the right and Stannard to the left. Nor did he see Gibbon's triumphant regiments rise from the stone wall to hold aloft their shot-torn flags, nor the retreat of Pickett's division and Pettigrew's and Trimble's shattered brigades, stumbling downhill past their own dead thick on the field.

For Otis the day would be remembered for his one last fearful encounter during the double bombardment, half a mile away from the stone wall on Cemetery Ridge and a full half hour before the Confederate regiments moved out of the trees to begin their fatal assault.

"Oh my God, Otis," shouted Seth, his voice hoarse above the roar of the guns, "it's not you."

Once again Otis felt his knees fail him. A nine-pound ball flew over their heads with a sucking sound and slammed into a tree. The tree exploded in splinters of shredded bark. The noise of the artillery was louder than ever, a perpetual thunder from the pieces massed along the ridge. Otis could not see the guns, but their red flashes colored the smoke like the flames of a burning city, and there was a sharp smell of bursting black powder and the over-heated barrels of the cast-iron guns. The entire force of the Federal batteries on Cemetery Ridge was roaring in concert, aiming a heavy fire across the valley, and solid shot kept falling into the trees from the guns on the other side. One shell shattered a rock not far from Otis, and the fragments spattered his face.

He cried, "No, Seth, no," and held up beseeching hands.

But tears were running down Seth's face as he lifted his rifle. He called out to Otis in anguish, "Charley's dead. They killed Charley Mudge. Tom Fox was hit. Tom Robeson isn't going to make it. Where were you, Otis? Where were you when they told us to cross that swale?"

Seth's rifle was shaking in his hands, but he was only four feet away and he couldn't miss.

Otis had no choice. He pulled out the six-shot Colt revolver he had won in a crap game—it had never before been fired by Otis Pike—and screamed, "Forgive me, Seth," and shot him dead.

PART VII

THE FIELD OF BATTLE

Years hence of these scenes, of these furious passions, these chances,
Of unsurpass'd heroes, (was one side so brave? the other was equally brave;) . . .
Of those armies so rapid so wondrous what saw you to tell us?

—WALT WHITMAN

STRANGELY
BEAUTIFUL

The Gettysburg battlefield was lovely and green, the shallow valley between the battle lines pleasantly rolling. A split-rail fence ran down and up again from the equestrian statue of Robert E. Lee to the road below Cemetery Ridge nearly a mile away.

It was a fine day. As they walked across the field Mary wondered if Pickett's and Pettigrew's men had been aware of the fragrance of the tall grass as they trudged in parade formation up the hill toward the Union guns, or if they had looked down at the wildflowers blossoming around their marching feet. But of course there was probably some other crop growing on the farmer's field that day, not blades of grass intermingled with daisies and yarrow and clover. And surely the brimstone smell of the solid shot and exploding shell of the two-hour bombardment would have overwhelmed the scent of whatever it was that some innocent farmer had planted on this sloping ground earlier the same year.

A five-rail fence ran along each side of the Emmitsburg Road.

Homer's bulk made climbing between the rails difficult, and he complained about being under fire at the same time.

"Well, why don't you duck?" said Mary, but it wasn't funny. She shuddered, remembering what she had read aloud to Homer on the long drive south, the whole story of the march across the valley by the rebel army, straight into the massed rifles and artillery fire of the Yankees behind the stone wall and the brutal raking bombardment of the guns on Cemetery Hill and Little Round Top.

But today there was no gunfire, nothing but the buzz of insects in the grass and the fluting whistle of a bird overhead. The sky was blue and the sun was warm. They climbed over the stone wall and settled down to eat the last of their sandwiches.

Then for a while they wandered here and there among the monuments. The inscriptions recorded the courageous actions of regiments of the seven corps of the Army of the Potomac on the first, second and third days of July in 1863. Moving from one to another, taking in the immensity of the sacrifice, Mary and Homer could think of nothing to say, until Homer groaned that he was still hungry.

"There'll be restaurants in the town," said Mary. "And bookstores. We could find some more books about the battle."

Slowly they walked back across the field. At the rise on the other side they headed for the bronze landmark of Robert E. Lee, still gazing magnificently past them at some vision of his brave regiments moving gloriously up the hill.

The car was parked along the road, in the shade of the trees. Here behind the stone wall there was another reminder of the battle, an endless line of artillery looking silently away from the road toward the gentle rise of Cemetery Ridge.

"They're beautiful," said Homer.

"Strangely beautiful, yes," said Mary. "It's odd to say so, but it's true."

THE SHOP

They ate an early supper in a jolly pub near a large square in the center of town. Then they wandered along the streets of Gettysburg to explore the shops selling books and Civil War memorabilia.

In one they bought a map of the town, and then, exhausted, they went back to the car, meaning to drive straight to the motel and go to bed. It was somewhere out of town, but where?

Mary turned the map this way and that, but it was no use. Folding it again, she said, "We'll have to ask." At the edge of town, they stopped at a store called Bart's Battle Flag Books to inquire the way—and then, of course, there was no harm in looking around.

Bart's was an antiquarian bookstore. A regimental flag hung in the window, a yellow banner with crossed cannon and the embroidered words *Seventh N.Y. Heavy Art.* The inside of the shop was dark and interesting.

"It's like Gwen's attic," murmured Mary. "I mean the way it used to be."

"You mean before Ebenezer came along."

They began with the books. "Surely," said Mary, "they can't all be about the Civil War."

"Well, they are. Look at this—*Gettysburg the First Day, Gettysburg the Second Day, Gettysburg Day Three.*"

"And look, Homer, every general has his own biography. I mean, it's not just Grant and Lee. Who's this handsome general?"

"John Gordon," said Homer. "One of the best of the Confederates."

"I must say, I like good-looking generals. This one must be a Yankee, Winfield Scott Hancock. Yes, I remember Hancock. Wasn't he in this battle?"

"Was Hancock at Gettysburg?" Homer snorted. "The only thing Hancock did at Gettysburg was win the battle almost single-handed. No kidding. He was everywhere, moving troops around in a hurry and filling gaps in the line."

"But why are there so many books about the Civil War? Why such a fascination with this one little piece of history?"

Homer stared at the crowded shelves. "It's because the stakes were so high. So much bloodshed, so many terrible battles. Every human emotion ratcheted up to its highest point. The normal laws of human behavior turned upside down."

"Still—"

Homer was carried away. "Civilization grinding to a halt. Primeval savagery taking over. The pitting of one snarling beast against another, thousands of men against thousands, the games of strategy, the weather, the mud, the bad luck, the colossal mistakes."

"But it's so terrible. There ought to be other ways to settle a dispute."

Homer wasn't listening. "And then there are all the fascinating details, the thousands of separate stories, one for every man who fought on either side. There's no end to it." Then Homer stopped ranting and said, "Well, look at this. What have we got here?" He was trying on a pair of old-fashioned spectacles, hooking them over his ears.

Mary laughed. "Oh, Homer, you look sweet."

"Can't see a thing."

"May I help you?" It was the proprietor, a thin bearded man in a Robert E. Lee T-shirt.

Homer put down the specs and grinned at him politely. "A rebel sympathizer, I guess?"

"No," said the man, "I don't take sides." He patted his chest. "Half the time it's Abraham Lincoln. Name's Bart. What can I do for you?"

Homer took Mary's arm. "We're from Massachusetts. Just tourists, looking around."

"Help yourself," said the proprietor. At once he was captured by another customer.

"Hey, Bart," said the customer, "you know the cavalry battle on the third day, Stuart and Custer? What've you got on the Spencer repeating rifle?"

"Got a book," said Bart. "Follow me."

Mary and Homer drifted to the front of the store and looked at a table covered with antiquities. The wall behind it was hung with looped flags and a pair of moth-eaten coats, one gray, one blue.

"Oh, Homer, look at this, an old stereoscope and a set of cards to go with it."

"I remember those things." Homer put a card in the holder. "Here, try it."

Mary lifted the contraption to her eyes and stared. "It's not working."

"You have to adjust the focus."

She moved the card holder back and forth, and exclaimed, "Oh, it's so real. Oh, Homer, we've got to have this."

"Well, how much is it?"

She found the price tag. "Twenty-five dollars. Oh, but Homer, it's so charming." They looked for Bart, but he was still busy with his customer.

Waiting, they lingered beside the table, inspecting a pair of gold-fringed epaulets in a metal box, half a dozen squash-fronted caps, the tall hat of an officer from Louisiana and a display of regimental belt buckles. There were cartridge boxes and canteens on the table, along with swords, knives and guns. Under a glass dome a small case held a photograph. "Oh, Homer," whispered Mary, bending close, "look at this."

"What?"

"The photograph, look."

Obediently, Homer peered at the little case, which stood open like a book. One side was padded with velvet, the other displayed a photograph in an oval frame. "Some soldier's wife?"

"But Homer, I've seen her before."

"In a book?"

"No, not in a book. In my house."

"*Your* house? You mean in Gwen's house on Barrett's Mill Road?"

"Yes, yes. I recognize her. It's a family picture. She's somebody in our family. Oh, Homer, we've got to have this too."

"Good grief. Well, all right, if it means so much to you." Homer turned to look for the proprietor, then jumped, because Bart was right behind them.

Mary pointed to the small case. "How much is it?"

Bart looked at her. He looked at Homer. They were outsiders, well-spoken tourists. "A hundred and fifty," said Bart.

Homer winced but reached for his checkbook.

"Actually it's part of a set." Bart extracted the little case, wrapped it in tissue paper and handed it over. "Belonged to a member of the Second Massachusetts Volunteer Infantry, a guy named Pike. Otis Pike—he died at Gettysburg."

"Pike?" Homer looked at Mary. "He's on the wall, remember? Otis Pike—his name's on one of the tablets."

"What tablets?" said Bart.

"Oh, Homer, so he is." Mary explained it to Bart. "In Memorial Hall at Harvard. There are a lot of tablets inscribed with the names of students who died in the Civil War."

"No kidding."

"It's part of a set?" Mary tried to sound casual. "What else is in the set?"

There was a pause. "Oh, a lot of things," said Bart. "I've got 'em out back."

"Well, may we see them?" said Homer.

The pause was longer. "Well, they're pretty precious. Because it's a whole collection, you see. For one thing, there's a letter." He looked at them to see the effect of this delicious item.

"A letter?" said Mary. "Who is it addressed to?"

Instead of answering, he listed something else. "And a play."

"A play?" Mary was puzzled. "You mean a play in a book?"

"Right, with the words for one part underlined."

"What play is it?"

But Bart had saved the best for last. "And a coat, a Union army sack coat."

"A coat!" Homer and Mary said it together.

He leaned forward and whispered, "Bloodstained."

Homer glanced at Mary, then asked again, "May we see them?"

Bart blinked. "Well, it would be a whole lot of trouble." Instead of leading the way to some treasury in the back of the store, he stayed put.

Mary controlled her irritation and said softly, "Would twenty-five dollars pay for your trouble?"

"Fifty," he said at once.

Disgusted, Homer jerked at Mary's elbow, but she reached into her bag and counted out the bills. "And twenty-five for the stereoscope."

Bart dropped the stereoscope and the set of cards into a bag. "Wait here," he said, walking briskly away. "I'll be right back."

Homer growled, "What a creep."

"Of course he's a creep," murmured Mary, "but I want to see what he's got. Because there's some connection with this woman, and I recognize her, I know I do."

"But she was Otis Pike's girlfriend. Are you people related to Otis Pike?"

"Not that I know of. But I do know her, I swear I do."

"Well, good for you."

When Bart came back he was carrying a dusty blue coat. He laid it gently on the counter, then lifted the chain pinned to the collar. "Identification tag." He tipped the metal disk toward the light. "Not government issue, they ordered them special."

They bent to look. "George Washington," said Homer.

"Other side." Bart turned the metal tag between his fingers. "See? *2 Reg Mass Volunteers.* That's the Second Massachusetts Volunteer Infantry. His name sort of curves around the outside."

"So it does," said Mary, turning her head sideways. "It says *Otis*

M. Pike." Trying not to show her excitement, she murmured to Homer, "Second Massachusetts, the same regiment. Seth Morgan was in the Second Massachusetts. Homer, they must have known each other."

"Mmm." Homer looked doubtfully at Bart. "You said the coat was bloodstained? I don't see any blood."

"Inside." The proprietor lifted one side of the coat.

They touched the fabric. It was true. The lining was stiff and stained brown where blood had clotted.

"How much for the whole collection?" said Mary boldly.

He answered promptly this time, having worked out the price in the back of the shop. "Two thousand."

"Two thousand!" She was shocked.

"Oh, come on," said Homer, pulling at her arm.

"Very rare," called Bart as they stalked away. "You don't get bloodstains every day. You don't get coats. By rights I oughta ask more."

"We forgot to ask him how to find the motel," said Mary as Homer pulled the car away from the curb.

"Well, I don't dare ask anybody now," said Homer grouchily, "or you'll find something else you've just gotta have."

But Mary was groping happily in the bag from the bookstore. As the car headed vaguely out of town, going in the wrong direction, she fitted a card into the holder.

It was a double image of dead men on the Gettysburg battlefield. The bloating of the bodies showed clearly in three dimensions.

PART VIII

THE SLAUGHTERHOUSE

That slaughterhouse! O well is it their mothers, their sisters cannot see them—cannot conceive, and never conceived, these things. One man is shot by a shell, both in the arm and leg—both are amputated—there lie the rejected members. Some have their legs blown off—some bullets through the breast—some indescribably horrid wounds in the face or head, all mutilated, sickening, torn, gouged out—some in the abdomen—some mere boys—many rebels, badly hurt—they take their regular turns with the rest . . . the pungent, stifling smoke—the radiance of the moon. . . .

—Walt Whitman

IT WAS THE
GENERALS

Almost fainting, Otis dragged Seth's body far into the underbrush. As he laid it down on its side on the ferny bank of a stream, a twelve-pound shell screamed through the treetops and dug a hole on the path where they had been standing only a moment before.

Otis reached out for support and his trembling hand found a tree, but his fingers refused to take hold. He slid down the tree and slumped to his knees. A second shell burst right over his head and another tree cracked and crashed down, but halfway to the ground it hung up in a crotch.

Otis no longer cared. It wasn't the danger that was enfeebling him, it was the shock of what he had this moment done to Seth. *Oh, Seth, it wasn't me, it was this war. It was the generals. They're out to kill us all.*

It was not good enough. There was no pardon, no excuse. Sobbing, Otis struggled to his feet and fumbled through the trees, the thorny undergrowth catching at his trousers. At the edge of the woods he stood panting and looking out on an open field. Gulping lungfuls of the sunlit air, he had the odd notion that he had seen it before, this field, only yesterday, when the regiments of the First Division had been summoned away from Culp's Hill and ordered south. Somehow his frantic gyrations around the battlefield had brought him back. He had come full circle.

And then there was a tremendous shock, and Otis shrieked as something knocked him flat on the ground. Rolling his head sideways, he saw that he had not been struck by a shell but by a maddened horse galloping away lopsided on three legs. Otis leaned up on his elbows and watched it plunge wildly away in the direction of the Baltimore Pike.

The boom of the guns had stopped. Pulling himself upright, he tried to collect his wits. Somehow the blow from the horse had knocked the sobbing out of him. As he walked back to the place where he had left Seth, a plan began to blossom in his head.

So far he had avoided looking at Seth's face, but now he forced himself to reach down with shaking hands and turn Seth over on his back. The sight was sickening. The cartridge of Otis's revolver had destroyed Seth's jaw and sent brain matter gushing from the side of his head. When a bottle fly buzzed down and landed on an open eye, Otis swept it savagely away. Then he hobbled sideways and bent over double, trying to control the shits, the upheaval in his stomach, the outpouring of saliva into his mouth.

But the convulsion passed, and a fit of cold dispassion took its place. Bracing himself, Otis turned back to look carefully at the body on the ground.

The front of Seth's coat was drenched with blood, but a white handkerchief was still jaunty in his breast pocket. Otis remembered that Seth had worn a handkerchief every day, whether in bivouack somewhere or in winter quarters.

The handkerchiefs! The men of Company E had teased their first lieutenant about his pretty handkerchiefs, each with its initial S embroidered in one corner. They had laughed and elbowed each other and called out, "Don't he cut a swell." But Otis knew they envied Seth his loving wife at home.

Now he took the handkerchief out of Seth's pocket and inspected it, finding only a little blood along one side. He folded it and put it back. Then, ransacking the rest of Seth's pockets, he found nothing but a small case containing a letter and the photograph of a pretty young woman.

She was Seth's wife, the one whose devoted hands had made the handkerchiefs. Otis looked at her hungrily and stroked the glass over her face. It occurred to him that her husband no longer had any rights in the matter. Why shouldn't Otis Pike be the possesser of this sweet creature? Hastily Otis snapped the case shut, tucked it into his pocket and sat down to get his tangled thoughts in order.

Before long it was clear what he must do. He would have to obliterate everything that made this piece of mortal flesh recognizable as First Lieutenant Seth Morgan of Tom Robeson's Company E in Charley Mudge's Second Massachusetts Volunteer Infantry. No enlisted man or officer in that regiment, no friend in another outfit must be able to recognize those mild blue eyes, that generous nose and what was left of that amiable mouth.

Steeling himself, Otis cocked his revolver and waited for another burst of cannonfire. It did not come. Sobbing again, he took aim and pulled the trigger.

Oh, Seth, oh, God forgive me, Seth. Blood was erupting in another fountain. Blubbering, Otis backed away, but the crimson gout soon stopped and he could see that he had been successful. No one would ever recognize that butchered carcass now.

The rest of the task was also brutally distasteful. By the time Otis had unbuttoned and removed Seth's sack coat and heaved the body back and forth and wrestled it into his own coat, his hands were sticky with Seth's blood. Then, flinching, he had to thrust his trembling arms into the sleeves of Seth's blood-drenched coat and pull it close and button it over his own chest.

The next task was harder still, the exchange of official identities. It was truly fortunate that both of them had invested in metal name tags. Seth's was pinned to his coat. Otis had his on a fancy chain. Gritting his teeth, he dragged the chain down over the hideous head and settled it around Seth's grisly neck. Then he unpinned Seth's star-shaped tag and threw it into a bushy tangle.

Finished at last, he collapsed a few feet away from the body and wept and cursed the generals, wept and cursed the war, wept and cursed himself. When the fit subsided he lay down exhausted and drained of all feeling, uninterested in the sound that floated toward him on the breeze, threadlike and delicate, the sound of cheering.

Stay put, he told himself. *Wait till it gets dark.* No living soul would be out there in that swale after dark. And anyway the presence of a man in a bloodstained coat carrying the body of a fellow soldier would seem perfectly natural.

The fact that this body was being brought *forward* rather than *away* would not be noticed in the dark.

And the air seemed to promise rain. The fierce moonlight that had poured down over the field of battle yesterday would tonight be lost in clouds. At midnight he would set down in the middle of the swale the remains of that gallant warrior, Otis Mathias Pike, a hero in the battle for the possession of Culp's Hill.

MORNING REPORT

Next day the morning report for the Second Massachusetts was as melancholy as that of any other regiment in all the seven corps that had fought in the three-day battle.

First there was an address by Major Morse, who had taken the place of Colonel Mudge as commander of the regiment. His speech was partly a congratulation to the troops for the courage of their assault on the trenches the day before. "Did you see that, boys? General Slocum, his whole staff, did you see the way they took off their hats?" But mostly his address was a eulogy for Colonel Mudge. The colonel's death was no news to the remaining members of the regiment. They had all seen Charley Mudge go down.

It was raining when the first sergeants called the roll. The men stood huddled under their blankets, wincing at the pauses when nobody answered. Although all the men in Company E knew about Captain Tom Robeson, they hung their heads when he failed to respond.

But there were surprises in the rest of the roll call.

"Lieutenant Seth Morgan?"

When there was no answer, the sergeant spoke up louder, "Lieutenant Morgan? Seth?"

There was still no answer. Seth's fellow officers looked at each other. The sergeant leaned toward a corporal and muttered a question. The corporal, who was acting as company clerk, consulted his sheet. "No, sir," he said. "He's not here no place among the wounded."

"Well, what about the dead?" whispered the sergeant.

"He's not there neither."

The sergeant whistled under his breath. The clerk moved his pencil to the column headed "MISSING" and scribbled, "1st Lt. Seth Morgan," and the sergeant continued to call the roll.

When he got down to the *P*s there was another pause after he called the name of Private Otis Pike. During the silence there were snickers. *Otis must have skedaddled.*

"Put the damn fool down as missing," said the sergeant, but then the corporal leaned toward him and whispered, "No, sir, that ain't right, sir. Otis Pike's daid."

"Dead!"

The corporal tapped his sheet and pointed to a name.

"Well, if that don't beat all. How did the poor bastard manage to get himself killed?"

The corporal looked around and whispered to another sergeant, then cleared his throat. "Sir, Sergeant Willow here was in the burial detail." The corporal wagged his head in the direction of Culp's Hill. "He found Otis layin' out there daid."

"Out there?" The first sergeant couldn't believe it. He raised his eyebrows at Sergeant Willow, who stepped forward and gave his report.

"Private Pike, that's right, his body was out there, sir. I didn't recognize it at first because his head was all"—the sergeant swept a hand across his face—"well, it was mostly gone, but he had a tag on him, and it was Otis all right. He was out there way in front."

"In front? What do you mean, in front?"

"Right behind Colonel Mudge, sir, that's where he was." Sergeant Willow looked uncomfortable. "Believe it or not, sir."

"Well, if that don't beat the devil." The first sergeant cleared his throat and called out the next name. "Alpheus Peterson?"

"Here, sir."

"Private Scopes?" The first sergeant looked more closely at his list. "Private Lemuel Scopes?"

No answer.

"He's daid, sir," said the corporal.

"What about his brother?" The sergeant read the name aloud, "Rufus Scopes?"

Again there was no answer.

"Both of 'em's daid, sir," murmured the corporal. "They was twins."

"I know they was twins," said the first sergeant angrily. Muddled, he looked fiercely back at his list. "Private Tatum?"

"Daid too, sir."

When the miserable morning report was completed, the regimental adjutant called out, "Company captains, I believe two of you are replacements? I hope both of you took down the names of the dead and missing, because you're supposed to write to their next of kin."

Then the first sergeant bent his head over the corporal's roll, signed his name, and handed it to the company's new captain, who also signed his name, and then the regimental adjutant gathered up all the morning reports and took them to his soggy tent on the outskirts of Gettysburg, there to be consolidated and sent on to the acting assistant adjutant general of the Second Brigade. From brigade level the expanded report would be passed along to the headquarters of the First Division and from there to the central command of the entire Twelfth Corps. At last the report containing the final official figures for all the regiments of the First Division during the Battle of Gettysburg would make its way to the staff of General Meade himself, to be tallied in his final battle report and packed off to the headquarters of the Army of the Potomac in Washington, where it would become part of the vast collection of papers documenting the land campaigns of the entire Union army and the maritime history of the navy.

General Meade's final battle report was of no concern to the staff officers of the Second Massachusetts Volunteer Infantry. But

Sergeant Willow, who had been in charge of removing the bodies to the place where they were to be temporarily buried—a pit was being dug for them beside the field hospital for the Twelfth Corps—was dissatisfied.

He should have piped up during roll call when Otis Pike was reported dead. He should have spoken up then, because he had something to say about the burial detail and the body of Otis Pike. After all, collecting corpses was not the jim-dandiest detail you could ever be on, because of the smell in the first place, and then you had to keep the varmints at bay, not to mention the grief of the thing, so he had only been doing his unfortunate duty, groping around all those swollen bodies into their pockets and so on, looking for personal possessions to be sent home to grieving wives and sweethearts. And then when he got to Otis's corpse he had been mystified by the small amount of blood on his coat.

Sergeant Luther Willow was an ardent reader of dime novels. He was familiar with the gallant exploits of the London police in their pursuit of dastardly criminals. And like the admirable police detective Benjamin Bone, Sergeant Willow always examined the pattern of the bloodstains on the bodies of the men he found dead on the battlefield. Of course they were battle casualties, not murder victims, but in making his own personal investigations he felt like a colleague of Detective Bone.

The rebel shell that had blown away the face of Private Otis Pike had left very little blood on the coat—that was the peculiar thing. You would have thought it would be soaked in blood, if not on the front, then on the back, where he was lying in it. Instead, there was only a little on the lining and some superficial stains on the front, almost like the prints of a hand. It didn't seem natural.

In his perplexity Sergeant Willow had removed the coat from the body and set it aside, along with the metal tag and the items from the pockets of both the coat and the trousers. He had written the words "PVT. OTIS PIKE" on a piece of paper and pinned it to Otis's shirt. Maybe tomorrow, he'd go around to wherever the Tenth Maine had settled down, the regiment of provost guards for the Twelfth Corps, and interest somebody in this little battlefield mystery.

Unfortunately he didn't get around to it for a couple of days, and by then it was too late. Tenth Maine, Second Massachusetts and

the entire rest of the army were on the move again. Pike's possessions, including his mysteriously clean sack coat, were carefully
ticketed and sent away to a collecting point in the city of Washington, along with thousands of other personal possessions of the men
who had died at Gettysburg.

Sergeant Willow never saw the coat again.

PART IX

THE NUTTINESS OF EBENEZER

THE HAIR
PRESUMPTIVE

It was even worse than they had feared.

They had not written to Howie "Ebenezer" Flint to tell him they were coming. They had not even phoned, in case he put them off.

Therefore when he opened his front door a crack and saw them standing on his sagging front porch, his jaw dropped and his face flushed, deepening from pink to purple.

Howie had never met Homer and he had not seen Mary since they were children. And yet he seemed to guess at once that they were a threat. "You can't come in," he whispered. "I am the hair presumptive."

"You're what?" Mary put out her hand. "Oh, come on, Howie, we're kinfolk. Remember when you came to Concord with your family? When we were children? I'm Gwen's sister Mary and this is my husband, Homer. We just want to talk to you."

Howie's eyes swiveled back and forth between the two tall people standing on the drooping floorboards of his front porch. His eyes were small and glittering behind little old-fashioned glasses. They failed to see Mary's friendly hand.

It was obvious that the idiotic boy Gwen had known as a child had fulfilled his early promise. "Actually," said Howie, keeping a firm grip on the door, "I am quite ill. Last week I was at the point of death." He coughed.

"Oh, look, Howie"—Mary adopted her best wheedling tone— "we've come all this way. You can't refuse to see your own third cousin twice removed."

Reluctantly Howie at last opened the door just wide enough for them to squeeze through.

Only when they were inside did the full glory of his whiskers burst upon their gaze. Howie's whiskers were full and dark, thick and hateful, a bushy growth eighteen inches long. Homer decided gleefully that they were a sort of statement—*I may be a total flop at everything else, but at least my chin is a genius.*

"Thank you, Howie," said Mary, trying not to exclaim at the extravagant growth of his beard nor stare around at the rubbish in the hall. The interior of Howie's house was a classic case of the newspaper headline, OLD COUPLE FOUND DEAD AMONG STACKS OF OLD NEWSPAPERS.

"My name's not Howie," growled Howie, "it's Ebenezer."

"But didn't it used to be—"

"Legally changed in a court of law. I have chosen to be known by the name of my great-great-grandfather."

"Your great-great-grandfather was called Ebenezer?"

The little eyes flashed behind the tiny specs. "Right. And he was not a traitor like *your* great-great-grandfather."

The shaft went home, and Mary winced. But perhaps this fool had found out something she didn't know. Quickly she said, "You mean Seth Morgan was a traitor? What kind of traitor?"

The little eyes shifted. "I don't know exactly. I just know it was something shameful."

Something shameful. It was the old family story. Mary was disappointed. The silly man knew no more about Seth Morgan than she did. "Listen here, Howie," she began boldly. "Oh, sorry, I mean Ebenezer. We'd like to see the things you"—she stopped just in time to avoid the word *swiped*—"the things you borrowed from my sister's house last month."

Ebenezer twiddled his fingers in his beard and said craftily, "I didn't borrow them. Actually, I took what is jurisdicially mine."

"Yours! But you removed them from her house without permission."

"Since we have the same great-great-*great*-grandfather," said Howie, jutting his chin forward stubbornly—a fearsome gesture because his whiskers jutted forward at the same time—"all family documents belong to the posterior equally. I am a legal derelict and posterior. Therefore I have as much right to them as she does. Or you neither."

Bewildered, Mary turned to Homer, who was keeping a firm hold on the muscles of his face. In a strained voice he said, "I think Ebenezer is referring to posterity."

"Oh, of course." Mary turned back to Ebenezer. "But surely that's not so. Those things have been in my sister's house for nearly a hundred and fifty years."

"I think you will find," said Ebenezer smugly, "that the entire specter of the law is on my side."

ONCE AGAIN, HER FACE

This was no time to quibble about who owned what. Homer nudged his wife. "Show him the photograph we bought in Gettysburg."

"Yes, of course." Mary rummaged in her bag and unwrapped the little leather case. Opening it, she said, "I don't know who this young girl is, but I recognize her. I know I've seen her before, perhaps in Gwen's attic. I wonder if you have her picture among the things you took away?"

Ebenezer stared at the photograph. At once his demeanor changed. He became the proud antiquarian. "Hey, you guys, you want to see what I got?"

"Oh, yes," said Mary.

"Follow me." Zigzagging between the piled-up boxes in the narrow front hall, he led them into a cluttered room.

"My Civil War museum," he said grandly, flourishing a pudgy

hand. From somewhere, as if by magic, there was music, fifes and drums.

His museum was a chaos of miscellaneous objects arranged on a couple of card tables and a sideboard. "Priceless," said Ebenezer, spreading out his arms. "My collection is priceless."

Homer bent to look at a crosscut saw and said, "You're into carpentry?"

Ebenezer chuckled. "Amputational instrument from Bull Run. Cut off thousands of arms and legs, I'll bet."

"Umph," said Homer, who had bought a similar saw at Vanderhoof's Hardware Store. Politely he moved on to the next item on display, a small box with a gold ring nestled in a bed of cotton.

"You won't believe my good luck," said Ebenezer, cooing over it. "This very ring"—his voice took on a reverent vibrato—"was removed from the finger of Abraham Lincoln by his grief-struck wife on the occasion of his decease." He rolled his eyes. "Pricey, it was very pricey."

"Mmm, I should think so," murmured Mary. The object in the box was obviously a fraternity ring from some jolly Greek-letter band of brothers.

"Oh, there's so much more." Ebenezer's enthusiasm bubbled over. He grew more and more excited, showing them one absurdity after another.

They looked on politely, but Homer was more interested in Ebenezer's euphoric state than in the exhibits in his museum. Enthusiasm was all very well—in fact he himself moved through life on cresting waves of euphoria—but Ebenezer's was completely out of control. Combined with stupidity and ignorance, it was positively dangerous.

"I've got John W. Booth's pistol here somewhere," he said. He scrabbled in the mess on one of the card tables, knocking aside a bag of groceries, which tipped over and fell with a crash.

"Whoopsie," said Ebenezer. With a hysterical giggle he dropped to hands and knees.

Mary helped him pick up the tumbled soup cans, trying to think of an excuse to get away. The day was getting on and it was a long drive home. But then under the last tin of chicken noodle soup she found another small leather case. It had fallen open, displaying the photographs of a man and a woman.

The glass over both pictures had been broken, but the woman on the right was the one whose likeness they had bought yesterday in Gettysburg.

Beaming, Mary stood up and showed the battered case to Homer.

"My God, you were right," he said. "It's the same woman. The man must be her husband. He must be Seth, your great-great-grandfather. Then the woman would be your great-great-grandmother."

"Well, perhaps that's who they are. Anyway, I remember the two of them together." Gently she laid the case on the table and set down beside it the one from Gettysburg.

"Goodness me," said Ebenezer, gazing at them. "Where did you get the other one?"

"In Gettysburg. What was the name of the shop, Homer?"

"Bart, the guy's name was Bart. Bart's Battle Flag Books, that was it."

"May I ask," said Ebenezer sweetly, "how much you paid for it?" Mary told him. His eyebrows shot up and he whistled.

"Oh, Bart was a scoundrel," said Homer. "All his prices were ridiculous. He said it was part of a set. He tried to sell us a whole bunch of other stuff that was supposed to go with it, but he wanted a couple of thousand for it, so we left."

"Other stuff?" whispered Ebenezer. "What sort of other stuff?"

"Oh, there was a uniform coat. He was really proud of the coat because of the blood on it, and—*ouch.*" Mary had stepped on his foot. "Oh, well, I dunno what else he had," he finished lamely. "We didn't offer to buy it. We couldn't afford it."

Ebenezer seemed to forget about the matching pictures, the bloodstained coat and Bart's bookstore in Gettysburg. He waved them across to the display on the sideboard.

And here Mary took alarm at another priceless piece of Lincoln memorabilia, a kerosene lantern labeled "THE LAMP BESIDE THE DEATHBED." Well, that was ridiculous. But so was the attached price tag: *$350.*

She looked at Ebenezer, scandalized. "Are these things for sale?"
He looked modestly down. "But you see, I am a well-known dealer in historical momentos."

Her heart sank. "Ebenezer, you're not selling the family things?" Before he could answer, she snatched up the little broken case again and turned it over. A price tag was pasted on the back. Ebenezer was offering for sale this precious photograph of two people related to the family—his family as well as hers—for $750.

There followed a nasty scene—rage on Mary's part, giggles and protestations on the part of Ebenezer and an attempt at rational argument by Homer.

Glowering at Ebenezer, he warned him that they were on their way to visit a friend in the local judiciary. This old friend would clap a restraining order on Ebenezer, forbidding him to sell a single solitary thing that had been removed from Mary's sister's house.

Ebenezer had an immediate change of heart. "Take it," he said, thrusting the broken pictures into Mary's hands. "Here, these too. And here's some more." He snatched up scraps of yellowed documents without looking at them and held them high.

Mary looked at his handfuls with scorn, but Homer accepted them graciously and folded them to his chest. "Come on, my dear," he said. "Thank you, Ebenezer. We'll come back another day."

"Homer," said Mary, as the door slammed behind them and they teetered across the sloping porch, "who do you know on the bench in Washington?"

Homer grinned. "Not a soul. But I don't trust old Ebenezer, that important posterior and derelict, any farther than I can see him. Somebody at home must know a practicing magistrate around here. In the meantime, I doubt Ebenezer will dare to sell a thing."

"Oh, good for you, Homer."

"But we're not going home yet."

"We aren't? Oh, Homer, I'm dying to go home."

"There's something we've got to do first. We've got to get back to Bart's Bookstore in Gettysburg before Ebenezer gets there first and snatches up that goddamned bloody coat." He unlocked the car, tossed Ebenezer's trash onto the backseat and got in behind the wheel.

Mary sighed and climbed in beside him. Then, while Homer lunged back down the highway in the direction of Gettysburg, she picked up the stereoscope, plucked another card out of the box of stereographs, tucked it into the wire holder and adjusted the gadget in and out until the two pictures became one and jumped into three dimensions.

At once the cluster of men in the foregound stood away from the tent in the background. What was going on? Then she saw the bare leg hanging from a table. One of the soldiers was holding a white cloth over the face of a prostrate patient. In the center, caught forever in the moment before amputating one of the patient's legs, stood a man with a saw.

PART X

IDA

There stood the surgeons, their sleeves rolled up to the elbows, their bare arms as well as their linen aprons smeared with blood, their knives not seldom held between their teeth. . . . Around them pools of blood and amputated arms and legs in heaps sometimes more than a man high.

—GENERAL CARL SCHURZ

THE SURGEON

In the vestibule of the courthouse the surgeon could not spare a hand to mop away the sweat on his face or the tears that kept running down his cheeks. The tears were partly from exhaustion and partly from the perpetual anguish of caring for an endless succession of mangled men.

Now his left hand held the forceps clamped on the severed end of an artery, and with his right he was trying to tie the ligature. His steward reached out to help, but his clumsy fingers grazed the forceps and the artery slipped back out of sight.

The woman was the last straw. When a shadow eclipsed the sunlight from the open door, the surgeon glanced around and saw her, then looked back angrily at the mess on the table, the wreck of a boy no older than fifteen.

He pitied these women, but he was sick of them, sick to death of their doleful questions, their weeping, their habit of swooning at the sight of a gangrenous leg. And then, of course, he had to stop whatever he was doing and take care of them first.

This one was obviously in a family way. She'd be more trouble than all the rest. In a minute she'd keel over when she caught sight of the basket under the stairs, or faint away from the smell of ether and chloroform and the reek of suppurating wounds combined with the general town stench of the dead horses that hadn't been buried yet.

Or maybe the wretched mother-to-be would venture past him into the courtroom, where hundreds of men lay naked on the bare floor with nothing but newspapers to keep off the flies. Even out here with the door shut, she could hear their whimpering cries.

The surgeon did not turn around again. He checked the tourniquet, tightened it a little, made another attempt to tie the ligature, succeeded, picked up his instrument, judged the line his saw would take—it was a single-flap amputation—and got to work.

But his strength was draining away, the nervous energy that had kept him going day after day when he had hardly paused for food, only sipping a little whiskey now and then, managing only a few hours of sleep, falling like a dead man on a horsehair settee in the judge's private chamber, now cluttered with waiting coffins.

He did not look at the woman, but knowing that she was there, he edged sideways to hide the back-and-forth movement of the tool in his hand. No doubt she could guess what was going on. She could see his right elbow driving back and forth and hear the brittle rasp of the saw. Any moment now she'd crumple to the floor and give birth.

Still she uttered no sound. When the last shred of skin was cut through and the severed leg tossed into the basket, he left the task of dressing the stump to his steward and turned around to glower at the woman.

She was deathly pale, but still standing. "Sir," she said quickly, seizing the moment, "I've come to Gettysburg to find my husband. His name's Seth Morgan. He's a first lieutenant in the Second Massachusetts. No one seems to know where he is. I tried to find Colonel Mudge, but they told me he was killed at a place called Culp's Hill."

"Oh, yes," said the doctor, who had received some of the wounded from that criminally stupid attack. His grim look soft-

ened. "There must have been a muster after the battle," he said
kindly. "Do you know who took Colonel Mudge's place? Surely
someone will have a list."

The boy on the table whimpered, and the surgeon spoke testily
to the steward, "Keep it up, keep it up." Obediently the young man
dripped more ether on the cloth over the soldier's face.

"Oh, yes, there was a list in the paper, the Philadelphia paper. I
saw it, the casualties for the Twelfth Corps, and my husband was
listed as missing. And I met a corporal in his company just now,
but he hadn't seen Seth since the fighting. I'm not sure, but I think
that's what he said. I believe the corporal wasn't very well."

Drunk, guessed the surgeon. "Well, of course the roster of the
wounded isn't complete yet." He looked at her doubtfully. "If your
husband was wounded, you might find him in the hospital for the
Twelfth Corps. You see, they sort them out by corps."

"Where?" she said quickly. "Tell me where to go."

For a moment he considered, looking at her silently. "Are you
sure? Perhaps it would not be wise for a woman in your—"

"Where is it? Tell me." Then she had to stand aside because the
next case was coming in, slung in a blanket between two young
women.

Carefully they rolled the new patient onto the table. It was a
head wound this time. The boy's face was flushed with fever. He
was thrashing from side to side.

With relief the surgeon dismissed the woman. "I believe the
Twelfth Corps hospital is in a barn somewhere south of town."

She said something, probably "Thank you," and he heard the
swish of her skirt against the frame of the door.

The poor woman is in for a shock, thought the surgeon, handing
the can of ether to the steward. If her husband's name was not on
the muster roll of dead and wounded after the fracas at Culp's Hill,
and if he hadn't been seen since the battle, most likely he was a
deserter.

The surgeon grimaced at Sally and Sarah. "Go on home, you
two. William and I'll get along first-rate."

Sally folded the blanket and shook her head. Sarah said softly,
"Sir, I'm afraid there's two more have died."

A TIDY LITTLE
VILLAGE

My, but the white went quickly. None of us had any white petti-coats as it was all cut up for bandages.
—NELLIE AUGINBAUGH, GETTYSBURG

Second Massachusetts?" The officer was in a hurry. His tent was being dismantled. There was a thump, and one of the canvas walls collapsed. "Here, ma'am, we'd better step outside." He took Ida by the elbow and led her out into the hay field, where the flattened grass was wet and and the harvest spoiled.

"The hospital for the Twelfth Corps, it's way south." He pointed. "It's Mr. Bushman's property, a big barn, way down the Taneytown Road, and then you go east." He gave Ida a sidelong glance. "In the morning maybe somebody'll be going that way."

"I can walk," said Ida. "Which way is the Taneytown Road?"

"Well, this here's Baltimore Street. You go south a little way and you come to a fork and you take the right fork, and then pretty soon there's another fork and you go left. Then you go on about three-quarter mile, and there's a track to the right. You turn there and pass the schoolhouse. It was a hospital, but not the one you want, missus, so you keep on and pretty soon there's a turnoff and you go right again. From there it's another mile or so, and after a while you'll see Mr. George Bushman's barn. That's the one for the Twelfth Corps."

"The right fork," repeated Ida. "Then left, then right and right again. Thank you."

"You'll wait till morning, won't you, missus? It'll be dark soon and you shouldn't be out there, not now, not all by yourself." When Ida merely smiled and turned away, his conscience must have bothered him because he said, "You're staying someplace, missus?"

"Oh, yes," said Ida.

"Well, good night then, ma'am."

The Taneytown Road was just where he had said it would be. Ida walked quickly. There was still plenty of light, but she must hurry because by the time she reached the hospital the sky would be dark.

She had no question about what she should do. Turning onto the Taneytown Road and tramping along in her sturdy boots, she felt no doubt at all. Ida was a tall, big-boned woman, and carrying the child seemed to have made her stronger. She felt well, rather than sickly like poor cousin Cornelia, back there in Philadelphia.

But Ida blessed Cornelia's lying-in. It was providential that Ida had taken the cars from Boston to be at her cousin's side just at this time, because no sooner had Cornelia been brought to bed than the Philadelphia paper had come out with the terrifying news of the battle. If Ida had been at home in Concord when she saw Seth's name among the missing, she might have despaired of making the long journey south to look for him. And her mother would never have let her go.

But in Philadelphia she was her own woman. Ida had dropped the newspaper, pinned on her money belt, packed her valise, embraced Cornelia, kissed the baby and set off. Now, by hook or by crook, by horsecar and railroad and a coach from the town of Westminster, she had found her way to Gettysburg. She was here, calmly purposeful, serenely resolved to search anywhere and everywhere. She would find him, she knew she would, she was certain sure, because it was just a matter of not giving up.

Stepping down from the coach and walking along the main street of Gettysburg, Ida had perceived at once that the entire town

was a hospital. She had seen litters carried into the Express Office
and a dead man carted off from the Eagle Hotel. Ambulances
swayed along the main street, their horses pulling up at house
doors. Ida had felt the urgency all around her. Men and women
were hurrying up and down the street and in and out of
dwellings—on desperate errands, guessed Ida. Even a boy driving a
cow along the street looked careworn and harassed.

Surely a missing man might be overlooked in this confusion,
wounded perhaps and not yet recorded, his name not written
down.

Ida asked the first person she met, a woman in a blood-spattered
apron, where she should begin to look, but the woman merely
shook her head and walked rapidly away with her tray of rolled-up
lint. When Ida saw the open door of a store with all its merchan-
dise painted on the side—DRY GOODS, NOTIONS, CARPETS, OIL-
CLOTHS, HARDWARE, IRON NAILS—she walked in. No dry goods or
carpets were visible anywhere, only boxes and barrels stamped SAN-
ITARY COMISSION.

From somewhere in the back came the shriek of nails being
clawed up from the lids of boxes. Ida sought out the man with the
crowbar and found him opening crates of clothing. She wondered
if any of the shirts in the crates had been made by Concord
women.

"Please, sir," said Ida, "I'm trying to find my husband. Can you
tell me where I should look?"

The man put down his crowbar and wiped his forehead. "Good
heavens, ma'am, you look in a fair way to need a chair." He swung
one out from behind the counter and Ida politely sat down. "Well,
there's all these people's houses you could look into, but my advice
is, try the churches or maybe the courthouse first. Big places like
that, they got a lot more."

"Thank you," said Ida, smiling at him and rising from the chair.
And so, following his pointing hand, she had begun with the courthouse.

Now, walking south as she had been told to do, she looked left
and right, curious about a village that only ten days ago must have
been very much like her own. The town of Gettysburg was now a
desperate resource in a time of crisis, a refuge for thousands of

battle-wounded men. It was clear to Ida that all its citizens had dropped whatever they had been doing last June. Now in this terrible month of July they were helping out however they could with the wreckage left behind by a war that had moved on someplace else.

She hurried on in the direction of the Taneytown Road, passing a flower bed that was now a butcher's refuse dump of sawed-off arms and legs, and a tannery that was shut up tight and a newspaper office from which no cheerful clatter of presses rattled out into the road. Only at an open shed belonging to J. H. GARLACH, CARPENTER, was normal business going on, if the making of coffins could be called normal.

Next door to Mr. Garlach, a wheelwright was hard at work mending the smashed wheel of a gun carriage. Down the road from his shop Ida could hear the clanging ring of a hammer, and soon she was walking past the dark cavern of a smithy, where the blacksmith was pounding a glowing iron tire on his forge.

She walked on, looking for the fork in the road, then stood aside for a girl in a floury apron who was running into town with a basket of new-made bread. Ida couldn't help exclaiming, "Oh, how good it smells!"

"It's my brick oven," said the girl proudly. She stopped running, eager to talk. "I've been baking all day for a week, all the loaves I can pack in my oven at once. There were twenty-five barrels of flour in the shed when I started that first day. Now there's only five, so Father cut the rest of the field today with his new reaping machine."

"Oh my," said Ida, wanting to praise her. "A reaping machine! Think of that!"

IDA ON THE BATTLEFIELD

A crude sign was nailed to a tree:

15 REBS
BURIED HERE

But the worst thing were the dead horses. Ida was surprised by the length of their swollen carcasses stretched out like that on the ground. The smell was very bad. She took out a handkerchief—it was of her own making—and held it over her nose. A little way off, a boy was robbing an animal of its saddle. He seemed undaunted by the overpowering stench, but he was having a hard time with the girth because it had been strained to the breaking point by the bloating of the horse's belly.

Ida tramped on over the deeply rutted road, imagining the traffic that had come this way last week, the trains of ambulances going and coming, the ammunition wagons, the horse-drawn artillery and the marching men. She had to pick her way carefully among the ruts and ridges to avoid the litter of battle—a dead mule, a caisson on a smashed limber, rags of clothing, blankets sopping from the recent rain, rotting pieces of salt pork and spongy masses of hardtack.

Her boots sank in where the mud was soft. But they were old and comfortable and her burdens were light, both the baby inside her and the valise in her hand. Ida strode along briskly, leaning a little backward. On the journey from Philadelphia her good dress had lost its crispness, but it swayed easily as she walked. Under the bulging skirt her money belt was comfortable, riding high under her bosom, keeping her banknotes safe.

She began passing clusters of men in uniform, mostly in their shirtsleeves because the day had been warm. Some of them stared open-mouthed at the strange sight of a woman in a family way walking alone on the battlefield. One of them spoke to her kindly. "Missus, do you need help?"

"No, but thank you," said Ida. Sturdily she walked on and on. Beside the road at one place was a half-ruined farmhouse where more dead horses lay, strung up by their bridles to the fence rail. In the field below the farmhouse stood a magnificent Pennsylvania barn, and she couldn't help wondering about the poor farmer whose crops had been trampled by the heedless ferocity of the two opposing armies. War, thought Ida, pitying him, was a cruel law unto itself, trumping the pitiful documents of righteous ownership, like the deed to their own Concord farm locked safely away in the bank on the Milldam.

It occurred to her that she was walking over property lines, although she didn't know the names of the owners. She didn't know that one of the hills on the left side of the road belonged to a farmer named Culp, where the Twelfth Corps had been heavily engaged in a bloody two-day battle, where her husband Seth had survived the carnage of the attack across the swale on the morning of the third day. She was not aware that the ruined cottage with the dead horses had been the home of a widow Leister until it was preempted by General Meade himself, nor that the great barn below it lay in the middle of the battlefield. Turning into the lane that led past the schoolhouse, she saw a weathered sign pointing to the outbuildings of another farm. Where was that poor farmer now?

When the schoolhouse came in sight, Ida was surprised to see that it was not like the small wooden schools scattered around the town of Concord. This one was made of stone, and instead of boys and girls, a few men and women were carrying cots and bedding to a wagon drawn up on the road.

One of the women had a basket of bloodstained sheets. As she set it down in the wagon, she looked up sharply.

Ida nodded at her politely, thinking, *Sanitary Commission.* But she hurried her footsteps, not wanting to be stopped, quelling an impulse to tell the woman that she had helped raise money for the Sanitary at a First Parish fair. She had knitted countless mittens for the Concord Soldiers Aid Society. She had made fifteen pairs of drawers.

"Pretty soon there's a turnoff," the officer had said. Yes, there it was, another narrow lane. But at once Ida had to move out of the way of a team pulling a heavily loaded wagon. Piled high on the wagon bed were crates of ducks and chickens, mounds of household things and a dozen pieces of furniture, including a chest of drawers with a mirror that gleamed with the last of the daylight. High above everything else, three children huddled on a mattress. A skep of bees wobbled in the back.

The two plodding horses were driven by a woman hunched forward on the seat. Ida smiled at her, but the woman in the sunbonnet was too caught up in her own misery to smile in return. She did not glance at Ida as the wagon lumbered to the corner of the schoolhouse road, its wheels creaking, the children swaying left and right.

Ida did not blame her. She knew how she would feel if their own farm had been blown to pieces, if their own peach and apple trees had been shattered by shot and shell, if she and Seth had been turned out to make way for a battle, along with their mothers, her younger brothers Eben and Josh and her little sisters Sally and Alice. Where on earth would they go with their high-piled wagon?

Soon it would be too dark to see. Ida walked faster, keeping her eyes on the road, fearful of stumbling or turning her ankle on a stone. But when she looked up she saw a looming shape off to the left. Surely it was the barn she was looking for.

How big it was! But all the barns in this part of the country were as big as churches, towering buildings on high foundations. Their size and bulk must mean abundant harvests. Beside them, the barns of her own little town, far away to the north, seemed modest and hardscrabble.

No cattle grazed around the Bushman barn, although the pasture was dotted with green clumps where last year's cowpats had nourished the soil. One field was yellow with timothy ripe for the cutting, as though Mr. Bushman's farm lay nowhere near a battlefield.

Two boards had been nailed to a fence post. In the darkening shade under the trees Ida could barely make, out the words:

$\longleftarrow$ HOSPITAL XII CORPS

HOSPITAL II CORPS $\longrightarrow$

A cart track led off to the right, but Ida obediently went left, and circled around the barn to the rear. Here a couple of horses stood saddled and bridled, their reins secured to a spike. There were ambulances under the trees, their humped white shapes visible in the half-light, their shafts resting on the ground.

Ida climbed the grassy ramp to the upper floor of the barn and walked through the high open door. At home this level of the barn would house the two horses and the cow. Here there were no horses and no cows. The livestock had been driven away.

At first, as she looked into the darkness, it was evident that this emergency hospital was in better case than the one in the courthouse. The men lay on cots, and in the darkness she could see their white bedding going back and back in orderly rows. But the smells of putrefying wounds and gangrene were the same, and there was a strange noise like a barking dog.

For a moment Ida stood in the high doorway, shy of entering without permission, knowing that she made an odd silhouette against the fading light. Pale faces turned to look at her, a few heads lifted and sank back. Someone at the other end was moaning. The yelping came from a bed close by, where a poor man was throwing himself up and down.

An orderly hurried forward and asked her brusquely, "What do you want, missus?"

Nothing could stop Ida now. "I'm looking for my husband," she said calmly. "First Lieutenant Seth Morgan, Second Massachusetts."

"Well, fine, ma'am, is his name on the list?"

"What list?"

"The muster roll. Every regiment had a roll call. You mean you haven't looked at the muster roll?"

"No," said Ida. "But the Philadelphia paper said he was missing."

The orderly was carrying a malodorous vessel. "Well, I'm sorry, ma'am," he said crossly. "We're busy here, I should think you could see that."

Ida persisted. "I only want to look for him. I just want to walk along here and see."

The orderly was almost weeping with exasperation. He gestured to the wide blue square of the door with his utensil. "Go and find yourself a midwife."

"It's all right, Sergeant." Another man appeared out of the dark. "I'm making my rounds. She can come with me."

MR. BUSHMAN'S BARN

There was a note of home in the doctor's voice. He introduced himself as Dr. Chapel. Gratefully Ida followed him from bed to bed, looking eagerly as he lifted his lantern over each face in turn. Soon she put out her hand for the lantern and he gave it to her, leaving his own hands free to remove a dressing or examine the stump of a leg.

He did not tell Ida to look away, nor did she wish to, although the suffering of one man was almost more than she could bear.

"Sam?" whispered the doctor, bending over the bundled shape on the last bed in the first row of cots.

The man called Sam stirred. Ida lifted her lamp and saw him blink and try to lift himself. When he was unable to sit up, he dropped back and rolled his head from side to side, staring at his shoulders, his face a mask of horror. "Not both," he cried. "It's not both."

"It's all right, Sam," murmured the doctor, laying a hand on his chest.

"One arm, they said it was just the right. Oh, Christ, it's not both." He was bellowing now, lifting up his two wrapped stumps. The bellow became a scream.

The doctor spoke softly to Ida and took the lantern. "Get Harry."

She ran to the man who was making a bed near the open door, the one who had told her to get a midwife. At once Harry snatched up a can and a wad of cheesecloth. Ida hurried after him as he lumbered back to the bed where Sam was shouting, "Kill me. Oh God, please kill me."

There were groans and curses from the other beds. Ida took the lantern again and held it high while the doctor loosened Sam's shirt and Harry folded the cloth into the right shape. Then the doctor took it, held the can of chloroform up to the light and poured out a few drops. He had to shout at Harry to be heard over Sam's screams. "Hold his head."

It was easier said than done because Sam was rearing up and throwing himself from side to side. At last Harry managed to get him by the ears and thrust his head down.

At once the doctor held the wad over his face, and soon, to Ida's intense relief, Sam's body softened and lay still, and they moved on to the next bed.

There were four rows of cots in the great hollow volume of the barn. Ida carried the lantern from cot to cot. Mingled with the medicinal smells was another smell, nearly overpowered by the sickening odor of rotting flesh—the familiar wholesome fragrance of the hay that was piled above the beds in the shadowy loft. Farmer Bushman had cut his fields before the battle. He had stored away his harvest in good time.

Soon they had made a complete circuit of the beds on both

sides. There were only a few more wounded men in the last row. Ida's hope faded. The third man from the end was not Seth, nor was the second man. The sleeping soldier in the last bed was a stranger.

Disappointed, she watched the doctor pull back the last sheet, lean down to smell an open shoulder wound then stand back, satisfied.

He turned to her and said, "Thank you, ma'am." Then with a smile on his worn face, he added, "We could certainly use you here. I don't suppose, just for a few days . . ."

In spite of her disappointment, Ida was pleased. She smiled and shook her head. "I'm sorry, but I've got to look for Seth."

"Well, too bad." The doctor stretched and arched his back.

"Perhaps you know where I might look?"

Instead of answering, he led her to a bench and they sat down. "I'm sorry, ma'am. I shouldn't have asked you to stay. Shouldn't you be at home? May I ask where you live?"

Ida did not want to seem stubborn, but she was calmly determined. "I'm fine. I'm really just fine. And I've got to find Seth. He was in the Second Massachusetts. Do you think—"

The doctor stood up and began walking away, because there was only one other place for her to look.

He murmured it over his shoulder. "Speak to Sergeant Woody outside."

"Thank you," said Ida. She rose from the bench and walked firmly to the door.

Harry was there, a bulky shape against the sky, his teeth showing white in a mocking grin. He said, "Good luck, missus."

Someone else appeared in the doorway, an officer, his coat hanging loose over his shoulders. He spoke to Harry, asking for a friend in the artillery reserve.

Ida stepped past him and walked carefully down the grassy slope. Then she had to walk three-quarters of the way around the barn before she found Sergeant Woody.

He was keeping watch over the bodies of the dead.

THE DEAD OF THE
TWELFTH CORPS

Alas! how many thousand mothers have been bereft at Vicksburg and Gettysburg, refusing to be comforted, because their children are not!

—MARY LIVERMORE

Sergeant Woody looked at Ida's shape and said, "Oh, ma'am, this ain't no place for a lady."

I'm not a lady, Ida wanted to say. *Pray God my husband isn't here.*

This time, the smell was like the gaseous stench from the dead horses, but it rose from the motionless forms lying on the bare ground, the bodies of men from the thirty-three regiments of the Twelfth Corps who had been killed in the recent battle. This time Ida did not take out her handkerchief. She stood still, trying to control her trembling.

"Looking for somebody, ma'am?" The other man stood up. "What name?"

Her voice shook as she told him.

"All right, missus, I'll show you around."

The chimney of his lantern was black with smoke. Ida followed it, steeling herself to look down, trying not to recoil from the sight of wrecked faces with staring eyes or skeletal faces with empty sockets where the eyes had once been. Some of the faces belonged to men who had been dead a day or two longer, and from them the skin itself had deliquesced away, revealing the bone.

Of course Ida did not know that in the first three rows lay the bodies of men of the 123d New York who had been killed on the second day in the battle for the peach orchard and men of the Twentieth Connecticut who had died at the angle in the stone wall on the afternoon of July third. Nor did Sergeant Woody explain that the remains in the fourth and fifth rows were from her husband's own regiment, the Second Massachusetts, and also from the Twenty-seventh Indiana, casualties of the garbled order at Culp's Hill on the morning of the third day.

The drenching rains of July fourth had plastered the dead men's uniforms to their bodies and washed away the bloodstains as though a regiment of laundresses had scrubbed them on a thousand wooden washboards. The creased and rumpled clothing was still damp from the rain. Damp too were the scraps of paper pinned to their blouses or to the fronts of their coats, the writing half-washed away.

To Ida it was horrible the way they had been laid out in perfect rows as if ordered to fall in. They were not toy soldiers, they were individual men, lying here so helplessly on their backs, side by side, row upon row. They had been fair and dark-skinned, tall and short, middle-aged and young, bearded and clean-shaven. More terrible still were the looks of suffering on some of the faces.

Shaken, Ida picked her way among them, afraid of what she might see, fearful of stepping on an outflung arm or a shattered leg with her big feet.

Sergeant Woody led her along, passing his lantern over each face, looking back at her with shiny inquisitive eyes, not wanting to miss the moment of recognition, the shriek, the swoon. But even in his coarse curiosity the man had enough sense to pause beside one body and drop a rag over what had once been a face.

But the body was wearing Seth's boots. Ida uttered a cry and fell to her knees. The boots were unmistakable. They had been specially made for Seth with elastic inserts on the sides by the cobbler on the Milldam. Seth's coat was gone. His shirt was wet, but some of the blood remained in a cloudy stain, brown like the stains on the apron of the amputating doctor in the town, like the bloody sheets carried out of the schoolhouse, like the apron of Dr. Chapel in the barn.

Weeping and whispering Seth's name, Ida stretched out her hand to lift the rag.

Enjoying this moment of melodrama, the ghoulish sergeant grinned, but then he said quickly, "No, no, missus." Pushing past her, he reached down and unpinned the paper attached to the cloth of the coat. "This ain't no Seth," he told her. "This here's an Otis." He showed it to Ida, who closed her eyes and whispered, "Thank God."

Gratefully she stood up and finished her tour of the fallen soldiers of the Twelfth Corps. Seth was nowhere among them.

"He's not here," she said eagerly to the guard. "And he's not on the muster roll. Where can he be?"

Sergeant Woody made a cruel suggestion. He pointed to a lighted tent across the lane and said, "Why don't you ask over there, missus?"

Ida set off at once. Having endured so much, she could endure a little more.

"You know what really happened to him," said the other guard, who had witnessed the woman's pitiful search.

Sergeant Woody laughed. "Naturally I do. He skedaddled."

THE EMBALMING
SURGEON

B etween the place where the dead men lay and the glowing tent across the way, the smell suffusing the air changed character. From the sickening stench of decaying flesh it became a chemical reek.

Ready for any horror, Ida walked sturdily forward. Heading for the line of light at the edge of the curtained opening, she stopped when she saw a burning ember among the trees at one side. It was a lighted cigar.

The cheroot made a bright arc as it was thrown away. A big man with an apron over his coat stepped forward into the light.

"Name?" he said to Ida.

She guessed at once that he didn't mean her own. "Seth Morgan," she said at once, struggling to speak above a whisper. "First Lieutenant, Second Massachusetts."

"I'll get my list," he said. "Excuse me." He lifted the tent flap and went inside.

For a moment Ida caught a glimpse of a naked man stretched on a plank. A rubber tube arched obscenely out of his chest and descended into a bucket.

"I'm sorry, ma'am," he said, emerging from the tent with a paper in his hand. "That name isn't here. When was the order sent?"

"The order?"

"By telegraph. Didn't someone send an order?"

Ida shook her head. Was it something she should have done? She was confused and ashamed.

The surgeon pitied the young woman. She should never have come. She looked far gone with child. "Forgive me," he said. "You mean you want to order it now? He was an officer? That'll be eighty dollars." He waved his hand in the direction of the rows of the dead. "I guess your husband's over there?"

"No, no, he's not. I can't find him."

"Well," said the embalming surgeon, embarrassed, "a lot of the deceased have already been interred." He pointed another way. "If you make out a requisition, Dr. Chapel will have your husband exhumed and sent home. You say he was Second Massachusetts? Good, because there's no list for the buried rebs." He chuckled. "Their kinfolk are out of luck."

Ida thanked him and turned away, heading vaguely in the direction of his pointing finger. But her courage and strength had given out. She reached out a hand to the dark ground and sank down.

LIEUTENANT
GOBRIGHT

NOAH GOBRIGHT
Class of 1860

First Lieutenant, Artillery Reserve, Captain
John Bigelow's 9th Battery, Massachusetts
Light, Lt. Col. McGilvery's Brigade

The moon that had shone so full and round over the entire battlefield from Culp's Hill to the Round Tops on the second of July
would not rise this evening until midnight, reduced to its last
quarter.

But it was midsummer, and the air was warm. There was a faraway rumble of thunder. Ida lay back and pillowed her head on her
valise and covered herself with her shawl. Her child tumbled for a
while and then was quiet. It had been a long and terrible day. Dozing, Ida dreamt about Seth's boots.

When a harsh light shone in her eyes, she blinked and sat up.

It was a man with a lantern. He withdrew it from her face and
lifted it so that she could see him. At once Ida recognized the soldier
who had come into the barn just as she was leaving it.

"Ma'am?" he said. "Mrs. Morgan?"

Laboriously Ida stood up, her bonnet awry.

"I came to find you." Bowing slightly, the officer introduced himself. "My name is Gobright, Lieutenant Noah Gobright." He nodded at the great pale side of the barn across the way. "I was there just now, visiting a friend, and Doctor Chapel told me you were looking for your husband." Gobright turned up the flame and set the lantern down on the ground. Then he said, "I know your husband, Mrs. Morgan."

Ida pulled her bonnet straight, her heart beating. Lieutenant Gobright was not crude like the sergeant guarding the dead across the way, nor awkward like the surgeon in the embalming tent. Oh, what was he going to tell her?

Hurriedly she explained. "The list in the newspaper, it said he was missing. I've come to find him. I've looked everywhere."

Instead of speaking, he reached inside his coat and drew out a bundle wrapped in a handkerchief. "I've been carrying this around," he said, handing it to her. "I meant to send it."

Ida quailed as she unwrapped the handkerchief, whispering, "But this is Seth's." Then she uttered a small cry, because one corner of the cambric square was red. She had hemmed and embroidered the handkerchief herself, but she had used no crimson thread. Fumbling with the things inside it, she murmured, "Oh, my letter, my last letter. Oh, please . . ." Ida's voice failed her, and she had to start again. "Please, Lieutenant Gobright, tell me where you found them."

Instead of answering, he began talking about his part in the battle, the struggle between Captain Bigelow's artillery and the Mississippians of General Barksdale's brigade, the way General Barksdale, with his white hair streaming behind him, had driven his men forward until he was brought down, there in the orchard of green peaches on the second afternoon.

But the story had nothing to do with the strange absence from duty the next morning of First Lieutenant Seth Morgan of the Second Massachusetts. Lieutenant Gobright stopped, and then with hesitating pauses, he spoke about comrades killed in action.

Ida waited. Why wasn't he answering her question? Her heart sank, but she vowed to maintain her dignity no matter what Lieutenant Gobright said.

His voice died away. For a moment there was nothing but the murmur of the hosts of summer insects, and then a scream from the direction of the barn. *Poor Sam,* thought Ida, *waking up again to the knowledge of his plight.*

But then Lieutenant Gobright began talking again, more cheerfully now. "I think your husband is most likely still alive. But—"

"Alive!"

"But perhaps he left the battle."

"Left the battle?" Ida didn't understand.

"You see, it's where I found the letter."

"Where you found it? But where was it?"

Lieutenant Gobright picked up the lantern. In the brighter light she could see that he had turned his head away. "It was beside the pike, the Baltimore Pike."

"Oh," said Ida with rising excitement. "Then he had been there?"

"I think so."

"But what does it mean?"

Gobright looked at her again and reached for her hand, not boldly, but kindly. "I'm afraid, Mrs. Morgan, it means he was trying to get away to Baltimore."

She stared at him, still uncomprehending.

"He was on the run." As she still didn't seem to understand, he put it more plainly. "He was deserting."

"No, no." With an impassioned motion Ida snatched back her hand.

Thinking that it would comfort her, Gobright took something else out of his pocket. "This was with the letter."

Startled, Ida took the little folded sheet and looked at it wildly. It was a sermon for men going into battle. She could see only the hymn at the end, and then at last she broke down and wept.

Holy Ghost, the Infinite !
Shine upon our nature's night
With thy blessed inward light,
Comforter Divine !

We are sinful: cleanse us, Lord;
We are faint: thy strength afford;
Lost—until by thee restored,
Comforter Divine !

AMERICAN TRACT SOCIETY,
28 CORNHILL, BOSTON

MY DEAR DAUGHTER

Lieutenant Gobright commandeered an ambulance and drove Ida back to town. But when he jumped down to inquire at the Globe Hotel, he came back shaking his head. "They say they're full up, but it's the bar that's full up."

A drunken man reeling along on crutches heard Gobright and shouted at him, "They dug it up, didja know that?"

"Dug what up?"

"Whiskey, two barrels of whiskey, two gin." The crippled man laughed so hard, he staggered and nearly fell. "Under the cabbages. They hid it under the cabbages."

"The sisters," said Lieutenant Gobright to Ida, climbing up again. "They'll take you in." He shook the reins and headed the horse back down Baltimore Street. "Saint Francis Xavier," he said. "It's another hospital."

"Oh, thank you," said Ida. "Forgive me, I've been so much trouble."

"Not at all, ma'am, not at all."

At the church, Gobright jumped down again and went inside. From the street Ida could hear his voice raised in powerful persuasion. Almost at once a woman ran out the door to help Ida down. At first in the dark Ida could see only her enormous white cap. She was a Sister of Charity, she said as she took Ida's arm. "We came from Emmitsburg with Father Burlando. Oh, we saw such terrible things on the way, dead men being buried in pits beside the road."

"Well, good night then, Mrs. Morgan," said Lieutenant Gobright. He clucked at the horse and the ambulance rolled away. Ida called out her thanks, but Sister Camilla was urging her inside.

The entry was another operating chamber with a prostrate patient, blood on the floor and a heap of arms and legs tossed to one side, but this surgeon was smoking a cigar and swearing as he flourished his saw.

Tut-tutting softly, Sister Camilla swept Ida through a door into the church and led her down an aisle, holding a candle high.

The straw under their feet was blood soaked, and there was the familiar stench. Never afterward would Ida be able to erase the scene from her mind. She trailed after Sister Camilla through a great congregation of wounded men lying on boards across the backs of pews, moaning and calling out, "Sister, Sister."

"In here, my dear," said Sister Camilla, opening a door at one side of the altar.

Ida whispered her thanks, but Sister Camilla did not stay to hear. As she whirled away, the cries were louder, more desperate, "Sister, please, Sister."

Sister Camilla called out to them cheerfully, "I'm coming," and closed the sanctuary's door.

Ida sank down on the floor, sobbing, and fell instantly asleep.

In the morning she woke early and sat up, listening. The hospital chamber was quiet, as though the men were all asleep, or perhaps they had all died.

Then she remembered the train. "The track's been repaired," the lieutenant had said. "There'll be a train for Baltimore at the depot at ten, but it won't be for passengers. They may not take you."

But they must take her. Ida stood up with difficulty and smoothed her rumpled skirt with her hands. She was thankful to find the priest's comfort stool behind a curtain, along with a bowl, a pitcher of water and a slop basin. She brushed her hair, did it up again, tied on her bonnet, wrapped herself in her shawl, picked up her valise and ventured outside by the priest's private door.

There was a small child on the street. Ida smiled at her and said, "Can you tell me the way to the depot?"

Instead of answering, the little girl wrapped her hand in Ida's skirt and dragged her along. At the intersection she kept a tight hold but pointed up the street with her free hand.

Ida thanked her, kissed her, unwrapped the small hand and watched her set off reluctantly, walking backward and waving. The children too, thought Ida, must have seen terrible things.

The approach to the depot was obstructed by loaded wagons. Baskets and boxes were heaped beside a building that had become a storehouse for the Christian Commission. Ida saw sides of beef packed in straw and ice, baskets of eggs, stacks of folded undergarments and piles of blankets. Iron cots leaned against the wall. Men and women were unloading hospital equipment—weights and scales, urinals and mortars, chests of pharmaceuticals. A couple of boys walked by in the direction of the station, trundling a steaming boiler of coffee.

The fragrance of the coffee was delicious, and so was the aroma of baking bread. Ida had eaten nothing since yesterday morning, but she did not want to bother the women who stood beside one of the wagons, heaving down baskets of crockery. They looked at her curiously, but she only nodded and walked on. *It's all right, I won't be any trouble.*

The blockage on the street grew thicker. Horse-drawn ambulances and crates of supplies were everywhere. When Ida worked her way past them to the depot, she found the platform lined with a long row of wounded men. Nurses were moving among them, both men and women, and so were town ladies, handing out slabs of buttered bread. Boldly Ida reached for one as the tray went by. From somewhere a brass band was playing "Home, Sweet Home."

The train had already come in, but it was not about to depart. Roustabouts were shouting and running around with crowbars. Officers bawled orders and a steam whistle shrieked. Ida could see a deep cut off to the left of the depot, but it was empty of track because Gettysburg was the end of the line. Since there was no way for the locomotive to turn around, it would have to push the cars all the way back to Baltimore.

Someone was shouting, a postboy with a mail pouch. All the heads looked up. Some of the men sat up and looked at him eagerly as he began calling out names in a shrill, nervous voice. Most of the names went unanswered, but a few letters were passed into outstretched hands. "Perley Wheeler? Here, give it to him, he's way in the back. Albertus Strong, you got a couple. Mrs. Ida Morgan?"

Everyone stared. Ida gasped, then went forward clumsily and took her letter while the postboy went on calling out names. "Private Schuetz? Private Doobey?"

Ida's letter was from her mother, who had addressed it in care of Ida's cousin Cornelia in Philadelphia, and then Cornelia must have put her baby aside long enough to forward it, vaguely addressing it to:

Mrs. Ida Morgan
Gettysburg Penna.

Reading the letter, Ida could almost hear her mother's firm confident voice:

My dear daughter,

Cornelia's letter shocked us all. When Eben finishes the cultivating that he promised to Mr. Hosmer I will send him to bring you back. How could you be so foolish. Poor Mother Morgan has taken to her bed.

Mrs. Weston of Lincoln has heard from George who was at G'sbg in 18th Mass reg't and is well. I hope you will inquire about Edward Chapin with 15th Mass. They have not heard from him and live in dread of the newspaper as do we all. Mrs. Ripley fears for Ezra who was at Vicksburg. Mother Morgan joins me in praying you will come home at once. Think of the health of your firstborn so soon to see the light if not your own. Please telegraph about Seth and self.

Yr devoted mother,
Eudocia Flint

Ida smiled. Cornelia must have written her Aunt Eudocia about her newborn baby and also about Ida, and then Ida's mother had snatched up pen and paper, and then the mail train carrying her letter to Philadelphia had made a record run, its whistle blasting all the way, and Cornelia had sent the letter on.

Of course Ida would not go home. And it was not possible to telegraph. She would write from Baltimore.

TO
BALTIMORE

But first she must get there. Ida found her way to the ticket window, but it was shut. She turned to a large woman in a mighty apron. "Please, ma'am, may I travel to Baltimore on this train? I have money. I can pay my way."

"Good heavens, girl," said the woman, looking her up and down, "what on earth are you doing here?"

Ida did her best to sound sensible. "But I'm really very well. I've been looking for my husband, Lieutenant Seth Morgan of the Second Massachusetts Volunteer Infantry. I'm told I may find him in Baltimore."

"Well, my girl," said the woman crisply, "you're not going to Baltimore on this train. There's no room for the likes of you."

"But I can help," pleaded Ida. "I can spoon-feed. I can change dressings."

"Oh, is that so?" said the nurse. "What about bedpans?"

Her question was sarcastic, but it did not seem so to Ida, who had been raised on a farm. She was acquainted with all that fell from the bowels of livestock, and she had performed this kind office for her dying father when he was crushed by a falling tree. She answered at once, "Oh yes, I can do that."

The big woman in the apron studied her, then scribbled out a chit. "Here," she said, "they need water. The dipper and butt's over there."

In the freight car Ida had not a minute to herself. Kneeling in the straw, crawling from one man to another, following the orders of the woman in the apron, she changed dressings and handed around slices of bread. When one patient handed her his Old Testament she found his favorite Bible story and began reading it aloud, but he already knew it by heart. "Oh, that's good," he said, laughing, "the way Goliath says, 'Am I a dog?' "

At Hanover Junction there was a rest stop where the Christian Commission had set up tables. They were serving out beefsteak and pastry. Ida stepped down from the baggage car into the fresh air, found a bench, took pencil and paper from her valise and began a letter to her mother.

> *Dear Mother and Dear Mother Morgan,*
>
> *As Seth is now in Baltimore, I have taken the cars to find him. If Eben has not started, tell him he need not come, because I am very well.*
>
> *I am sorry I could not telegraph, as the instrument in G'sbg was only for official use. I could not find Seth, but I believe him to be in Baltimore. I am told it is half-Secesh.*
>
> *Most sincerely, y'r loving Ida*
>
> *P. S. I am really very well.*
> *P. P. S. I am told there is a railroad hotel. I will write again from there.*

PART XI

THE BLOODSTAINED COAT

THE GUN THAT
WON THE WAR

Three thousand," said Bart.

Homer was scandalized. "But you said two thousand when we were here before."

"Maybe I didn't show you the whole collection. There's this letter, it's extra. And this rifle here"—Bart stroked the gleaming walnut stock—"it's a Spencer repeater. Mostly it was the cavalry at Gettysburg got Spencers, Custer's brigade." Bart picked up the beautiful gun and showed them the magazine that held seven cartridges. "Breech loader—you could fire fourteen rounds a minute. So they didn't have to reload after every shot and ram the cartridge down."

Doubtfully, they stared at the gun.

"To be honest with you," said Bart, lying in his teeth, "I've already got an offer for this rifle, but I hate to break up the set. If this genuine Spencer repeating rifle straight from Gettysburg was on TV, God knows what it would bring."

Homer smelled a rat. By returning to the shop they had become sitting ducks. He had seen the look in Bart's eye as they walked in—*The suckers are back.*

He asked a skeptical question, "Where did you get this collection anyway?"

"Government auction. Unclaimed relics removed from the bodies of Civil War victims. Collectors, they bid against each other. I won this time, but it was pretty—"

"Pricey, I'll bet," growled Homer.

"Your assumption is correct." Then Bart ended his sales pitch with a masterly stroke. "This is the gun that won the war."

Homer gave in. So did Mary. Five minutes later they walked out of the shop with the gun, Otis Pike's identification tag, and the bloodstained coat with all that its pockets contained, leaving behind in the hands of the proprietor a check for $3,150.

Grinning, Bart watched them go, congratulating himself on his quick wit, because the rifle had been a last-minute inspiration. In the back room, running his eye over his shelves of miscellaneous relics, he had recognized the gun at once as Otis Pike's own personal firearm. And the yarn about winning the war always worked like a charm.

It was time to lock up. But just as Bart hung the CLOSED sign on the door, another customer turned up, a whiskery man so out of breath he could hardly speak. "I feel sure"—puff, puff—"you will not want to close your door because, you see, I am here"—puffity puff—"to purchase a few things that I understand you are offering"—gasp, choke—"for sale." The new customer bent himself double, panting to recover his breath.

Generously Bart reopened his shop door and let him in. And then of course Ebenezer was disappointed in his quest because his third cousin twice removed, or perhaps it was his second cousin three times removed, had beaten him to it. But his wild drive to Gettysburg was not entirely wasted.

The wily proprietor of the shop spread other delectable items before his goggling eyes—a pair of drumsticks that had belonged to a famous drummer boy, a feather cockade that might once have adorned an artilleryman's dress cap, and a dirty little bottle possibly containing a few drops of the tincture of laudanum, that precious old standby in the pharmacopoeia of the Civil War surgeon.

The jewel was a .44-caliber Remington revolver, the gun that had won the war.

All of these things were pricey, very pricey, but Ebenezer snapped them up.

Afterward, as he approached his car with his bag of precious things, he fell prey to another huckster.

It was a smiling elderly woman peddling salvation, handing out pamphlets. She appeared before him on the sidewalk as suddenly as though descending from above.

Ebenezer stood stock-still beside his car and stared at her.

Fixing her pale eyes on his face, she handed him a pamphlet and said softly, "Good afternoon, dear friend. Tell me, wouldest thou be perfect?"

He gaped.

She toddled a little closer. "Wouldest thou inherit eternal life?"

Ebenezer was still transfixed. His mouth opened in wonder, a pink O in the cataract of his whiskers.

She crept still closer. "Wouldest thou, dear friend, have treasure in heaven?"

"Oh, yes," said Ebenezer. "I would, I certainly would."

THE POCKETS

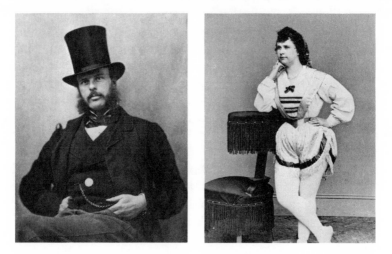

In the motel they laid the Otis Pike collection down on the bed—the identification chain, the coat, and the articles taken from the pockets. Mary also put down on the bed the two little cases of photographs. Homer leaned the gun in the corner, having ceased to believe in it.

"Of course Bart cheated us," he said. "We were babes in the wood."

"Of course we were," said Mary dreamily, "but just the same"—she touched the coat—"it brings it so close."

They pulled chairs up to the bed and sat down to look at everything carefully.

"I'll make a list," said Mary, pawing in her bag.

They began with the blue coat. "Not much blood on the outside," said Homer. "Strange the way the stains look like fingerprints." He undid the buttons. "Most of it's on the lining. You know, if we were paying so much per ounce of blood, we didn't get our money's worth."

"Don't be such a ghoul," said Mary, but she scribbled it down. An hour later there were ten items on her list.

1. Brass tag on a chain identifying Otis M. Pike of the Second Massachusetts Volunteers (Seth Morgan's regiment).

2. Union army sack coat, no stripes on sleeves (probably meaning a private). A few bloodstains on front of coat, lining somewhat stained.

3. Contents of left front pocket—folded note, very mysterious—

FOR GOD'S SAKE, OTIS, IN THE NAME OF FAIRY BELL,
    THE YOUNG SCAMP AND THE FEMALE SMUGGLER,
        DON'T DO IT AGAIN.
                THE CONCORD ROSEBUD

Extracting the next item, Mary burst out laughing.

4. Right front pocket, oilcloth packet containing photograph of curvaceous woman in tights, name printed below, "LILY LEBEAU."

5. Also in packet, dapper-looking man in top hat.

Homer gazed at the splendid mustachios and sideburns, the top hat, the prosperous-looking coat and vest, the watch chain. "Do you suppose he's Otis Pike?"

"I doubt he's my great-great-grandfather," said Mary. She picked up the last thing in the oilcloth packet. "Oh, Homer, it's a fan letter."

6. Also in packet, a letter:

Dear Miss LeBeau,

How often have I worshiped thine image from afar! I write now from the battlefield by moonlight amid the cannon's roar. Should I survive the perilous action of this day, I hope soon to soften your Marble Heart.

Enclosed, the likeness of—
A Passionate Admirer

"They go together," said Homer. "The man who had his picture taken in the top hat wrote the fan letter to the woman in the fancy rompers in the middle of a battle. Only he never mailed it because he died that day. What about the inside pocket?"

Mary picked up the little book that lay on the bedspread, turned the pages and handed it to Homer.

7. Taken from an inside pocket a small book, a play, the top edge bloodstained—*The Marble Heart, or the Sculptor's Dream.*

"*The Marble Heart?*" said Homer. "It goes with the fan letter."

"Right! Lily LeBeau was a famous actress, I'll bet. He must have seen her in this very play."

Homer took the little book and leafed through it. "It's just an old-fashioned melodrama. But look at this"—he showed a page to Mary—"some of the lines have new versions on the side."

"Oh, Homer, how interesting, the stuffiness is gone. Look what he's crossed out—The eyes which coldly view thy tears.' It's so much funnier in the margin—'All you need is a couple of beers.' "

Mary laughed, Homer laughed, and they went on to the next item.

The next letter was not in a coat pocket. They were through with the coat and its contents.

8. Unfinished letter, salutation in a clear hand:

My dear wife,

I am well, my dear, but I regret to say that many in the reg-
iment were lost this morning. Charley Mudge and Tom—

The last items were the two little cases of photographs.

9. Case bought on first visit to Bart's shop, with familiar photograph of a woman.

10. Case stolen by Ebenezer from Gwen's attic, with two pho-
tographs—the same woman and a man, probably her husband.
Glass over photographs broken. NOTE: THIS IS NOT PART OF
"THE OTIS PIKE COLLECTION."

That was it. They hovered over the bed, looking from one thing
to another.

One thing was clear. Homer put two of the letters side by side,
then declared firmly, "The dear wife letter and the fan letter to Lily
LeBeau were written by different people."

"Mmm," said Mary. "You're right." She reached across the bed
for the strange note that began "For God's sake, Otis," and set it
down between the two letters. "What about this?"

Homer studied them, then tapped the letter addressed to "My
dear wife." "It's in the same hand. So it wasn't Otis Pike who wrote
to his wife, it was somebody else. Someone who also warned Otis
about something—'For God's sake, Otis . . . don't do it again' "

"We know another thing," said Mary. "The fan letter to Lily
LeBeau was written before the battle in which Otis was killed. The
'dear wife' letter was written afterward. And we know from the
tablet in Mem Hall that both Otis Pike and Charles Redington
Mudge died at Gettysburg. So the 'dear wife' letter must have been
written by a survivor in the same regiment, the Second Massachusetts."

"Your great-great-grandfather's regiment." Homer picked up
the case with the single photograph of a young woman. "This was
in the Otis Pike collection, but she was related to you somehow,

not to Pike. Could Otis have gotten it from Seth?" Homer picked up the case with the two photographs side by side. "So here she is again, and the man with her must be your great-great-grandfather Seth Morgan, who survived the battle and wrote the unfinished letter to her and also the crazy letter from the Concord Rosebud."

"Well, he's certainly not Otis Pike, because Otis must be the dashing guy in the top hat." Mary studied the sober faces of the bearded man and the young woman in the double case. "But of course they may be different people entirely. A great-great-aunt and a great-great-uncle. Maybe the man is the *brother* of my great-great-grandfather. Oh, God, Homer, maybe they belong to Ebenezer after all."

EBENEZER'S TRASH

The landscape of southern Pennsylvania moved slowly past the car windows—fields and farms and forests. Mary was bored. She stretched her arms and worked her shoulders up and down. "Oh, Homer, it's such a long way."

Homer kept his eyes fixed on the highway. "Is any of that junk food left?"

"A few crumbs." Mary found the bag of potato chips.

Homer fumbled in it blindly. "How many more miles before the next tack?"

She looked at the map. "A long way yet, about forty miles, I think." She yawned, and in a fit of restlessness, reached into the backseat and picked up a bundle of the wastepaper that had been dumped on them by Ebenezer.

As a collection of historical documents it was absurd. "What's this?" She was staring at a sixth-grade essay written by a child named Mary Morgan: "Leanardo Davincy was born in 1452."

Angrily she tossed one piece after another over her shoulder. "Oh, Homer, that exasperating man. How could he be so gullible?"

"Mary, dear, settle down. Why don't you drive for a while?"

"Oh, yes. Good idea."

He pulled over, stopped the car and opened his door, while trucks lumbered past on the highway. The breeze swept up the chip bag. Mary got out with relief, letting Ebenezer's papers scatter from her lap. "Whee," she cried, "look at 'em go!"

"My God, woman," said Homer, laughing and chasing the chip bag.

"Don't call me woman," said Mary, but she raced after the flying rubbish, and together they rescued every worthless scrap. But when they climbed back in the car, another piece of paper fluttered up and plastered itself against the windshield.

"Oh, let it go," said Mary, turning the key and looking back at the racing traffic.

"No, no, stop." Homer stared at the scrap of paper, which was still flattened on the glass as though insisting on being read. With the engine revving, Homer opened the car door and reached for the scrap with a long arm. He brought it in and showed it to Mary, pointing to a single word.

She whispered, "Mudge."

"It's some sort of promotional handout for Hasty Pudding in the year 1860. I didn't know that nutty Harvard dramatic club went back so far."

Mary was enchanted. "I suppose they were putting on their ridiculous farces and dressing up in drag just the way they do now."

"No longer, I'm afraid," said Homer. "And I don't suppose they called it drag in the 1860s."

"Oh, Homer, what a find."

!!!!!!!!!!

** !! HASTY PUDDING !! **

!! STRAWBERRY NIGHT !!

!! JUNE 17, 1860 !!

LADIES WILL BE AS
WELCOME AS THE FLOWERS IN MAY!!
(OR RATHER IN JUNE!!!)

*

THOSE ALIVE TO THE TRUE SUMMONS
OR WHISTLE OF ART WILL WITNESS
IN THIS, THE SWAN SONG OF THE CLASS OF 1860,

THE SUMMIT AND NADIR
OF TRUE GENIUS!!!

Triumphs of Moral Desperation!!
Novel Effects!!
Great Tragico-Comico-Melodramatico Burlesques,
Accompanied by Astonishing Feats of Acrobatics by
those world-famous artistes of the trapeze,

MUDGE AND GOBRIGHT!!

PART XII

LILY LeBEAU

A LITTLE PIECE
OF BAD NEWS

Ida wrote her mother again from Baltimore. She did not mention her alarming reception in the hotel.

Ida had never stayed in a hotel before, although she and Seth had once heard Professor Agassiz speak in the Parker House. On their wedding day they had settled down at once in the family place near Mr. Barrett's sawmill. Ida's father had been dead only a few months, struck down by the falling tree, but her mother had cheerfully given up her bedchamber and hung the windows with new curtains.

This hostelry was large, ugly and run-down. The lobby was embowered in potted plants and furnished with brass spittoons and grubby tufted sofas. Ida couldn't afford anything more luxurious. Her banknotes were still plentiful, but she had no idea how much longer they would be needed.

She had chosen this hotel because it was near the depot, a handy lodging for a runaway soldier. Ida hoped with all her heart to find

Seth quickly, but she was determined to stay in Baltimore until she found him, even if it took every cent of her precious nest egg.

The money had been intended by her father to pay for a year in a female seminary. The thought of further education had been pleasing to Ida, but she had abandoned it gladly upon her marriage to Seth. Therefore she was free to use the money any way she chose. And this way was more important than any other.

She carried her small valise to a desk where a portly man in shirtsleeves leaned on his elbows and stared at her. If Ida had been of a more shrinking nature, she would have faltered, but she was not timid. Firmly she said, "I would like to see your guest book."

He stared at her figure and said, "Do you desire to register in my premises?"

"I don't know," said Ida. "I'm looking for my husband. He was at Gettysburg. I'd like to see if he is staying in this hotel."

"He was in the late battle?" The face of the proprietor assumed a knowing smirk. "We got many paying guests from those parts." He grinned at her. "Several hundred, I calculate."

Stubbornly Ida said again, "Please, sir, may I see the register?"

He pulled a heavy ledger from a desk drawer and slapped it down. "Help yourself, missus." But he watched as she ran her finger down the names.

When she came to the end, he pretended to feel sympathy. "He ain't there?"

"I guess he must be in another hotel," said Ida sadly. "Or perhaps he's staying with a friend." But why hadn't he let them know?

The proprietor leaned over the counter confidingly. "Sometimes, you know, missus, they change their names."

"I see," said Ida, refusing in her dignity to admit that they understood each other. "Well, I'll just look again."

This time she was more careful. And now, with a skip of her heart, she came upon Seth's name, and nearly burst into tears of joy. "He's here," she said, looking up, exulting. "He's here in this hotel."

The proprietor craned his neck. "Oh, him. Is he your husband?" He stared at her again, disbelieving. "I must say, I wouldn't have thought it."

Ida looked back at Seth's name, and felt a moment of doubt.

"It's strange. It doesn't look like his writing. That's why I missed it at first."

"Well, some people write different after they—" The man shrugged his shoulders and didn't finish, but Ida knew he meant *after they skedaddle.*

"You know him?" said Ida eagerly. "He's still here?"

"Oh, sure, he's here." The man behind the counter had a coarse joking way about him, and now he took pleasure in passing along a little piece of bad news to Seth Morgan's pregnant wife. "He's here all right, and so's his lady friend."

CALM THY FEARS

Ida had endured a number of hard blows, but this was one of the worst. She closed her eyes, feeling a lurch from the child under her skirt. After a moment she said softly, "Is he in?"

"Oh, no, I suppose he's at the theayter. Minute he checked in, he was off. Keeps going back."

Disconcerted, Ida said, "Which theater?" Surely there was some mistake.

"Holliday Street, I guess." Then the proprietor looked past Ida and his face broke into a huge grin. "Well, here's the lady in person. I bet she can tell you."

"I can tell her what?" Seth's lady friend was a tall, buxom woman in a towering bonnet. She leaned her bulk against the desk, reached up her gloved hand and cupped Ida's chin. "Such a sweet face."

"This here's Seth's Morgan's wife," said the proprietor gleefully. "She's come looking for her hubby. And this, missus, is our fair queen of the dramatical arts, Miss Lily LeBeau."

Ida did not know what to say or where to look. But Lily LeBeau cried out at once in horror, "I didn't know the damn fool had a wife." She put her arm around Ida. "My dear, I swear on the Bible, he didn't tell me he was married. Oh, what a beast."

They were a mismatched pair. Ida was pale and demure, Lily rosy as a sunrise. Imperiously she led Ida to one of the sofas and made her sit down. Then she settled beside her, nestling close, pushing to one side the springs inside her massive skirt. "My dear child, you should be at home. When is it to be, the blessed event?"

In spite of everything—in spite of her headlong journey to Gettysburg, in spite of the terrible things she had seen in the town and in the Bushman barn, in spite of her search among the windows of dead soldiers and her grisly glimpse of the embalming surgeon's tent and in spite of the painful news that her dear Seth was now a deserter—Ida's stern resolve melted before the kindly concern of the woman who had taken her place in her husband's affections.

To Lily she whispered, "In two months. But really, I feel just fine." Then Ida lifted appealing hands. "Please, oh, please. I've got to see him."

"Well, of course you've got to see him." Lily reached up to tuck a strand of hair back under Ida's bonnet. "Now, my sweet thing, you just comfort yourself. Lily will take care of everything." Her skirt boiled up as she leaned closer. "That mean old Seth of yours, he appeared at the door of the theater, Holliday Street—well, I must say as shouldn't, it's the best in Baltimore—and asked for Lily LeBeau. It was just only last week. Well, to me he was a perfect stranger, but, my dear, how that man of yours can talk. Of course if I'd known he was married! But he never let on." Lily put a tragic hand on her bosom. "But there!" She brightened. "Right now we're playing in *The Marble Heart*. You know it, don't you, honey?"

Miserably Ida nodded that she did.

"I've just got a little part. I'm only a slave girl, but I get to sing." Lily cocked up her face and trilled, "Love on, love on, calm thy fears! Time will bring happier hours!" She stopped and grinned at Ida as the proprietor guffawed.

Then Lily gave Ida a squeeze. "As it certainly will bring happier hours for you, my dear. Now where was I? Oh, yes, there he was in the theater, your husband, and he said he'd made a lot of improvements in the parts. And really, it was God's truth, they were first-rate, so comical." Lily's chuckle was delicious. "And he expanded my part so it was really important. Well, naturally I liked that, so I took him to Jacko, and Jacko, he liked the changes, so, oh dear me"—Laura groaned and rolled her eyes—"now there's all these more rehearsals. Of course we don't know what his nibs will think, but he's way up in Boston, so who cares? Anyway, Seth's worked himself into the company well enough, fast too, I'll say that for him, giving credit where credit is due."

"Thank you," murmured Ida, trying to take it all in.

Lily slapped her knee, and her springy skirt bounced. "Tell you what we'll do. I've got to be in the theater for a spell, but you can lay down in my room for a couple of hours—that's all the longer I'll be. And then, I swear, I'll take you to the theater and you can look that naughty man straight in the face."

Lily stood up and led the way, billowing toward the staircase. "This way, dear. Can you still climb stairs? My off cousin, she got so big, she just laid there on the bed in the front room."

"Was her baby all right?"

"Oh dear, no. The poor thing got so big, it wouldn't come out. How she took on!"

"But what happened?"

"They were both taken. It was sad."

HER WIFELY
DEVOTION

Lily bustled into her hotel room ahead of Ida and thrust something under the bed. "Now, dear, just you lay down and rest yourself. Oh, the heat." She snatched up a fan and flapped it in the heavy air. "Here, I'll just draw the shade."

Then with a wild salute of her fan, she was gone.

Ida took off her dusty boots, lay back on the bed and closed her eyes. But instead of sleeping she thought about Seth. She had found him, and in a little while she would see him, but then, dear God, what would she say to him?

Through the open window came the rhythmical hammering of a rolling mill and the shriek of an incoming train.

What was a husband, after all?

Ida turned heavily on her side and thought about this simple question—because Seth was not simply the lover who had so pleased her with his tenderness on their wedding night in the big parental bed, although that night had been astonishing to Ida, who had so far witnessed only the coupling of the hog and the sow, the bull released from the bull pen among the cows, and the fiery cock rushing at the hens.

Nor was it only the marriage vows that had bound him to her that morning in the First Parish Church with all the town looking on.

A husband was more than that. Seth had been her companion in all the pressing tasks of the family farm. He had taken over her father's duties in the peach and apple orchards, cultivating the soil and pruning the water sprouts and at last, with a couple of hired hands, relieving the bowed branches of their heavy weight of fruit. He had also performed a thousand other duties in field and woodlot, house and barn, and kept the winter school in District Two.

Ida was proud that, even so young, her husband had become a personage in the village. Already he was a deacon in the church and a trustee of the public library. He had even spoken in the Lyceum on the *Odes* of Horace.

For her part, Ida kept all the farm records smartly up-to-date, noting down in her ledger the expenditures for seed and feed, for the spring pig and the new batch of chicks, and the outlay for the patent cultivator and the digging of a new well after the old one went dry.

It was astonishing the way outgo sometimes overwhelmed income, as when the proceeds from the sale of a couple of bull calves had been transformed into a smart four-seater spring wagon—Seth had brought it home from Brighton the very same day as a surprise for the ladies. At once Ida had taken up her ledger and set both items down on the blue lines with meticulous care.

In addition there was her calico-covered journal for the orchard, its pages sewn together by hand and ruled with pen and ink. Here Ida kept track of flowerings and ripenings, failures and successes, and the price each bushel brought on the Boston market, the sturdy northern peaches and the apples—the Sweet Winesaps, the Ben Davises, the Baldwins, the Seek No Furthers.

But she and Seth were not only partners in a common enterprise. After all, they had grown up in the same town, their minds were stocked with the same recollections and they had the same views on matters small and large. And like all contented couples they shared a private language. Playfully Seth called Ida "the cynosure of all eyes," and she teased him with noble names from Sir Walter Scott.

And of course Concord was a celebrated village. Like all the rest of their fellow citizens, they revered Mr. Emerson and shared in the gossip about the other colorful citizens of the town—the philosophical farmers, Mr. Alcott and his daughters, Judge Hoar and his sister Elizabeth, Mrs. Thoreau and her boarders, not to mention her clever daughter and the famous eccentric son who had died last year.

It was true that Seth was far more learned than Ida, because it had been he, not she, who had taken the cars to college in Cambridge. Ida envied him his Latin and Greek, but she herself was no ignorant country girl. In the public schools of Concord a forward girl like Ida Flint could pick up more than a scrappy education. And among her elders at home there was Yankee wit aplenty, pumped up with a new sort of yeasty exaltation.

Therefore Seth did not have to temper his speech to the understanding of his young wife. They possessed in common the whole of the village and all the compacted and sifted wisdom of its people.

Perhaps Mrs. Thoreau's late and lamented son had not spoken extravagantly when he called the town of Concord "an earthly paradise." It had not occurred to the newlywed pair to think of themselves as residents of the Garden of Eden, and yet perhaps it was so. And if Ida was Eve, Seth was certainly her Adam.

This was the husband she was seeking, the one whom no temporary madness could ever change for long.

THE BURIAL PARTY

But of course she would not find him. The change to Seth Morgan was of a very different kind.

As Ida lay asleep on the bed belonging to Lily LeBeau in the hotel beside the railroad in Baltimore, a burial detail on the battlefield of Gettysburg moved slowly among the bodies beside the Bushman barn. Stooping over the sad wreckages of once-living men, they tried with meticulous care to name them. Reaching into coat pockets, vest and trouser pockets, they removed the things to be sent home—a pipe, a watch, a pocketknife, a letter, a Bible. Sometimes a daguerreotype or a bloodstained photograph had to be tugged from the clutch of a dead hand.

When two members of the burial party came to the body of Seth Morgan they found no coat and therefore no pockets. There was only a note pinned to the shirt, "PVT. OTIS PIKE."

The name was not on the embalming surgeon's list of the officers and enlisted men whose bodies were to be preserved and sent elsewhere.

The burial party could not wait. They lowered Seth into a trench among the other men of the Second Massachusetts Volunteer Infantry who had been killed while trying to recapture the rebel works on the lower slope of Culp's Hill.

Their bodies would lie there only a little while. Before long they would be exhumed, enclosed in wooden boxes and buried in the new cemetery set aside for the dead of the Battle of Gettysburg. At the time of its dedication, months from now, the two speakers would be illustrious.

If only on that day their voices might be shovels to burrow into the earth, picks to smash the box lids, augurs to drill open the deaf ears. Then the dead of Gettysburg might hear the eloquent phrases about a nation conceived in liberty and dedicated to a certain noble proposition, they might then be sharply heedful of the stirring words about devotion and consecration and high resolve.

Would they then be resigned, proud to have fallen in the Battle of Gettysburg? Perhaps they would, perhaps they would not.

ANOTHER SKEDADDLE

Lily minced no words. "Seth, you swine, why didn't you tell me you've got a wife?"

Otis looked at her in consternation. "Wife? I've got a wife?"

"Well, for goodness sake, of course you've got a wife. She's come all this way by herself, looking for you. And she's—" Lily made a bulging shape in front of her skirt. "How could you abandon that sweet girl at a time like this?"

Christ Almighty. To his horror Otis understood that it was Seth Morgan's wife who was here in Baltimore, and she would take one look at him and scream and shriek and want to know what he had done with her beloved husband, and then the whole game would be up. "My God, you've seen her? You mean she's here?"

"She certainly is here. She's in my room in that fleabag hotel. She's crazy to see you."

Otis put his head in his hands, remembering the little case he had found in Seth's pocket, with the pretty young girl inside it,

Seth's loving little wife, who had made him handkerchiefs with her own little hands. "Oh, for Christ's sake, Lily, shut the door."

She slammed it so hard it shivered in its frame.

The scarred surface of the table was dusty with face powder and cigar ash, but Otis, staring down, saw the theater on Holyoke Street, the jolly old theater that belonged to the Pudding. He saw Charley Mudge plunking his banjo and singing a witty song, then staggering and falling at Culp's Hill. He saw Tom Robeson flounce across the stage in bonnet and false curls, then drop to the ground in that same godforsaken swale. He saw Henry Farrar prance onstage as Mr. Snoozle, then drag at a fallen horse in a hail of shot and shell. He saw Seth Morgan merrily intoning one of the best lines Otis had ever invented, then falling, his face smashed into a smear of blood.

And then Otis saw the face of Noah Gobright. He looked up and said, "Lily, don't bring her here."

Lily tore off her bonnet and unhooked her chemisette, staring at him reproachfully. "Why on earth not? The poor sweet thing."

"I didn't tell you, Lily. I skedaddled."

She widened her eyes in mock horror as her skirt dropped to the floor. "Why, Seth, you naughty boy."

"No, no, you don't understand. It was the fourth time. If they catch me, they'll shoot me." Otis stood up, the voice of Gobright ringing in his head, calling after him, *Otis, Otis.* "They'll collect a firing squad and shoot me."

Lily was tying ribbons around her plump ankles and crisscrossing them up her legs. "But your wife won't tell on you. Surely you'd be safe with your little wife?"

"If I go home with my wife, they'll find me. I can't go home."

Swaths of rose-colored muslin swirled around Lily. "What a fool you are, Seth. Why don't you change your name? If you're so afraid of your wife, why do you still call yourself Seth Morgan?"

What could he say? Keeping Seth's name alive was a kind of painful tribute, a debt of guilt and honor—as if honor meant anything in this war, which of course it didn't. They were always talking about glory and honor, the generals. "Oh, God, Lily, I killed someone."

"You killed someone? Well, for heaven's sake, Seth"—Lily tied the ribbons under her knees—"isn't that what you were there for, to kill as many Johnny Rebs as possible?"

"It wasn't a reb."

Lily's face disappeared behind a powder puff, and she began fussing with her curls. Hairpins showered around her chair. Thoughtfully she said, "I know what you need, Seth, a new name, something striking. Adolfo—what about Adolfo?"

Otis laughed. "No, not Adolfo."

She pinned her hair into a Grecian knot. "But, Adolfo dear, we're forgetting your little wife. Any minute now she's going to have a blessed event."

"Oh Christ." Otis picked up his silk hat and stroked it, remembering uneasily the way it had been paid for. He had skedaddled from Gettysburg in the remnants of two uniforms—Seth's grisly blood-drenched coat and his own trousers, grubby from two days of scrambling all over the shot-torn battlefield. After the dangerous encounter with Gobright, he had hotfooted it away down the pike as fast as he could run in the pouring rain. Then, miles away from Gettysburg, he had made a last inspection before tossing Seth's coat away in a ditch. Thrusting his fingers into an inside pocket, he had come upon the wad of banknotes.

What a piece of good luck! Next morning in his rented room in the Baltimore boardinghouse, he had swabbed the notes clean, the words *blood money* throbbing in his head.

But blood money or not, he had to look like a gent before presenting himself to Miss Lily LeBeau. The new suit was only ready-made, but even so, it had been costly. He had also bought a gold fob and a chain for his watch.

"Really, Seth," said Lily, "I've got to tell her something."

Otis threw up his hands. "If she's expecting, she shouldn't be here. Tell her to go home."

There were shouts in the corridor. Jacko thumped on the door. "Oh, Seth," urged Lily, "she's so determined. She's not going to leave without seeing you. How can you be so heartless?"

Otis made up his mind. "If she won't go, then it's up to me." He began pulling things down from the hooks on the wall. "I'm going to light out of here in a C-spring shay. There's a train in half an hour. I'll see you in Washington, Lilybelle."

The thump on the door was louder this time. Lily stood up tearfully to be embraced. "Oh, Seth," she whimpered, "what shall I tell her?"

"Tell her anything. I don't give a damn."

When the curtain rose on the first act of *The Marble Heart,* Lily bounced onstage right on cue, and then as she trilled her plaintive song, she thought what she should tell poor Ida.

Seth was gone, she would say. She had arrived at the theater and found him gone. His battle wound had flared up, that was what she would say. He was recovering somewhere in the country, away from the bad air and noise of the city. And then she would urge the dear child to leave at once and give birth to her adorable baby at home.

Love on, sang Lily happily—

—love on, calm thy fears!
Time will bring happier hours!
The eyes which coldly view thy tears
Will warmly greet sweet flowers!
Love on, love on, love on!

PART XIII

OUT OF THE DARK

FAMILY ALBUM

Home at last from their long triple journey to Gettysburg, Washington and Gettysburg again, Mary and Homer went straight to bed. But next morning, refreshed, they drove across town to see Gwen.

"Did you visit Ebenezer?" she said, as they walked in the door with their arms full of loot.

"Wait till you hear," said Mary.

"The man's a nutcase," said Homer.

"Look what we've got." Mary set everything down on the dining room table. "But most of this stuff comes from Gettysburg."

Patiently Gwen listened and looked at all the expensive relics they had bought in Bart's antiquarian bookshop, the coat and the other things from his "Otis Pike collection," including the small leather case with the photograph of a sober-looking young woman in a white-ribboned cap.

"Oh, I remember her," said Gwen. "But doesn't she have a husband?"

"Here," said Mary. "Ebenezer stole it, but we got it back." She opened the other little case, the one that had been tipped off the table and smashed under Ebenezer's soup cans.

Looking at the pictures beneath the cracked glass, Gwen recognized the husband and the wife. "Poor things," she said, "but who are they? Flints or Morgans, I'll bet, but which ones exactly?"

Mary looked at her and said slowly, "Isn't there a—"

"Family album!" cried Gwen. "Of course there's a family album."

"I'll bet Ebenezer grabbed it," said Homer.

"He did not. It wasn't in the attic, it's right here in this room. At least I hope it is." Gwen went to the china cupboard. "I hope to God he didn't find it." She opened the glass door and peered past a teapot in the shape of a thatched cottage. "Oh, good, it's still here." She pulled the big book out carefully, rattling the teacups.

It was a heavy volume bound in stamped leather. The spine was cracked, but a pair of brass latches were still fastened over the thick pages.

Gently Gwen set it down on the table and undid the clasps.

"I'd forgotten all about it," said Mary. "It's in terrible shape."

"I'm really ashamed," said Gwen. "We should have taken better care of it." She opened the front cover. The first page was headed with the words "Index to Portraits," but it was not a list of portraits, it was a genealogical record.

"I didn't know you people had a family tree," said Homer.

"Oh, Gwen," said Mary, "I'm ashamed too. We haven't been keeping it up. Well, neither did Mother. She's not in here, and neither is Father. Your marriage isn't here, and neither is mine."

As an outsider, Homer felt no Morgan family guilt. "Look," he said, pointing to the family tree. "The woman in the pictures must be up here at the top somewhere."

It took them an hour to determine who was who. Gwen and Mary pored over the faded names and figured out the lines of descent, and Homer copied them down.

<u>Alisha Mary Snow</u> + <u>James Elisha John Morgan</u>   <u>Joseph Flint</u> + <u>Clara Mary Holborne</u>
m. Oct. 1812 | (Grandfather d. 1850)

<u>Augusta Henrietta Wilkes</u> + <u>Pliny Morgan</u>   <u>Bartholomew Flint</u> + <u>Eudocia Fanning</u>
m. June 18, 1833 | (Father killed by falling tree, 1856)

(Ida, Eben, Sarah, Joshua, Alice)

<u>Seth Morgan</u> + <u>Ida Flint</u> + <u>Alexander Clock, M.D.</u>
my dear husband, my dear husband,
m. 14 April. 1862 married 11 June, 1866

<u>Horace Bartholomew Morgan</u>   <u>Eudocia Mary</u>   <u>Augusta Alice</u>   <u>Rebecca</u>
b. Wash. D.C. Sept. 28, 1863   b. 11 May '67   b. 2 July, '68   b. 7 Oct. '69
(our dear child taken 2 Aug. '67)

"It stops there." Gwen ran her finger up the selected list in Homer's notebook. "Here at the top Joseph Flint is called 'Grandfather,' so this whole thing must have been written by his granddaughter, Ida Flint, who married—" she ran her finger sideways, "Seth Morgan, and then somebody named Alexander Clock later on. I don't remember any Clocks."

"Because they only had daughters," said Homer. "One died, and the two surviving daughters married other people, so then there were no more Clocks." He tapped the name of Seth Morgan. "Here he is, your great-great-grandfather, Ida's '*dear husband*'—I mean, her first '*dear husband.*' "

Mary looked at the name and felt a pang, remembering the blank page in the Harvard album for the class of 1860, the missing face of a young man deemed unworthy of his peers.

Heartlessly Gwen said, "Seth Morgan, he's the shameful one nobody ever talked about. What happened to him afterward? There's no death date, but Ida married again, so maybe he died in the Civil War."

"Unless she was a bigamist," said Homer.

"Our great-great-grandmother?" Mary pretended to be shocked. She turned the page. "Let's see what these people looked like."

Only a few of the pictures were accompanied by names. "Too bad," said Homer. "The trouble is, everybody knew what Grandpaw and Aunt Milly looked like, so there was no need to write their names down."

The first two were daguerreotypes. They were dark, as though the old gentleman in a neck cloth and his wrinkled old wife were peering out of a closet.

The next husband and wife had been taken after the daguerreotype era. These were *cartes de visite,* photographs on cards slipped into openings in the thick pages.

"This one says 'Father,' " said Gwen. "So I'll bet he's Bartholomew Flint."

"Ida's father," said Homer, "the one killed by a falling tree. So the woman must be his wife Eudocia, Ida's mother."

"Oh wow," said Mary, turning the page, "who's this old sour-puss?"

Gwen turned the book sideways. "There's writing—wait a minute. It says 'Mother Morgan.'"

Homer flipped back to the family tree. "She must be Seth's mother Augusta."

"I disown her," said Gwen firmly.

"So do I," said Mary.

"I'm sorry to inform you," said Homer, "that you can't disown an ancestor, good or bad. Without grumpy old Augusta you two wouldn't be here at all. Who's next?"

Mary turned the page, and they all said at once, "There she is."

It was the young woman in the white-ribboned cap. "And she's written her entire name under it." said Gwen. "'*Ida Flint Morgan Clock.*' She's the young woman in those two little cases."

"So which of her two husbands is with her in one of them?" said Homer. "Is it Seth?"

"Maybe it's her second husband, Alexander Clock." Gwen turned the page to a pair of children. On the left side a small boy looked out of the cardboard frame; on the right a baby lay on a pillow, its small hands folded on its breast.

"Oh yes," said Mary. "I remember the dead baby."

They studied Homer's list again. "The little boy may be the son of Ida and Seth," said Homer. "Horace Bartholomew Morgan."

"And the baby must be little Eudocia Mary," said Homer, "the first child of Ida and Alexander Clock. See? She lived only a few months."

The last photograph was different from the rest.

"I remember this," said Mary. "It's a bunch of men in uniform. Look, Homer, it's labeled. It's the Second Massachusetts"—she squinted at the date—"on May thirty-first, 1863."

"Not the whole regiment," said Homer. "Probably just one company. See if Seth is there."

The faces were small, the photograph faded. Gwen ran for a magnifying glass.

It was a happy-go-lucky group, jolly comrades gone a-soldiering. Rifles were stacked at one side, but some of the men

were clowning for the camera. One of them lolled in the fore-
ground, grinning because his ears were being tickled by feathers in
the hands of a couple of boys kneeling behind him, obviously a
pair of twins. The only sober face was that of the captain, who was
looking gravely to one side, his hand on the pommel of his sword.
Homer noted the sideburns, the look of tired intelligence.

They bent over the picture, hunting for the young bearded face
that lay under the cracked glass in the folding case, then shook their
heads, agreeing that it wasn't there.

"May thirty-first, 1863," said Homer. "It was after Antietam
and Chancellorsville but before Gettysburg."

They gave up on the picture in which Captain Thomas Rodman Robeson stood gazing at the horizon and First Lieutenant
Seth Morgan looked cheerfully straight into the lens of the camera,
his hat in his hand.

Nor did they recognize Private Otis Mathias Pike, hilariously
tickled by Lemuel and Rufus Scopes as he lay grinning on the
ground in the very forefront of the fighting men of Company E,
Second Massachusetts Volunteer Infantry.

GLORIOUS LIBRARIES

The next step was libraries.

"You take the Archives department this time," said Mary. "I'll try the Theatre Collection."

Mary Morgan and Homer Kelly had spent their honeymoon in the Concord Library—well, part of it anyway. Libraries were their saloons. They had visited these intoxicating pothouses all over their native New England and in far-flung cities across the Atlantic.

None of these grogshops was more inebriating than the small and sequestered storehouses in the Pusey Library, where the bartender librarians served up precious vintages from days gone by.

Homer liked everything about the Archives library. He fell in love at first sight with the pretty slips one filled out to ask for things in the HUP category (Harvard University Picture collection) or HUG (texts relating to Harvard University graduates). Once you had filled out your slip and placed it reverently on the counter,

Angelica Doyle picked it up and glided silently away. A moment later, lo! the thing appeared like magic on your table.

Each of the HUP photographs came in its own slipcase. Homer was moved every time he reached his hand into an envelope and pulled out the face of a young man who had served in the Civil War. Perhaps it had been hidden from view for 140 years, or at least since the invention of these charming acid-free envelopes.

Otis Pike, class of 1860, was the first to emerge from the dark. Homer stared at the amiable young face. Pike's suit was jaunty and his mustache and sideburns were neatly trimmed. He was clearly a younger version of the man in the top hat.

Only three years after this picture was taken, he had been killed in the Battle of Gettysburg.

Homer thrust back his chair and returned to the desk to ask a question. "Is there any record of the battlefield experiences of the men whose names are on the tablets in Memorial Hall?"

"Of course there is." Angelica whisked around the counter and plucked a pair of books from a shelf. "*Harvard Memorial Biographies.* They're in here, all of them."

The two volumes were a gold mine. Homer found the entry for Otis Pike at once among the memoirs for the class of 1860. The writer of this one must have cudgeled his brain and chosen his words with tactful care—

OTIS MATHIAS PIKE

Pvt. 2d Massachusetts Vols. (Infantry) July 12, 1862.
Killed at Gettysburg, Penn., 3 July, 1863.

Otis Pike's life is an inspiring study in the overcoming of obstacles. It is an example of the triumphant achievements that can sometimes arise from unpromising beginnings.

Private Pike was born in Worcester, Massachusetts, September 2, 1839. Orphaned when a small boy, he was taken into the household of a bachelor uncle. Entering Harvard as a freshman in 1856, he soon became one of the most popular members of his class.

Though several times admonished for inattention to his studies, and once in danger of suspension in consequence of a practical joke at the expense of the college steward, he was permitted to continue his undergraduate career. Thereafter, his less-than-perfect record as a scholar was offset by his brilliant participation in the dramatic society known as the Hasty Pudding Club. Pike's unique contribution was the authorship of witty farces and songs, many of which are still remembered.

On the death of his uncle, Pike found himself without family, but as the heir to his uncle's estate he was able to graduate in 1860 with his class. His enlistment in the army was somewhat clouded by circumstance, but his friends in that celebrated regiment, the Second Massachusetts Volunteer Infantry, were pleased to accept him into their distinguished ranks as a private.

In the Army of the Potomac, Pike once again wrested glory from doubtful beginnings. Although three times chastised for leaving the ranks, he was in the very forefront among his gallant classmates as the regiment surged over the breastworks on the morning of July 3, 1863, in an attack on Culp's Hill during the Battle of Gettysburg. Next day, his body was found farthest forward in the field, in company with that of his heroic classmate, Lt. Col. Charles Redington Mudge, his regimental commander.

Another classmate, Capt. Thomas Bayley Fox, was mortally wounded in the same attack, as was the commander of Private Pike's company, Capt. Thomas Rodman Robeson, class of 1861.

Their memorials will be found in these pages.

Well, good for Otis Pike. But what about Seth Morgan?

Homer looked for Seth's name in the table of contents, but it was not there. Well, of course it wasn't there. These were the histories of men who had given their lives for the Union cause. In the elegiac biographies written by their friends and comrades, every dead soldier had been *gallant, stalwart, chivalrous, heroic.*

Seth Morgan had served in the same regiment, but Mary had found only a blank page for him in the album for the class of 1860. Had there been something shamefully wrong with his army career? In contrast to the gallant sacrifice of Private Otis Pike?

PART XIV

THE MARBLE HEART

NO WIFELY CLAIM

When Ida woke from her nap, she heaved herself out of bed and poured water from the pitcher into the bowl on the washstand. Then she scrubbed her face with soapy fingers and unpinned her hair.

Her baby was awake too, thumping and bumping inside her. Ida smiled, because surely no girl would kick like that. Seth would be pleased to have a boy. And surely he'd be glad to see her, and if he were not—but Ida could not bear to think what she would do if he were not.

It occurred to her as she brushed her hair how odd it was that Seth's new lady friend would permit his wife to see him. Perhaps in all her alluring splendor as an actress on the stage, "the cynosure of all eyes," Lily had no fear of competition from a plain little fustian wife. And perhaps—Ida winced—perhaps Seth would be mortified by the public display of his wife's condition, angry at her for interfering in his thrilling new life.

Miserably Ida remembered a day of pouring rain last spring
when Seth had been spending his furlough catching up on chores
left undone by the women and children. Ida had popped open her
mother's umbrella, splashed out to the barn and found Seth and
Eben forking up the manure pack, breaking through the dry crust
to shovel the foul-smelling mess into a tipcart. Oh, yes, perhaps
she'd been a fool to follow him. Perhaps he would be justified in
telling her to go away and let him alone.

But when she heard Lily's key in the door, her heart bounded up
again, and she ran to pull the door open. Eagerly she said, "I'll get
my shawl."

"Oh, my dear," said Lily, "just let me catch my breath." She scur-
ried past Ida, pulling off her bonnet. To Ida's surprise a yellow braid
came with it. Lily saw her astonishment and laughed. "A diadem
plait, it's all the rage. Just wait till you see what a fair charmer I'm
going to make of you, with those raven tresses and that pretty face."

"Please, Lily, oh, please may we go now?"

"Ida dear, there's no point in going to the theater now. I've just
heard the news. He's gone out of town. They say he needs a change
of air."

"A change of air?"

The scream of the rolling mill had begun again. "Oh, you
know, dear, away from the stench and noise of the city. Just listen to
that." Lily bustled to the window and slammed it down.

"But where?" cried Ida. "Where did he go?"

"Dear me, I don't know. It's just for a few days."

"A few days!"

"His battle wound," babbled Lily. "It was bothering him."

"Oh," cried Ida, "he was wounded? Seth was wounded?"

"On his neck," decided Lily quickly, rejecting leg, arm, shoulder, chest and back. "It's flared up again."

"Oh, but he needs me," burst out Ida. Then in her distress, she
said, "Please forgive me, Lily," because in this new shape of things,
it might be discourteous to make any wifely claim. Perhaps it was
Lily, only Lily, whom Seth needed in his time of suffering.

But Lily was still scurrying around the room, plucking up pieces
of clothing. A corset with crisscrossed lacing sailed into the air. She
threw open her trunk, tumbling the contents, holding things up for

inspection, dropping them and then tugging at something else. Finally she pulled out a gossamer scarf and ran across the room to drape it over Ida's shoulders.

"Oh, how perfect," she said, clapping her hands. "And, my dear, it hides your—come see how sweet you look."

She swept Ida across the room to the looking glass and they stood side by side in front of it, Ida's drawn face pale in the mirror beside the rosiness of Lily.

"We'll go shopping tomorrow," said Lily firmly. "There's crinolines on Broad Street. Just wait till you see."

"But I don't wear crinolines," said Ida. She was desperately confused. "Hardly anybody in Concord wears crinolines."

Lily laughed. "Oh, praise be to Concord, the Paris of the North."

A LETTER FROM
EUDOCIA

My dear Ida,

Eben has set off & should arrive in city of Balt, by the time
you read this. I have told him to ask for you at hotel so please
look out for him. He has strict instructions to bring you home.
Now Ida I know that at 19 you are a grown woman but I
request nay order you to come home at once. Mother Morgan
although somewhat enfeebled as you know joins me in this
entreaty. Think of the child's welfare if not of self.

I send photograph of Alice taken in Watertown. Eben's is
from a gallery in Brighton while selling Mr. Hosmer's horse.

Yr devoted mother,
Eudocia Flint

Alice has made you a penwiper.

BABIES THAT
GET STUCK

The uncertainty was hard to bear. Ida waited day after day for the arrival of her brother Eben and for news of Seth's return from the fresh air of the country.

At night she slept on a settee in Lily's hotel room. By day she walked out on the streets of Baltimore looking for Seth, studying the faces of the companies of soldiers as their regiments marched to the depot and searching among the crowds gathered around the food tables of the Christian Commission. On the back streets of the city the colored people of Baltimore looked at her and smiled and called out, "Bless you, missus. When's that chile a-comin'?"

But Lily LeBeau kept saying she had heard nothing from Seth. Sick at heart, Ida pleaded, "Lily, he may be very ill. Doesn't anyone know where he is?"

"No, dear, I'm afraid not." Lily was weary of Ida's questions, weary of repeating the same old fable. Impulsively one day she changed her story. She sat down beside Ida and looked at her gravely. "Now dear, I have something hurtful to tell you. The fact is, your husband skedaddled."

Ida looked blank.

"You know, dear, from the battle. He skedaddled from the battle."

Hastily Ida said, "Oh, yes, I know, but I don't care about that."

"Good gracious, child, surely you can understand that your dear boy don't dare take a chance. They'll shoot him if they find him. That's what they tell me."

"But Lily—"

Whenever Lily's logic failed her, she had ways of skipping aside. The first way was a change of subject.

Boldly she patted Ida's bulging skirt and told her she really must go home. Didn't she know the truth about babies? Hadn't she been told there was often trouble with the first? Lily had heard such terrible things about babies that came out in pieces and mothers who died shrieking with pain. "I told you about my off cousin, how her baby got stuck."

When Ida merely set her jaw and said nothing, Lily tried another fib. "The hotel, Ida dear. Mr. Kenney knows you're here but his wife don't, and it's against the rules. If she finds out there's two of us, she'll throw the both of us out."

Quickly Ida said, "I'll pay you more, Lily." She patted the place where her money was tightly pinned under her dress.

Lily softened. "No, no, my honey, never mind. I'll talk to Jesse. He's sweet on me."

Her other resource was vivacious action. Failing in argument, Lily jumped up in a swirl of ruffles and feathers and bounced across the room to attack her trunk. Flouncing back with a sash, a fichu, a mantilla and a bonnet, she thrust them at Ida. "Now dear, just help me dress."

In a miserable state of agitation, Ida tied the sash around Lily's corseted waist, hooked the fichu, adjusted the mantilla and straightened the bonnet.

"Your turn now," said Lily. Once again she plunged her arms into the tumbled clothing in her trunk. "Because this evening you're coming with me. I won't take no for an answer. Remember, dear? It's the last performance. *There ain't gonna be no more, no more."*

She hauled out an enormous shawl and draped it around Ida. Then, standing back, she laughed at Ida's hugeness and sashayed around her, swishing her skirts from side to side. A curl came loose and fluffy bits of swansdown escaped from her bonnet and drifted to the ceiling, buoyed by a warm breeze from the blowing curtain.

Gloomily Ida stood stock-still, admitting to herself that Lily was bewitching. Her arms and bosom were plump with girlish chub, and most of her fair hair was real. Her eyes were blue and sparkling and her manner adorably coquettish, even with clumsy Ida, even with Mr. Kenney at the desk, even with the colored man who swept the stairs and the pretty dark-skinned chambermaid, even with the half-starved cat in the alley. Ruefully Ida told herself that Seth could not be blamed for being swept off his feet.

Obediently she accompanied Lily to the Holliday Street Theatre to witness her performance in *The Marble Heart.* Of course Ida already knew the tragic story of Phidias, the noble sculptor, and the three beautiful statues that came alive. Although Lily seemed to think of Ida's hometown as a far Northern outpost of civilization, the people of Concord were not completely out of touch with the dramatic arts. Ida herself had taken part in swashbuckling home-spun performances in the Alcotts' dining room. Some of the productions of Seth's Pudding Club had been burlesques of famous dramas like *The Lady of Lyons* and Shakespeare's *Othello.* No one in the family had heard Jenny Lind or seen Edwin Forrest, but the newspapers carried daily intelligence of the theaters and music halls of Boston.

This evening the living statues in *The Marble Heart* were astonishing. It was wonderful how still they stood on their pedestals and how thrillingly they melted at last and spoke. But how strange! The play was not tragic at all, not here in Baltimore, it was hilarious.

Ida was in no mood to laugh. She applauded when Lily sang her slave girl's song, but she was grateful when the curtain came down for the last time. Wearily she moved up the aisle in a crush of other people, the women in their ballooning skirts, the men adjusting their silk hats. In the lobby of the theater she waited, but it was a full half hour before Lily appeared, flushed and glowing, to walk back with Ida to the hotel.

The letter about Eben had been a milestone. Ida read it over and over, homesick for the first time. Oh, yes, it would be a relief to go back with Eben as her mother had requested—*nay, ordered*—her to do.

But she couldn't. She could not possibly go back with him now, not with Seth somewhere nearby, perhaps sick unto death.

AROUND THE PIANO

Mother Morgan sat in the corner, her head down.

Ida's mother sat at the piano, with Alice in her lap. Sally and Josh leaned on either side.

Eudocia flipped a page, poised her fingers over the keys, and said, "Ready?"

They were a singing family, and they launched into it with gusto. Even Alice pretended to sing.

Mine eyes have seen the glory of the coming of the Lord;
He is trampling out the vintage where the grapes of wrath are stored;
He hath loosed the fateful lightning of His terrible swift sword;
His truth is marching on.

I have seen Him in the watchfires of a hundred circling camps;
They have builded Him an altar in the evening dews and damps;

I can read His righteous sentence by the dim and flaring lamps;
His day is marching on.

He has sounded forth the trumpet that shall never call retreat;
He is sifting out the hearts of men before His judgement seat;
O be swift, my soul, to answer Him! be jubilant, my feet!
Our God is marching on.

> *Glory, glory, hallelujah!*
> *Glory, glory, hallelujah!*
> *Glory, glory, hallelujah!*
> *His truth is marching on.*

They were starting the fourth verse when Sally nudged her mother. Still singing, Eudocia swiveled around on the stool to look at Mother Morgan, who was weeping.

"Stupid," sobbed Mother Morgan. "Stupid, stupid."

"There now, Augusta," said Eudocia, springing up. "It's just a song. Here, why don't you put in the new pictures?" She opened the album to an empty page and showed Augusta how to tuck in the cards.

Augusta glowered at the young faces of Alice and Eben and muttered, "Stupid," again, but she bent to the task while they sang the last verse.

In the beauty of the lilies Christ was born across the sea,
With a glory in His bosom that transfigures you and me;
As He died to make men holy, let us die to make men free!
While God is marching on.

Later on, with Mother Morgan napping in her room, Eudocia talked about the song in the kitchen. Standing at the stove with a long fork, extracting peaches from a boiling kettle, she said it was all very well for Julia Ward Howe to say they should all die, but was Mrs. Howe about to die in the war? She was not. Did she have a son in the army? She did not. So she had no right to talk about dying. Eudocia pierced a floating peach. "Well, never mind. It's a good song anyway."

Heaps of overripe and bruised fruit lay on the table. Sally and Josh peeled and sliced and said nothing. Alice ate the juicy skins.

Jam was in the making, but it came to a halt when a wasp crawled out of a peach and stung Sally, who screamed, causing Josh to cut his thumb.

Eudocia dabbed baking soda on Sally and bandaged Josh and complained to nobody in particular, "When in the name of heaven is Eben going to write? When, oh when, is that sister of yours coming home?"

But a letter from Eben came next day.

Dear Mother,

I can't find Ida anyplace. I went to a lot of hotels and rooming houses but there are so many. The one where you said she was, the lady didn't have her name in the book. I went to a hospital the way you said and asked for somebody having a baby but they just laughed. They pointed to the beds and there must have been a hundred lined up in one big ward with wounded men and they said none of them was a maternity case. So then I looked for a lying-in hospital like you said but it was full of men too except for two babies crying and they weren't Ida's.

Now Mother don't worry but I have joined up. The recruiting office hardly asked me anything they were so glad to get me. I told you before how I wanted to go only you said I was too young but they said sixteen was all right. Now Mother don't worry about me, I'll write as soon as I know where we're off to. It's 2d Maryland. Tomorrow I get a blue coat with brass buttons—you know what they look like— and an Enfield rifle with a cartridge box and knapsack and all the fixings, just like you say at Thanksgiving.

Your loving son,
Eben

A GIGANTIC FIREARM

Seth did not return from the country, and Eben did not come. Afraid of missing her brother, Ida took to spending hours at the B&O depot, unaware that it was not a point of arrival for trains from the North. Every day she patiently waited on the platform, watching the passengers come and go. Sometimes entire regiments jumped down from the cars and with shouted orders were gathered into companies and marched away. Some of the trains carried wounded men, but Ida could see that these hospital cars were better equipped than the one in which the men had lain upon straw. One hospital train carried wounded colored soldiers shipped north from Battery Wagner. Others brought sick men, feverish with disease, from anywhere and everywhere.

But Eben did not appear. Ida was unaware that she had missed him. She did not know that he had gone straight to the hotel and asked for her. Nor did she know that the proprietor, Jesse Kenney, had been drunk that day, so dead to the world that his place at the desk had been taken by his prim and proper wife, who had not been informed that a woman in a very shocking condition was sharing a room with that tawdry actress Lily LeBeau.

But Jesse himself was at the desk when Lily said good-bye and put a greenback on the counter. "This is to pay for my room for the next two weeks. Now Jesse, take good care of my friend."

Jesse was surprised. "You're leaving, Lily dear?"

Lily leaned forward with her charming smile and whispered, "Hush, Jesse, she's not supposed to know. The dear child's eight months gone. I hope to God she'll have the sense to go home."

Jesse winked and nodded and watched Lily flow out of the hotel with hatbox and carpetbag, a tall colored porter wheeling her trunk behind her.

Ida was at the station, continuing her vigil for Eben, when Lily appeared on the platform and climbed aboard a waiting train.

For a moment Ida was too astonished to think. But then, dismayed, she ran to the stationmaster. "That train, quick, quick, can you tell me where it's going?"

"That train, ma'am?" The stationmaster was a dignified old gentleman. "That there train is heading for Washington, D.C. If you intend to behold the greatest city ever seen by mortal eyes, you better get on board toot sweet."

Once again Ida did not falter. Without stopping to regret the valise she had left behind in the hotel, she pushed through a thick crowd of soldiers and ran clumsily to the last car on the train. A porter was just lifting the metal step, but he lowered it again when she called out, "Oh, sir, please wait," and then helped her aboard.

The steam whistle shrieked, and the great wheels began to move. Ida lurched into the car and found a seat. The painful truth had struck her like a thunderclap. Seth was not recovering his health in the peace and quiet of the country. He was in Washington, and Lily was on her way to join him.

Ida's seat was on the wrong side. Therefore she did not see her brother Eben on the platform, moving with the rest of his company in a slow tide toward another long line of cars.

Now that he had joined up, Eben did not need cash anymore, so with the last of the money his mother had given him he had bought an enormous horse pistol and stuck it in his belt. He had

seen pictures of dashing Union soldiers decked out like that, sometimes with two pistols crossed over their chests.

There were a thousand men on the platform, edging forward
little by little, waiting to board the train, funneling slowly into the
cars. In the middle of the crush Eben was shoulder-to-shoulder
with a first lieutenant in his company. The lieutenant looked down
at him and backed away in terror. "Oh, by Jesus, will you look at
the boy! He's got a gigantic firearm. He'll surely kill us all."

Eben laughed, but he guessed that the pistol was a mistake. He
should have bought a squirrel gun, because that was a weapon he
knew how to use.

PART XV

THE CONCORD ROSEBUD

A TRIFLE FISHY

The Theatre Collection was right across the hall from the Harvard Archives library. Through the glass door, Homer could see Mary at one of the tables. She looked up as he approached and pushed back her chair. Buzzed outside, she came running up to him, flapping her papers and whispering, "Oh, Homer, such discoveries."

"Well, let's amaze each other over lunch. I could eat a yellow dog. Nothing so weakens the human frame as scholarly research. Well-known scientific fact."

The passage of time had swept away their favorite eateries in the square, Elsie's Lunch, the Wursthaus and Grendel's Den. So they had to make do with a chic little place on Church Street. The modish ingredients in the salads and sandwiches were elaborately described on the menu. Mary chose a mysterious salad of apricot couscous, shaved jicama and mango puree wrapped in prosciutto, Homer a puzzling dish featuring anchovies, Gorgonzola, sun-dried tomatoes and brandied lentils. With the waiter hovering over him, he studied the wine list and said, "Let's have some of this Shiraz."

"A bottle?" suggested the waiter.

"Certainly," said Homer grandly while Mary fumbled her notebook out of her bag.

The waiter hurried away, returned with the bottle, extracted the cork, and threw up his arm like a pianist flinging out an arpeggio.

Mary grinned and held up her glass. "Pricey, very pricey. Will you start, or shall I?"

"Me," said Homer. "Listen to this. There's a set of memoirs about all the Harvard men who died in the war. You know, the ones whose names are on the tablets. That nice librarian took them right off the shelf and handed them to me."

"Oh, yes, Angelica Doyle, she's great." Mary sipped her wine and laughed. "Memoirs, of course. All those fellow soldiers, naturally they wrote memoirs about their heroic friends. Oh, good for you, Homer. We should have thought of it before."

Their oddly assorted plates appeared, and they tucked into them like good sports.

"So I looked up Otis Pike," said Homer, "and he was there all right, among all the other men from the class of 1860 who died in the war."

"Like Mudge," said Mary. "Oh, just wait till I tell you. No, never mind. Carry on." She looked at the pink object on her fork and popped it into her mouth.

"What's more," said Homer dramatically, "I found his picture. Look at this."

Mary stared at it. "But we've seen him before. Surely he's the man in the top hat."

"I think so too. So the man in the top hat, the one who wrote the letter to his sweetie pie—remember the fan letter we found in the inside pocket of the coat?—you said he couldn't possibly be your ancestor, and you were right. He's Otis Pike."

"Well, I'm glad my great-great-grandfather wasn't two-timing my great-great-grandmother." Mary munched her sandwich and gazed at the amiable young face of Otis Pike.

"But what on earth was Pike doing with a picture of Seth's wife Ida? She doesn't fit with that blowzy lady in satin rompers at all. Surely a respectable girl like Great-Great-Grandmaw wouldn't have been to the taste of a man like Pike, not if he liked his women fat and winsome like that lady in tights."

"Well, for Christ's sake," said Homer, "adultery isn't exactly a recent invention."

It was an unfortunate remark, because not very long ago there had been a lapse from conjugal fidelity on the part of his wife. Embarrassed, Homer tried to pour another glass of wine and managed to knock it off the table. "Oh shit," he said, jumping up and moving his chair. "I'm sorry."

The waiter rushed up with paper towels and got down on his knees. His back looked unforgiving. "I could order another bottle," suggested Homer brightly.

"No, no, Homer," said Mary, "don't be silly. Here, you can finish mine." She smiled apologetically at the waiter. "Coffee! We'll both have coffee."

"Mary dear," said Homer, "it's your turn now."

"Oh, Homer, I found such wonders." She was dizzily triumphant. "It matches, it all matches." She scrabbled in her notebook. "Look at these. They're Hasty Pudding playbills." She put a photocopy on the table and tapped her finger on a name.

Homer read it, then looked up, astonished. "Seth Morgan, the Concord Rosebud? Your great-great-grandfather, he was playing a rosebud?"

"Oh, Homer, they were all just being silly. Hasty Pudding has always been like that. They were just having fun. But go ahead, read the rest of it."

Homer studied the playbill. "Fairy Bell and the Female Smuggler, we've seen them before. And also the Young Scamp."

"Of course we have. They were in that strange letter in Otis Pike's coat, the one addressed to Otis. It was signed 'The Concord Rosebud,' remember, Homer? 'In the name of Fairy Bell, the Young Scamp and the Female Smuggler, don't do it again.' "

Homer thought about it. "So it was a letter from your great-great-grandfather Seth Morgan, pleading with Otis, reminding him about Fairy Bell, who was really . . . um, Steve Driver, and the

CLASS OF '60

Mudge, Hayden, Wetmore, Howland, Driver,
Hopkins, Niles & Welds

MINSTRELS

BUSINESS MANAGER. . . . . LOV TAPPAN

*This Highly Acclaimed and Abominable Libretto Is the
Frightful and Extraordinary Work of That Illustrious Knight of
the Inkwell, Sir O. Pikestaff Programme for this Evening*

Program for This Evening

Grand Introductory Overture . . . . FULL BAND
Opening Chorus. . . . . COMPANY
Johnny Is a Shoemaker . . . . JOHNNY HAYDEN
Fairy Bell . . . . STEVE DRIVER
Female Smuggler . . . . CHARLEY MUDGE
Good Old Friends . . . . H. HOWLAND
Listen to the Mockingbird . . . . JOHNNY HAYDEN
Concord Rosebud . . . . SETHIA MORGAN
French Maid, Fair, but Alas! . . . . NOELLA GOBRIGHT
Rondo . . . . ORCHESTRA

INTERMISSION OF FIVE MINUTES

Violin Solo Descriptive of a bird that has escaped
from its cage, hopping from tree to tree . . . HOWLAND
Quartet . . . DRIVER, MUDGE, HAYDEN, HOWLAND
WHISTLING SOLO . . . . Sig. WHEELOCCO

	Mr. Schermerhorn	J. HAYDEN
YOUNG SCAMP	Mr. Williams	LITTLE HOP
	Young Scamp	STEPHEN WELD

Ballad, with invisible chorus. . . . . MASTER HOWLAND
Nubian Acrobats. . . . . MUDGE AND WETMORE
Banjo Duet. . . . . HOWLAND AND MUDGE

Female Smuggler, who was really Charley Mudge, and the Young Scamp, who was—wait a sec—Stephen Weld."

Silently Mary pointed to four lines in the middle of the playbill.

"Aha, I see. '*This Highly Acclaimed and Abominable Libretto Is the Frightful and Extraordinary Work of That Illustrious Knight of the Inkwell, Sir O. Pikestaff.*' " Homer looked up and grinned. "Our Otis again, the knight of the inkwell. He must have written all this sophomoric silliness."

"I don't know whether to be glad or sad that they were having so much fun prancing around in women's clothes and singing hilarious songs, with no idea at all about what was going to happen to them."

"Of course not," said Homer. "It was 1860. The war hadn't started yet."

"So they had no idea that two of them were going to die only three years later at a little town in Pennsylvania—the Knight of the Inkwell and the Female Smuggler. It seems so sad. But I suppose it's a good thing they had fun while they could."

"Of course it is. So why not be glad?"

"Let me see that memoir again," said Mary, "the one about Otis Pike."

As Homer handed it over, a shadow fell on the table. It was the waiter. In glacial tones he inquired if they would like dessert.

"Uh-oh." Mary looked around and saw a crowd of waiting customers glowering at their empty coffee cups. "No, no, we're finished. Come on, Homer."

So she had to read the memoir for Otis Pike on the sidewalk. The weather had gone downhill. Mary did her best to shield the pages from the rain while avoiding the umbrellas bobbing along Church Street and swarming around the theater.

"It's interesting," she said, batting at the paper, "this passage about being chastised three times for leaving the ranks. What does that mean, leaving the ranks?" She looked up at Homer. "Doesn't it mean deserting? So when Seth told Otis not to do it again, wasn't he warning him not to desert again?"

"Maybe." Homer mopped his wet hair. "If so, then the letter worked, because instead of deserting, Otis was killed. What does it say about that?" He bent over the damp page. "... *in the very fore-front among his gallant classmates . . . farthest forward in the field.*"

The subway entrance was a refuge from the rain. Thumping down the steps, they wrestled with the oddities surrounding the person of Otis Pike.

Mary put it into words as they dropped their tokens in the slot and bumped through the turnstile. "It was Seth who wrote the warning letter," she said dreamily as they walked up the ramp to the outgoing trains. "And yet he's the one who is supposed to have been the deserter."

"Fishy," said Homer, "it's just a trifle fishy."

THE

SCRAPBOOK

Thereafter, they scuttled this way and that, following one lead after another.

"Brown," said Angelica Doyle, "that's what you need, Professor Kelly. Francis Brown's roll of Harvard students in the Civil War."

"Call me Homer," said Homer. "You say there's a roll of students? But I've already got the memoirs."

"No, no. This is a list of all the men who were in the war, not just the ones who died."

"Oh, I see."

Opening the roll of students, Homer understood at once that Francis Brown had been one of those diligent record keepers whose labors are of so much more value than those of geniuses in the literary line—writers and historians and stuck-up professors like, for example, himself.

ROLL
OF
STUDENTS OF HARVARD UNIVERSITY
WHO SERVED IN THE
ARMY OR NAVY OF THE UNITED STATES
DURING THE WAR OF THE REBELLION.
PREPARED AT THE REQUEST OF THE CORPORATION,
BY
FRANCIS H. BROWN, M.D.
CAMBRIDGE:
WELCH, BIGELOW, AND COMPANY,
PRINTERS TO THE UNIVERSITY.
1866.

Homer turned over the pages of Brown's 1866 edition with
awe. At the request of the Harvard Corporation, Francis Brown had
scampered around collecting information about every student who
had joined up or been drafted during the Civil War. He had winnowed information from the Academical Department, the Medical
School, the Law School, and the Scientific School. He had written
it all down, he had made lists, he had sorted them into classes, and
he had put sad little asterisks beside the names of the men who had
died. His roll was a masterpiece of industry and attention to detail.
He had finished his list in 1866, but did he then rest? No, no, he
kept right on, adding new names and scrounging for more, produc-
ing an expanded version in 1869.

Homer exulted to Mary. "Your great-great-grandfather's in it. I
found out that he was a first lieutenant, but now he's more mysterious than ever."

"He is? Oh, Homer, what does it say?"

" 'Present at Gettysburg, further history unknown.' "

"How strange! Do you suppose it means he deserted at Gettysburg?"

"Could be. It might explain all the dark looks and raised eyebrows in your family."

"The shame, you mean. Oh, I'm sick and tired of the shame."

"Well, you'll like this. A lot more of those jolly men on your Hasty Pudding playbill are in Brown's list. They were in the war too."

"They were? Oh, show me, Homer."

In the end she put it all together in a scrapbook, with regimental histories from Francis Brown's *Roll of Students of Harvard University Who Served in the Army or Navy of the United States During the War of the Rebellion.*

CIVIL WAR HISTORIES
OF PERFORMERS IN
HASTY PUDDING

★Charles Redington Mudge, 1860

(Female Smuggler and Nubian Acrobat)

First Lieutenant, 2d Mass. Vols. (Infantry), May 28, 1861; Captain, July 8, 1861; Major, November 9, 1862; Lieutenant Colonel, June 6, 1863. **KILLED AT GETTYSBURG, July 3, 1863.**

★Otis Mathias Pike, 1860

(Despised and Celebrated Knight of the Inkwell)

Private, 2d Mass. Vols. (Infantry), July 12, 1862. **KILLED AT GETTYSBURG, July 3, 1863.**

Seth Morgan, 1860

(Concord Rosebud)

Second Lieutenant, 2d Mass. Vols. (Infantry), May 25, 1861; First Lieutenant, November 9, 1862. **"PRESENT AT GETTYSBURG, further history unknown."**

Noah Gobright, 1860

(French Maid, Fair, but Alas!)

First Lieutenant, Artillery Reserve, Captain John Bigelow's 9th Battery, Mass. Light, Lieutenant Colonel McGilvery's brigade. **IN ACTION AT GETTYSBURG.**

Horace John Hayden, 1860
(Listen to the Mockingbird)
Second and First Lieutenant, 3d U.S. Artillery, August 5, 1861;
Brevet Major, October 2, 1865. **HAYDEN'S BATTERY
WAS AT GETTYSBURG.**

Stephen William Driver, 1860
(Fairy Bell)
Acting Assistant Surgeon, USA., April–November 1863.
PROBABLY AT GETTYSBURG.

George Gill Wheelock, 1860
(Whistling Solo)
Acting Assistant Surgeon, USA, January 13–July 8, 1865.
TOO LATE FOR GETTYSBURG.

Stephen Minot Weld, 1860
(Young Scamp)
Second Lieutenant, 18th Mass. Vols., January 24, 1862; First
Lieutenant, October 24, 1862; Captain, May 4, 1863; Aide to
General Reynolds at Gettysburg; Lieutenant Colonel, 56th
Mass. Vols, July 22, 1863; Colonel May 6, 1864: Brevet
Brigadier General, U.S. Vols., March 13, 1865; mustered out,
July 12, 1865. **HUGELY IMPORTANT, FIRST DAY
AT GETTYSBURG!**
Order from General Reynolds in Weld's diary:
"Ride at once with your utmost speed to General Meade.
Tell him the enemy are advancing in strong force,
and that I fear they will get to the heights beyond the town before I
can. I will fight them inch by inch."

★Thomas Rodman Robeson, 1861
(Polly Ann and Augustus Tompkins)
Second Lieutenant, 2d Massachusetts Vols. (Infantry), May 28,
1861; First Lieutenant, November 30, 1861; Captain, August
10, 1862. **DIED AT GETTYSBURG, July 6, 1863.**

Oliver Wendell Holmes, Jr., 1861
(Ludovico, a Respectable Gentleman)
Private, 4th Battery Mass. V.M., April 1861; First Lieutenant, 20th Mass. Vols., July 10, 1861; Captain, March 23, 1862: Lieutenant Colonel (not mustered), July 5, 1863; A.D.C., mustered out, July 17, 1864.
WOUNDED BEFORE GETTYSBURG.

*William Yates Gholson, 1861
(Great Lyric Tragedienne)
First Lieutenant, 106th Ohio Vols., July 16, 1862; Captain, July 24, 1862; killed at Hartsville, Tennessee, December 7, 1862.
DIED BEFORE GETTYSBURG.

Henry Pickering Bowditch, 1861
(Brabanto, a Hasty Old Codger)
Second Lieutenant, 1st Mass. Cav., November 5, 1861; First Lieutenant, June 28, 1862; Captain, May 13, 1863; discharged, February 15, 1864; Major, 5th Mass. Cav., March 26, 1864; resigned, June 3, 1865. **PROBABLY IN CAVALRY BATTLE AT GETTYSBURG, JULY 3, 1863.**

Henry Weld Farrar, 1861
(Mr. Snoozle)
Vol. A.D.C., staff of General Sedgwick, March 1863; Second Lieutenant, 7th Maine Vols., April 10, 1863; First Lieutenant, March 15, 1864; Captain, June 7, 1864; Brevet Major, October 19, 1864; Brevet Lieutenant Colonel.
PROBABLY AT GETTYSBURG.

John Bigelow, 1861
(Montano, caught in a row but not disposed to fight)
Captain, 9th Mass. Battery, February 11, 1863: Brevet Major, U.S. Vols., August 1, 1864; resigned December 11, 1864.
HERO IN BATTLE OF THE PEACH ORCHARD, July 2, 1863, AT GETTYSBURG!

NOTE!!! In the first Hasty Pudding production of this 1861 class in March 1860, Sir O. Pikestaff was again responsible for "These Tearfully Comical Sidereal Abominations Involving Gaulish Chieftains, Druids, Bards, etc., Which Have Been Got Up with Utter Recklessness as to Pecuniary Considerations!!"

"Well, it's a very nice collection," said Homer, looking at Mary's pasted pages, "but are we any closer to exonerating your great-great-grandfather?"

"Oh, I suppose not," said Mary. "I was carried away, that's all."

PART XVI

FINDING LILY

THE B&O

Lily LeBeau had boarded the train several cars farther forward. Ida told herself to keep a sharp lookout at every stop and be ready to jump down if Lily got off, because if she lost Lily, how would she ever find Seth?

Oh heavens! For a moment, everyone in the car bounced and swayed as the train floundered over a rough place on the track. Ida guessed that the rails had been torn up by the enemy and patched together again. The car wobbled and lurched, and its occupants lurched with it, their possessions rolling in the aisle.

Ida clung to the back of the seat in front of her and thought about the safety of the infant growing so rambunctiously inside her. She didn't really worry. The child had given her no trouble so far. But some of the other passengers glanced at her in concern. She smiled confidently back, and when the rails smoothed out, she devoted her attention to the view racing past the window.

She was fascinated by the size of the fields, so much bigger than the rocky tracts of arable land at home. Every one of these endless rail fences must enclose a dozen acres or more. The corn was tasseling everywhere. There were long slatted barns and broad fields of tobacco. She saw a woman in a sunbonnet sitting high up on the seat of a cultivating machine in one field, the reins of the plodding horses in her hand.

Leaning against the glass to look back, Ida wanted to jump off the train and tell her that it was the same at home. Her father was dead and her husband was in the war, so now it was up to the women and children to carry on.

Last fall, it had been Ida and Eben, Sally and Josh who had wandered around the apple orchard, picking up the windfalls. Their mother had followed after them, helping little Alice gather good ones in her pinafore. Of course, thought Ida, smiling to herself, Mother Morgan had never helped at all, being too sickly, or so she said.

This summer, who would load the wagon and carry the peaches to market? Hired help was hard to come by, and it was a grueling drive in the middle of the night. Perhaps this year they would take them in on the cars. It was strange, thought Ida, how little she blamed herself for staying away from home in this busiest of all seasons. Perhaps being with child had made her selfish. But child or no child, she was determined to find Seth, no matter what terrible thing he had done, no matter how cruelly he had chosen another way.

"Your ticket, ma'am," said the conductor, appearing beside her.

"Oh, I'm sorry, I don't have a ticket. May I buy one?" Ida held out a five-dollar bill, hoping it would be enough.

The conductor shook his head. "Well, ma'am, we ain't supposed to sell tickets on the train, but everything's topsy-turvy anyhow." He handed her the ticket with her change.

Ida smiled and said, "Thank you."

But the conductor was in a conversational mood. Taking hold of the brass loop on the back of her seat, he explained why things were topsy-turvy. "First of all, there's all them crates of medical supplies for the hospitals down there."

"Hospitals?"

"In Washington. The whole city's turned into one whopper of

a hospital. And then there's all them trucks of coal. Look, missus, quick now. See 'em there on the siding? Abe Lincoln, he says they'll all be dark as pitch if we don't get 'em there in a hellfire hurry."

"Goodness me," said Ida.

The conductor expanded in the warmth of her interest. "Biggest problem is the men. Mr. Garrett, he's commandeered ten locomotives to carry ten thousand men, that's a thousand apiece."

Ida was happy to have someone to talk to. "Who's Mr. Garrett?"

"You don't know Mr. Garrett? Why, he's the most important man in Baltimore. He owns this here railroad. And if Mr. Garrett says ten thousand men's going out today, ten thousand men *will* go out today. Did you see them fellers back there at the depot in Baltimore? Couple thousand, he said they was all supposed to go out today, heading for some godforsaken place."

"I see," said Ida.

"Well, thank Gawd, ma'am, this here's only a passenger train with decent folks like you on board."

"Can you tell me when we'll arrive in Washington?"

He pulled out his watch. "Couple hours yet. When the train pulls in, I'll help you down with your things."

"Oh, no, that's all right," said Ida, uncomfortably aware that she had no things. "I won't need any help, but thank you just the same."

IDA FORLORN

As the time of arrival grew near, Ida gathered her strength for the ordeal ahead. Whatever happened, she must not miss Lily. She would keep her place in the cars and watch all the passengers as they moved along the platform below her window.

The outskirts of Washington were ugly with cattle yards and wagon sheds. An enormous corral held thousands of horses. The smell of a slaughterhouse seeped into the car. Ida was disappointed. Could they really be approaching the great capital city of the United States? She had seen photographs of splendid marble buildings like temples in ancient Rome, but so far, it looked more like a stockyard or cattle market.

With a hiss of steam and a squealing of brakes, the train slowed down and chugged into the station. At once all the other passengers stood up and collected their bags and bundles and moved along the aisle. A moment later they appeared on the platform below Ida's window.

The station was an imposing building with a tower that rose high above the track. Ida watched intently as streams of passengers from the other cars flooded slowly toward an open door—well-dressed businessmen, or perhaps they were congressmen, sharp-looking salesmen with heavy cases, shabby women in untidy bonnets, handsomely dressed ladies, whole families with children and babes in arms and strolling clusters of men in uniform, black soldiers as well as white. Some of their uniforms were outlandish, with baggy red trousers and tasseled fezes—like pictures in *The Arabian Nights*.

In the sodden August heat even the fashionable women looked disheveled, their crinolines tussled in the push and shove of other people's baggage. One well-dressed man took off his tall hat and mopped his bald head, and Ida thought he must surely be a senator. A boy with a tray hanging from his shoulders was selling iced lemonade, and for a homesick moment Ida wondered if the ice had come from one of the ponds at home, packed in the hold of a ship that had sailed all the way from Boston harbor, the great blocks keeping each other cold.

She caught her breath and leaned closer to the window. Was that Lily's pretty parasol?

No, it tilted sideways and the face beneath it was not Lily's.

"End of the line," said the conductor. "May I help you, missus?"

"Oh, thank you." But Ida was grateful for his hand as she stepped heavily down to the platform.

She had missed dozens of people. Hungrily Ida stared right and left, looking for Lily. But the crowd was thinning, the train was gathering steam and blowing its whistle and the powerful rods on the driving wheels were beginning their mighty seesawing motion. The great wheels turned slowly at first, then faster and faster and faster. The locomotive whistled and thundered out of the station, followed by its rattling train of cars, leaving no one on the platform but a couple of baggage porters, a stevedore with a cart piled with mailbags, the lemonade seller packing up his ice—which came, perhaps, from the North Pole—and Ida, forlorn.

Only then did she see that there were two doors into the station. Lily must have gone into the farther door, never passing Ida's window at all.

Almost running, she made her way through the other door. In the lofty waiting room a few people were sitting on benches and a few more were heading out the wide portal into the street. Ida hurried after the departing passengers, looking for a pretty plump woman in a soaring bonnet and a fetching outfit. When she had boarded the train in Baltimore, Lily had been wearing her favorite gown, her "Clothilde," with its lacy little cape.

Outside on the broad avenue, cab horses were ranged along the curb. One had a nose bag, and Ida was reminded that she had not eaten a morsel since a hasty breakfast in the station at Baltimore, and then it was only a bun.

People were climbing into the hacks, the men handing in their wives, the wives gathering up their billowing skirts and settling down.

Ida hurried along the row as the drivers flicked their whips across the broad backs of their horses and set off at a trot, heading for splendid lodgings or magnificent hotels somewhere else in the city. Soon all the cabs had sped away in the direction of an imposing marble building a little farther up the avenue. The dome of the building was covered with scaffolding. Ida had seen pictures, she knew what it was. It was the Capitol of the United States.

Painfully disappointed, she sagged down on a bench beside the door of the depot. Every one of the passengers from the Baltimore train had left the station, including Lily LeBeau.

THE NEW SHAPE
OF THE WORLD

Only a few weeks ago, Ida had trembled on the verge of finding her lost husband. Now she was alone and friendless in a strange city. She had only one harum-scarum acquaintance, and now Lily LeBeau had become a needle in a haystack. How would Ida ever find her in this labyrinth of unknown streets? Where might she have gone? To some nameless hotel or boardinghouse? To a theater? Was she dashing helter-skelter to a rendezvous with Seth?

Despairing, Ida stumbled away from the station. Turning her back on the Capitol, she began walking up an avenue, heading away from the glaring sun. Tramping along heavily, she was the object of inquisitive stares. But by now, Ida was grimly accustomed to being "the cynosure of all eyes," and she ignored the curious looks and the knowing grins.

And in the open air she soon recovered her spirits. Ida, after all, was a fatalist of the sturdiest New England kind. She was the daughter of a farmer who had endured one natural disaster after another—the wild winds that had torn the apples off the trees, the demented sow that had devoured her piglets, the gripe that had seized the milking cow, the early thaw that had brought along too soon the blossoms on the fruit trees, the lightning stroke that had set fire to the barn, the rainy spring that had flooded the lower field, the wasting disease that had taken Aunt Clara, the strange troubling of Seth's mother's mind and, most terrible of all, the tree in the woodlot that had twisted on Father's ax and crushed him where he stood.

In the last few weeks, blows like a dozen falling trees had fallen on his eldest daughter. They might have broken any other young woman, but Ida's mental habit had always been to absorb harsh tidings and step forward briskly into the new shape of the world, whatever it might be.

She stepped forward now, looking about her, curious to understand a city in which marble temples alternated with shanties and weedy vacant lots. The faces on the street were both white and black—the colored were free now. When a middle-aged white woman smiled at her, Ida spoke up boldly. "Excuse me, ma'am, I wonder if you know of a boardinghouse nearby?"

The woman was in mourning dress. "Why, yes, my dear, I certainly do. There's my own."

What good luck. Walking along with her, Ida learned that Mrs. Broad had been forced to take in lodgers after Mr. Broad was killed by a runaway horse while crossing New Jersey Avenue, only just around the corner from this very spot, and how in the blink of an eye poor Mrs. Broad had found herself a widow, forced to turn her home into a respectable boardinghouse. "Of course, I only take in folks of the better sort. You know, dear, what I mean."

Ida didn't know, but she said, "Oh, yes."

"I have six spare rooms but only four ladies at present, and one gentleman and wife, because Mrs. Poff got so wearied of working in the Dead Letter Office, she went home." Mrs. Broad took Ida's arm and whispered, "My dear, when are you expecting?"

"Next month," said Ida gratefully. "But I'm fine. I'm here for just a few days, and then I'll go home."

"Well, I have a woman friend experienced in the healing arts who could be of assistance, just in case."

Mrs. Broad's was a neat wooden house on G Street. She showed her new tenant around, starting with the parlor, where two women looked up from a checkerboard and an anxious-looking man lowered his newspaper.

Mrs. Broad introduced them as Mr. and Mrs. Tossit and Miss Whitley. "Mrs. Morgan is here just for a little spell," she explained, "before returning to . . ."

"Massachusetts," said Ida. She bobbed politely, then followed Mrs. Broad up the carpeted stairs.

"Here's your room," said Mrs. Broad, throwing open a door.

The room was small but neat, and the bedding was clean. A shining white bowl and pitcher sat on the washstand and a matching vessel was visible under the bed.

"It will do very well," said Ida.

She pulled off her shawl while Mrs. Broad explained the rent and mealtimes and gossiped about the other lodgers. "The Tossits, they're here from Maryland. One of those battles, his barn got burned down and so did his cornfield. He's here to get compensation, three thousand dollars he feels like he's owed, so every other day he goes to his congressman to present his case, and next day he goes to the quartermaster general. Miss Whitley, she's on night duty in the Capitol."

Ida was interested in the lives of people in other places. "Does Miss Whitley work for a congressman?"

"Oh, laws, no." Mrs. Broad laughed heartily. "She's a baker. All the soldiers in the city, thousands of them, they got to be fed, and there's thousands of poor wounded men. So there's a big

bakery down there in the basement of the Capitol. Another of my boarders is in the Sanitary."

"The Sanitary Commission? She's a nurse?"

There were screams from outdoors. Mrs. Broad lifted her hands in a gesture of dismay. "It's Annie's boy, she does the wash." Mrs. Broad went to the window, threw up the sash and shouted into the backyard, "You there, Jacob. Those sheets, you leave them be."

Ida looked out too. The backyard was full of laundry. A small black boy and girl were running in and out. One sheet sagged to the ground.

"You hear me, Jacob?" screeched Mrs. Broad. "You peg up that sheet."

"Mrs. Broad," said Ida anxiously, "you say the city's full of wounded men?"

Her landlady closed the window. "Oh, my goodness, yes. There's hospitals all over. They ship them upriver from Virginia or carry them down from the North in the cars. That big fight in Pennsylvania, those poor young soldiers, they're dying all over this town."

THE LIVING STATUE

Ida's first impression of the nation's capital was renewed next morning when she began a pilgrimage to the city's theaters, following the directions of Mrs. Broad. Blocks of marble cluttered the grounds of the Capitol, there were coal and lumber yards along the Mall and a muddy canal ran through the heart of the city. Often she saw cattle being driven along the grandest streets, and Mrs. Broad complained that there were more pigs than cats.

The four theaters were not far apart. Ida was a tall young woman with strong bones. Even carrying a robust infant eager to be born, she could walk for miles, pausing only once in a while to lean against a picket fence or rest on a marble stairway.

One afternoon she was glad to board a car of the Washington Horse Railroad Company on Seventh Street, although she wasn't sure where it was going. The only sign on the car was not helpful:

COLORED PERSONS
MAY RIDE IN THIS CAR

But the horse was plodding in the right direction. On the Avenue, Ida descended and walked over to Tenth Street to try the last of the theaters on Mrs. Broad's list. At the first three, Grover's National and the two music halls, the Varieties and the Canterbury, no one had heard of Lily LeBeau.

In front of the fourth theater, there was a crowd on the street. They were all staring up at a man stepping carefully along a tightrope stretched between two buildings. Ida watched too, holding her breath until he reached the other side. Then she turned to the gaping man beside her and asked her question about Lily LeBeau.

At once he turned with a theatrical gesture, swept off his feathered hat and said, "Dear madam, come with me."

Ida followed him gratefully through the darkened theater into a maze of dark passages. At the end of a narrow corridor he nodded at a closed door and said, "In there, dear lady," and vanished.

Ida knocked. A woman's voice called out, "*Un momento.*" Then the door was flung open by a white marble statue.

Ida gasped, but the statue laughed and pulled her inside. "Oh, dearie, it's just *The Marble Heart*. You must have heard of it? Well, here I am in person, a marble goddess come to life." She struck a statuesque pose, dropped into a chair, then jumped up again and pulled out another chair for Ida. "Here, dearie, sit down. What can I do for a sweet mother-to-be?"

Ida opened her mouth to ask for Lily LeBeau, but the loquacious living statue kept right on talking, crossing her white legs and lighting a cigar. "Oh Jesus, you can't imagine what it's like. I have to stand on that pedestal without moving a muscle for twenty blessed minutes before I come to life at last, and then I'm stiff all over. But fortunately, my dear, guess what? The new writer, he's changed the lines, so when I wake up, I get to stretch and yawn and say, 'Three long years of marble servitude!' " The living statue jumped up, stretched, yawned, then plumped herself down again. "And then I've got another line that really brings down the house." The actress raised a limp white arm to her white forehead and closed her eyes in anguish, " 'I'm so hungry, I could eat a horse.' "

Ida smiled and the actress laughed and slapped her knee, but at once she stopped laughing and said, "Well, I don't know how long the big boss will let us go on being silly like that. When he gets back from Boston, we'll be all la-di-da again. 'Gold cannot buy genius!' What twaddle."

There was a rustle of skirts in the doorway and a squeal. "Ida! Oh my God, it's not Ida?" Ida stood up awkwardly and smiled at Lily, who held out her hands and cried, "Oh, Ida, what on this earth are you doing here?"

Ida didn't know how to soften the truth. "Oh, Lily, I followed you. I saw you board the train in Baltimore and I figured you must be coming after Seth."

"Oh mother of God." Lily was wrapped in filmy layers of lavender gauze. Her face was heavily made up, but her dismay showed through the pink powder and the patches of sweat. She dropped Ida's hands and said faintly, "But my dear, it's not so."

"You've got to tell me, Lily," said Ida, determined to have the truth at last. "Is Seth here?"

Lily looked around desperately for an excuse to get away. "Wait, dear, wait for me, because it's just not so, what you said. Dearest girl, wait." With a flutter of gauzy veils, she was gone.

"So when are you due, sweetie?" said the marble statue, leaning back in her chair and getting down to business.

"Oh, not for ages yet," lied Ida, sitting down again in confusion.

"Well, I must say, you look ready to pop. My sister, you should've seen her. We thought she must surely have three on the inside, but it turned out to be only one, and, unfortunately it died. Then she died too."

"I'm sorry," murmured Ida, but the statue was off on another fascinating discourse, this time on the subject of disastrous labors she had herself personally witnessed, accompanied by advice on the care of the newborn. Ida was instructed to give her infant lots of titty.

"Oh, Ida, I'm sorry." Lily bustled in again. "Now, my dear, let me tell you what *actually* happened."

At once the living statue jumped up, said, "Ta-ta," bounded into the corridor and slammed the door behind her.

"Ida, dear," said Lily, "I wasn't following Seth. We had already broken up. The whole company was coming to Washington for this engagement, so of course I came too."

"Then Seth isn't sick?" Ida leaned forward, her heart in her mouth. "He was never sick in the country?"

"He was never what?" Lily had forgotten her earlier story. "Oh, sick in the country. Yes, dear, he was, but then he got better. I heard he was here, but it's not true that I followed him, no indeed. And then I heard that his old wound was troubling him."

"Oh, Lily." Ida reached out and caught at her hands. "What wound? Tell me. Please tell me."

Lily had forgotten that Ida's precious husband was supposed to have been wounded in the neck. Impulsively, she gave him a new affliction. "Jaundice," she said wildly. *Whatever that might be.*

"Jaundice!"

Well, no, on second thought, perhaps jaundice was not just the thing. Lily changed her mind. "I think that's what they said." She dithered around the room, snatching up a heap of tumbled curls and adding them to the torrent pouring down her back. "Maybe it was pneumonia."

"Oh, Lily, Lily, where is he?"

It was another impossible question. Lily caught up a mirror and twirled to see the toss of her curls and the sway of her gossamer gown. "Oh, in some hospital or other. There are so many in this horrid city." Then Lily put down the mirror and stopped lying. Looking Ida in the face, she said, "My dear, how can you bear to be away from home when your time is so near? Honestly, Ida, you look ready to burst."

Fiercely Ida said, "I'm all right," and then the thought of her suffering husband was so compelling and terrible that she could no longer sit still. Heaving herself to her feet, she said passionately, "Oh, Lily, don't you see? I've got to find him."

"Oh, my dear girl." Lily lifted protesting hands, but Ida turned and lumbered into the corridor, striding away from the frightening distortions and artful half-truths of poor foolish Lily LeBeau.

Poor foolish Lily dropped her hands and watched Seth's

unhappy wife fade clumsily down the hall. The poor child was almost running.

Lily felt put-upon. What else could she have said? She had been as good as gold, she had done everything a mortal soul could do on this earth to guard the safety of that skedaddling scamp Seth Morgan. His poor little wife would soon give birth, come hell or high water, whether she was still adrift in the city of Washington or at home way up north where she ought to be. Either way, a screaming baby might put some sense into her head, and then at last she'd forget about her heartbreaking struggle to find a husband who had no intention whatever of being found. A husband for whom *she,* poor bullied and self-sacrificing Lily LeBeau, had been forced to humiliate herself time and again.

Lily felt more and more aggrieved. This hateful pretense had been forced on her entirely against her will. In order to prevent the entire force of the law from pouncing on Seth and hanging him from a sour-apple tree, she'd been forced to tell terrible fibs to his wife, poor sweet little Ida, because Seth kept saying that somebody had it in for him, the snooping bloodhounds of the War Department and somebody else who was even worse. So it had been entirely on his behalf that Lily had been forced to tell all these awful lies. It had been extremely painful and difficult, and she was thoroughly ashamed of herself.

So when Otis looked in the door and raised questioning eyebrows and said, "How did it go?" she screamed at him and threw the mirror at his head.

IDA'S DRAWERS

We now give some new patterns in linen, which have been sent out to us from Paris. As everybody is talking of economy, many ladies, who have heretofore put out their linen work, will now make it up for themselves. In this way every subscriber for "Peterson" will be able to save three, four, five, or even ten times the price of subscription.

—*Peterson's Magazine,* November 1861

W hen Ida had jumped impulsively on the train in Baltimore, she had brought nothing with her but her shawl, the money belt sewn tightly around her rib cage and the tasseled bag attached to the high waistband of her dress. She had crocheted the "Lady's Work-Bag" herself, but it was small, holding only a purse, a comb, a handkerchief, and a powder box with a swansdown puff. Thus she had nothing to wear in the city of Washington but the clothes on her back.

They were not enough. She must certainly have a change of underwear. Ida had discarded her stays long ago, but she surely needed another chemise and an extra pair of drawers.

Ida confided her problem to Mrs. Broad. At once that kind woman bundled a couple of old sheets out of a cupboard.

"They've been side-to-middled already," she said, "so they're no use to me anymore."

Ida accepted them gratefully, and begged the loan of scissors and pincushion, needle and thread. In a single long night she turned the sheets into a chemise, an enormous pair of drawers and a night-dress.

Next morning she heated a kettle on the stove and got to work in the backyard, using Annie's scrubbing board and her cake of brown soap, then cranking everything between the rollers of the mangle. She washed out her bodice too, and her lace collar. Then, instead of pegging everything up on the line, she spread them out in her bedroom to dry. She didn't want to take up space in the drying yard, because it was always like a ship in full sail. That night she went to sleep in her new nightdress, her wet things cooling the warm air.

When Mrs. Broad appeared at her door next morning with a length of upholsterer's fringe, Ida laughed, because she knew what it was for. At once she reached for her purse and insisted on paying a few pennies, because Mrs. Broad had bought it from the ragman.

The fringe matched Ida's skirt exactly, and she looped it twice around the lower edge to hide the muddy hem. The effect was perfectly in the mode, because the magazines were full of fashionable ladies in wide-spreading gowns trimmed at the bottom in the same way.

"Well now, ain't you smart," said Mrs. Tossit. "Just like a fashion plate."

Of course it wasn't true, but even in her swollen skirt, Ida felt almost elegant as she began her new quest. "There's hospitals all over this town," Mrs. Broad had said. So all over town Ida would go. She would visit them all, even though she had little faith in any of Lily's lame stories. Hope was all she had left, the slim hope that she might find Seth somewhere, no matter what he was suffering from—a wound received in battle, a feverish inflammation of the lungs or an attack of yellow jaundice.

THE HOSPITALS

*Here in Washington, when these army hospitals are all filled . . .
they contain a population more numerous in itself than the whole
of Washington of ten or fifteen years ago. Within sight of the
Capitol, as I write, are some thirty or forty such collections, at
times holding from fifty to seventy thousand men . . . amid the
confusion of this great army of sick, it is almost impossible for a
stranger to find any friend or relative. . . .*

—WALT WHITMAN

Seventy-five by forty, my barn was," said Mr. Tossit as he buttoned his frock coat before stepping out the door for another frustrating day in the office of the quartermaster general.

"How dreadful," said Ida. "Surely they owe you compensation."

"Not to mention the cornfield," said Mr. Tossit, clapping on his bowler hat. "A whole forty-acre field of growing corn." Mr. Tossit's face was red and weathered. Ida could almost see a hay fork in his hand. "It wasn't my fault they had a fight on my farm."

"My poor William," said Mrs. Tossit when he had gone. "He's beginning to lose hope." But she sat calmly on the sofa, toeing and heeling a sock.

It was old Mrs. Starkey who told Ida where to look for her wounded husband. "If I were you, dear, I'd begin with Harewood Hospital. It's the biggest." Mrs. Starkey spent her days in the Treasury, counting ragged bills before they were sent to the furnace. She had been at Mrs. Broad's for over a year. "It was even worse last year, my dear, all the wagons and ambulances coming up from the wharves. Oh, it was dreadful. At first, I couldn't help crying, but now I'm ashamed to say I'm used to it."

"They're talking about closing the hospital in the Rotunda," said Miss Whitley, who baked bread in the basement of the Capitol.

Ida was astonished. "There's a hospital in the Capitol?"

"Oh, yes, and for a while the Rotunda wouldn't hold enough of the wounded, so they set up cots in the halls."

"They've put up lots of new hospitals," said Mrs. Starkey. "There's Armory Square and Campbell. Oh, my dear girl, I hope you find your husband soon. You shouldn't be running around alone, not now, my dear, not now."

It was the usual advice. Ida smiled and set off stoutly every day, her tasseled bag stuffed with cakes and apples pressed on her by Mrs. Broad. Whenever the street railway went in the right direction, she climbed on board. Otherwise she walked.

Harewood was a collection of immensely long one-story wooden buildings. Ida walked into a dining room where the plank tables seemed to stretch forever.

Lunch had been spread and the men were at table, all the ones who could leave their beds. Ida walked down the center aisle, trying to keep out of the way of the men and women carrying pots of soup and setting down pitchers of water.

As usual, her swollen shape attracted attention. Heads turned as she approached. Ida didn't care. Mockingly she told herself again that she was the cynosure of all eyes.

The joke brought an ache, a vision of Seth's smiling face, wasted now perhaps and hollow with disease.

It was only a vision. Seth's face was not to be seen at any of the far-flung tables. Nor was he lying on a cot in any of the long wards or sitting up in a wheelchair. Ida saw only strangers among the patients, row upon row, with hospital stewards and nurses in hurried attendance. Often she saw other women—wives and sweethearts who had managed to find their men.

Some of them nodded kindly to Ida. Others whispered behind her back. Sometimes men called out to her, but never in derision. Ida suspected they had wives at home in the same condition. One man in delirium lunged upright, reached out his arms and called out, "Rose, Rose."

Ida smiled and passed by, sorry not to be his Rose.

At Campbell Hospital, the story was the same—long wards, long rows of cots and hundreds of young men suffering from battle wounds or sick with fever, coughing or tossing from side to side or lying very still. Out-of-doors a row of veterans sat in the sun, each of them missing a leg or an arm. Perhaps they felt lucky to be alive. At least they would never stand apart as pitiable oddities. For the rest of her life, Ida knew, she would see battle-scarred men on the street everywhere.

If only Seth were one of them, honorably wounded in his country's cause. Ida had begun to think that perhaps it was from shame that he had left his family and abandoned his wife. How terrible if he should die before she could tell him that she felt no shame at all.

Deserters, after all, were commonplace. On Ida's first afternoon in the city she had seen a troop of men in dirty blue uniforms tramping along the Avenue with armed guards marching beside them. She had asked a woman on the street why Union men should be under guard.

The woman's sneering answer had delivered a pang. "Deserters, look at 'em, it's a wonder they's any good men left, the way thousands skedaddle every time they have a fight." Leaning over the curb, she spat into the gutter.

Ida had backed away, feeling ashamed but relieved at the same time, because her husband was not the only man who had run away from a battle.

She had watched the huddled men in their filthy uniforms as they marched away. Some were shame-faced; others looked defiantly left and right, their bloodshot eyes gazing straight back at the staring people on the street. *You laugh at me? I'd like to see you try it. I'd like to see you walk so smart, right up to the cannon's mouth.*

SOMEONE KNOCKING

Even though her hospital visits in the daytime were full of sorrow, Ida preferred them to her theatergoing in the evening.

Of course it was bizarre to think of her dear Seth, that sober Concord citizen and classical scholar, posturing on the stage in costume. Sometimes it seemed impossible to Ida that he could have chosen an exotic career behind the footlights over the idyllic quiet life of his own family at home.

But then she would remember his stories about the club he called the Pudding, when he and his friends had romped onstage, singing hilarious songs composed by one of their classmates. Painfully, she remembered the laughter of her young brothers and sisters whenever Seth had wrapped himself in a shawl and sang his Rosebud song—"Thou Hast the Petals, I the Thorns."

Perhaps by comparison, his old Concord life had not really been so idyllic.

Uncomfortably, Ida recalled a winter evening in the parlor, with

Seth sitting at the table trying to translate the *Odes* of Horace, while her mother sat at the piano, battling her way through "The Tic-Tac Polka," Alice banged her fists on the keys, Josh and Sally bickered in the kitchen and Seth's own mother sat whining in the corner.

It would not be surprising if domestic life had failed to measure up to those happy old times when he and his classmates had been ridiculous together, performing their comic farces and singing their nonsense songs.

So perhaps the theater was the right place to look for him after all, in spite of Lily's sorry fables about battle wounds and a possible case of jaundice. In running away from the war, perhaps Seth had run straight toward the dazzling excitement of an actor's life.

In the *National Republican* and the *Evening Star,* there were theatrical notices, and everywhere on the street small boys hawked playbills:

LAURA KEENE'S VARIETIES!!
CHARLOTTE CUSHMAN AS LADY MACBETH!!

Ida reached for the playbills and studied them eagerly. Lily's name appeared on the playbill for *The Marble Heart,* but Seth was not listed anywhere.

But perhaps, thought Ida, doing her best to imagine his strange new career, he had taken a stage name. If so, then the playbills were not enough. She had to see the players with her own eyes.

Therefore, nearly every evening she made her way to one of the theaters—Grover's National, the new Ford's or the Washington Theater. But when none of the players turned out to be Seth she would stand up, brush past the whisky-smelling men, step carefully over the puddles of tobacco juice, and make her way home to Mrs. Broad's.

The plays did not interest her. They all seemed posturing and melodramatic, although occasionally there was a spark of wit that made her laugh.

But it wasn't the dramatic productions themselves that made playgoing so disagreeable, nor even the tobacco juice. It was the necessity of showing herself among the queenly women who came to the theater in carriages, resplendent in their coronets of flowers and voluminous skirts of white silk.

Often the magnificent women were escorted by officers who rivaled them in splendor. The full-dress uniforms of colonels and major generals were adorned with sashes and fringed epaulets, and the swashbuckling cavalry officers swaggered in short jackets and buccaneering boots.

Ida could not help comparing their sparkling regalia with the ragged coats of the miserable deserters on the street or the blood-stained bandages of the men who lay in those endless perspectives of suffering white cots. How strange that the theatergoers seemed so happy and carefree, as though Washington were not a city of hospitals, as though the war were not grinding on and on, as though battle would not forever follow battle.

And no matter how accustomed Ida had become to inquisitive stares, it was hard to bear the looks of shocked disgust on the faces of the women in the glorious gowns whenever she stepped into the lobby of a theater. And then, after heaving herself up the stairs to the furnace heat of the topmost balcony and finding a seat among the boldly staring men and looking down at the women as they flowed into the boxes and removed their shawls and bared their white arms, she could almost hear them whispering, *A woman in a family way alone on the street at night, imagine!*

The hurried walk back to Mrs. Broad's was troublesome too. In the neighborhood of the National Theater Ida had to run the gauntlet of Rum Row. Sometimes she made a wide circuit to Harvey's cheerful Oyster Salon on C Street or to the glittering magnificence of Willard's Hotel. Of course she never ventured far south of Pennsylvania Avenue, because Mrs. Broad had warned her about the dreadful things that went on down there in "Hooker's Division," things that she, Mrs. Broad, would not stoop to mention.

But all the hard walking and humiliation would be worth it if only Ida might find Seth's name on a printed program or see him appear when the curtain rose, estranged from her and playing a part, but alive and well.

The days went by. Ida saw *Macbeth* and *Othello* and *The French Spy* and *The Apostate*. Some of the performances were fine, and some perfectly inane, like the posturing of the actors in *The Marble Heart*.

From her high balcony Ida watched as Lily LeBeau warbled her slave girl's song. Another young actor had a farcical speech: "Naturally, Diogenes, gold cannot buy genius, at least not that much gold. How about coughing up a little more?"

In the sweltering gloom near the ceiling, Ida peered at the damp program in her hand to see who was playing the part so absurdly. At once, she was startled to see that the funny fellow was one Adolfo Sethius O'Morgan. Dizzily she dropped the paper and leaned forward to stare, then sat back, limp with disappointment.

The actor was nothing like Seth. He was heavier for one thing, and surely Seth would never have spoiled his good looks with side whiskers and a drooping mustache.

She had seen enough. Gathering her strength, Ida rose and excused herself to her neighbor, then edged along the row of seats while Lily, the singing slave girl, wrung her hands and informed Adolfo Sethius O'Morgan that slaves, alas, had no right to love.

The journey back in the dark was grueling. Slowly and heavily, Ida put one foot in front of another. At the house on G Street she found Mrs. Broad waiting up for her, a candle in her hand. "Oh, dear girl, I've had such qualms."

Ida was almost fainting. For the last quarter mile she had lumbered along, trying to run, aware that two burly men were moving up behind her. Now Mrs. Broad caught at her arm, pulled her into the house and helped her into the kitchen. "Sit down, my honey," she said tenderly, pouring sherry into a teacup. "Another letter's come from your poor mother."

Ida sipped the sherry and leaned back and closed her eyes. "I know what it will say."

"Dear child, don't you think it's time? Shouldn't I send Annie for Mrs. McCool?"

"You sound just like Mother." Ida smiled and sat up. "No, no, dear Mrs. Broad. I'm finished with the theater, and there's only one more hospital I mean to see. If I don't find my husband in the Patent Office, I'll start for home, I promise." She pushed down on the table with both hands and struggled to her feet. "I'll be fine, Mrs. Broad. I won't need Mrs. McCool."

But Ida was aware that under the mounded bulk of her skirt someone was urgently knocking.

PART XVII

INVITED BACK

TOO FANTASTIC

Homer Kelly had taken to the written word at infancy, chewing *Peter Rabbit* in his crib, licking the cookbooks and sniffing the bottles of CINNAMON and NUTMEG, gaping at fluffy words in the sky and running his small fingers over letters carved on the trunks of trees. At last, when the Hardy Boys came Homer's way—blond-haired Joe and dark-haired Frank—he had never looked back.

Therefore by now, as an aging professor dreading retirement, Homer could squeeze a book like a lemon, mash it like a potato, press it like a clove of garlic and extract all the good stuff in a hurry. He worried about the fact that his brain was losing thirty-thousand molecules of gray matter every day, or maybe thirty million, but the technical know-how of an experienced scholar was still alive in his head. His fingers could twiddle swiftly through a card catalogue, and he had at last abandoned his rage at the computer reorganization of Widener Library. His wife had taken him by the hand and led him through it like a little child, and now Homer preened himself on his magisterial command of Hollis, the computerized catalogue of all the libraries in the university.

He also continued to receive bolts of revelation from on high, or wherever bolts of revelation come from—music, dreams, snatches of conversation, birdsong, rainbows in the twirling spray of lawn sprinklers, glimpses of young women with golden hair. Homer's inspirations were sometimes wrong, but often they came straight from the horse's mouth.

These days, while patching together a set of lectures for the coming semester, Homer took time out to ponder the Otis Pike/Seth Morgan connection and the mysterious relation between the Hasty Pudding Club of 1860 at Harvard College and the Second Massachusetts Volunteer Infantry in the Battle of Gettysburg.

There were books, any number of books, whole libraries full of books about that single three-day battle. Homer had discovered the remote corner of the Widener stacks where they could be found. Every moment of those three terrible days in July of 1863 had been recorded, and all the separate actions on every part of the field had been documented, from the exact placing of General Henry Hunt's two hundred pieces of Union artillery to the position of every regiment in the seven corps of the Army of the Potomac, from Culp's Hill on the north to the Round Tops on the south.

Like Mary, Homer was moved by the fact that Mudge and Robeson, Pike and Morgan had all been revelers in the comical productions of Hasty Pudding before finding themselves members of the same regiment in the Union army. But it was only Mudge, Robeson and Morgan who had risen in rank—Charles Redington Mudge becoming a lieutenant colonel, Thomas Rodman Robeson a captain and Seth Morgan a first lieutenant. Poor old Otis Pike, who had been recruited into the regiment as a special favor after a serious scrape in civilian life, had remained a private.

And then at Gettysburg, Robeson and Mudge had fallen on the morning of the third day. And so had the often-absent Otis Pike, if his regimental history was to be believed.

So what about First Lieutenant Seth Morgan, Mary's great-great-grandfather, who had been cited for bravery before Gettysburg, who had been *mentioned in dispatches?* In a history of the regiment written by its chaplain, Homer found Seth's name and an account of the part he had taken in the Battles of Cedar Mountain, Antietam, and Chancellorsville. His story began well but came to an abrupt end—

Missing; dropped from the rolls at Gettysburg, 4 July, 1863.

There were many more shelves to ransack in the Widener stacks, but today Homer was staying at home. He had a horrible cold. And in the slight mental imbalance that accompanies a cold, it occurred to him that war itself was something like a cold, an occasional affliction on the body of the human race. A poor wretch with a cold inhales a few shuddering breaths, waits a few seconds in fearful anticipation, and explodes in a violent convulsion. Perhaps the eruption of war was like that, a sort of global sneeze.

In Homer's abnormal state it seemed perfectly plausible. And then another weird notion occurred to him.

He explained it to Mary. "You know what we said before, how fishy it was. Well, now it looks fishier still. How could a man like Seth Morgan change character like that, from a tried-and-true soldier to a deserter? And how could a totally irresponsible runaway like Otis Pike die at the very front of the battlefield?"

"Well," said Mary doubtfully, "maybe he had a change of heart, like the soldier in *The Red Badge of Courage.* Remember, Homer? He ran away at first and then in the next attack he was filled with reckless daring. Maybe it happened that way with Otis Pike."

Homer brushed away *The Red Badge of Courage.* "Listen to this. I've got a theory. Instead of being inflamed with suicidal courage, Pike ran away again from the fight at Culp's Hill on the morning of the third day. Remember, this time it was his fourth desertion, and the punishment for that was death. Especially at Gettysburg, because General Meade had issued an order to that effect. So Otis took off—wait a sec. I made a map. Look, here's Culp's Hill where the battle was, and right nearby, this is the Baltimore Pike. One of the books says deserters ran away down the Baltimore Pike."

"Mmm," said Mary, looking at the map.

"Okay, so here comes Otis, trotting away along the pike, scared to death of being caught as a deserter and shot, when he comes upon the body of First Lieutenant Morgan, your Grampaw Seth, killed during the rebel bombardment. Terrible shame, his good old classmate lying there, all shot up."

"You're dreaming, Homer. You can't possibly know that."

"So," continued Homer, paying no attention, "what does he do? He exchanges identity tags with Seth. Coats too. In a bloody coat he'll look like a wounded man, not a deserter."

"But Homer, Pike died on the field at Culp's Hill. If the body was Seth's and not Otis's, how did it get back on the field of battle?"

"It's part of my theory," babbled Homer. "Not only does Otis intend to get away from the battle without being shot, he means to be declared a hero too. In the dead of night he drags the body onto the battlefield and leaves it there way up front, the mortal remains of gallant Private Otis Pike, his promising young life sacrificed to the glorious Union cause."

Mary shook her head sadly. "Don't you think, Homer, his old friends in the regiment would have recognized the body? They would have known it was Morgan, not Pike."

Homer rose to this challenge too. "Face blown off. Pike obliterated Seth Morgan's face. How about that?"

Mary winced. "Oh, Homer, you're making it all up."

"Of course I am. But if it's true, then your ancestor is exonerated. The shame of desertion would be attached to Otis Pike, not Seth Morgan, your heroic great-great-grandfather."

"I'd like to believe it, Homer, but it's just too fantastic."

THE SMASHED GLASS

Of course it was too fantastic, but while Homer followed his will-o'-the-wisp theory, Mary tried to make sense of the articles in hand. They were solid objects with nothing wispy about them.

So while poor Homer was seized by fits of sneezing in the bedroom, Mary took the two little photograph cases out of her desk drawer, set them on the mantel side by side, and folded her arms on the mantelpiece to study them once again.

They looked back at her gravely, Ida all alone in the left-hand case, Ida with one of her husbands in the case on the right. Was it husband number one, Seth Morgan, or husband number two, Alexander Clock?

The smashed glass looked terrible, and it occurred to Mary that the sharp splinters might scratch the precious pictures. Impulsively she picked up the little case, fastened it shut with its tiny hook and slid it into her bag.

At Vanderhoof's Hardware, they would know what to do. Those

good people were old hands at repairing broken windowpanes. They would replace the smashed glass in a jiffy. And then Ida and Seth/Alexander would be safe and sound. They would gaze serenely out of their little case at every succeeding generation of the family from now to the end of time.

But before driving off to the hardware store on the Milldam, she put her head in the bedroom door and said, "Oh, my poor dear."

Homer was convinced that his cold was the fault of a student who had come to a conference wheezing and blowing his nose. He had handed the idiot boy a box of tissues, but by then, of course, it was too late. The powerful explosions had already sprayed their hooked germs isotropically in all directions, and they had landed on walls, ceiling and floor and attached themselves to Homer from head to foot.

"Can I get you anything while I'm out?"

"More tissues," groaned Homer, mopping his nose. "Oh, God, I'm going to flunk that kid, I swear I am."

Vanderhoof's Hardware had occupied the same premises on the Milldam for as long as Mary could remember. As a child she had reached up to the tall cupboards with their drawers of latches and screen hooks while her father bought a hacksaw or a bag of ten-penny nails from Grandfather Vanderhoof. Emersons had still been living on Lexington Road when *Great*-Grandfather Vanderhoof had come from Holland to found the family business.

Now it was his great-grandson who sold tenpenny nails at the same old store, along with electric fans and lawn mowers, cof-feemakers and paring knives, outdoor grills and lawn chairs, ham-mers, paint and turpentine, who cut keys and repaired window screens and handled a glass cutter with nimble precision.

"I'm glad you guys are still here," said Mary, taking the little case from her bag. "The town has changed so much. I mean, except for you people, it's all boutiques and gift shops now."

"I'll tell you a secret," said the young proprietor. "The only rea-son we're still here is, we own the building. All those other people are paying fantastic rents. Well, what have we got here?" He took the case from Mary and looked at the faces under the broken glass. "No problem. Want to wait? It'll take me five minutes."

Mary watched as he got to work, gently prying the gilded frames loose with the narrow blade of a screwdriver. "Funny," he said. "This one doesn't fit very well. This man here, his side sort of sticks up."

"So it does," said Mary, leaning over to look.

"There now, you see why? There's another guy underneath." He showed her the buried photograph. "You want me to put them back the same way?"

Seth

A stranger's face looked out at Mary, but in the space below his likeness, someone had written a single word.

"Oh, no." Mary pulled off her scarf and wrapped it around the second photograph. "Just put the top one back."

"Well, okay, if you say so. It'll fit better anyway."

Mary watched him cut two new squares of glass and fit them over the faces of Ida and Alexander Clock. In her bag, tucked away securely in its deepest recess, lay the secret photograph.

As a loyal wife, Ida had displayed to public view the likeness of her second husband, but she had not wanted to forget her first. Whatever shame had been attached to First Lieutenant Seth Morgan of the Second Massachusetts Volunteer Infantry, his wife had not abandoned him.

Climbing back in the car, Mary had a crazy notion. She opened her bag, unwrapped Seth's picture and turned it over. The other side was smeared with faint brown streaks.

At home she found Homer fast asleep. She closed his door softly and went to her study to look for the photocopies she had brought home from the Harvard Archives library. She found the pictures of Mills and Mudge and, with them, the nearly blank page bearing only Seth's name and his regiment at the bottom—plus a few random streaks of paste.

If they matched the streaks on the back of the long-buried picture, it would mean that Seth's photograph had not been removed by his classmates in disgust; it had been taken—perhaps stolen?—by his devoted wife.

Mary put the photocopy and the photograph on the table and compared the two sets of streaks. They were the same in reverse.

There were stirrings in the bedroom, mutterings and soft whistles. Mary found Homer sitting up in bed. He was obviously feeling better. He was amusing himself with the old-fashioned stereoscope they had bought from Bart in Gettysburg, fitting one card after another into the wire holder.

He glanced up at her long enough to say, "Did they fix the glass on those pictures?"

"Oh, yes, and you'll never guess what turned up."

But Homer was back in the sepia world of the 1860s. Mesmerized, he said, "Here, look at this one."

Mary put the stereoscope up to her face and adjusted it until the two faded brown images jumped together. "It looks so real. What is it, that big stump?"

"Washington Monument, half-finished. Here, try this one."

This time it was the Capitol building, its round dome half-hidden under a network of timber.

"Wonderful." Mary gazed at the three-dimensional thrust of the scaffolding. "It's as though nineteenth-century Washington were popping right up into our own space and time."

Homer handed her another card. "This one's the best, the Patent Office."

"Oh, yes," whispered Mary, awestruck by the blocky effect of the enormous building with its templed portico. "But you know, Homer, I'm wrong. It isn't as though the past were coming into the present. It's more like being invited back, as though we were joining the woman in the picture."

"What woman?"

Mary handed him the stereoscope. "See her there on the sidewalk? A woman looking up?"

PART XVIII

THE PATENT OFFICE

THE SURPRISING
PATIENT

Ida would not soon forget the hospitals of the city of Washington—
the shattered men sunning themselves at Campbell Hospital, the four-
horse wagons rumbling up from the Sixth Street wharves with their
loads of wounded men, the one-legged boy bouncing along the
Avenue on crutches, the woman praying beside her dying husband at
Armory Square, the devotion of the army surgeons, the kindly care of
the men and women of the Sanitary and Christian Commissions and
the quiet courage of the wounded wherever they lay.

Surely it would be the same in the Patent Office. Too much the
same, Ida thought unhappily, fearing that once again she would not
find Seth. Perhaps she had been on the wrong track from the
beginning. It was not only her false friend Lily LeBeau who had
led her astray. Her own foolish hopes had deceived her.

Therefore she had now made up her mind. Her confinement
was near. As her hope of finding her husband faded, the concern
for his child grew stronger. If she failed to find Seth today, she

would go straight to the depot and take the cars for Baltimore, transfer to the other station and continue her journey home.

She had paid her weekly rent to Mrs. Broad and packed up her belongings. Her store of banknotes was almost gone.

At this early hour in the morning Seventh Street was nearly empty, except for a man in a bowler hat, fussing with a boxlike contraption on the sidewalk. On the other side of the street a woman at a newspaper stall stared at her, but Ida paid her no mind. Undaunted, she strode along the sidewalk toward the monumental staircase of the United States Patent Office.

Her healthy frame could still carry her swollen body any number of miles on flat ground, but the staircase was a challenge. Pausing to rest halfway up, she gazed at the massive columns soaring above her, amused by the hit-or-miss dignity of the city of Washington, its marble edifices alternating with acres of squalid debris. The portico of the Patent Office looked like the Parthenon.

Recovering her breath, she climbed the rest of the way and pulled open a massive door. At once she was confronted by another grandiose set of stairs. Slowly Ida made her way to the second floor, hauling herself up by the banister.

Here the door to the hospital ward stood wide open. But she waited, breathing hard, recovering her strength. At last she crossed the marble floor and paused on the threshold to take in the enormous room.

It was a magnificent chamber with a high vaulted ceiling. Glass cases rose from the floor, filled, Ida knew, with models of inventions. There was a gallery, and it too was lined with glass cases. The Patent Office was proof of what people always said, that American boys liked to tinker. Even the president, they said, had invented something.

The ranks of glass cases were arranged in alcoves like chapels in a church, but instead of altars, they held hospital beds. More beds ran down the length of the central corridor, the head of one butting up against the foot of another.

Like most of the other hospitals in and around the city of Washington, this one seemed in good order. The marble floor shone, the bedding was clean and white. A surgeon was moving among the beds and a number of nurses hurried in and out of the alcoves.

Some were middle-aged women, others were young men, convalescents themselves or medical cadets.

Ida walked into the room, but she was stopped at once by a bustling matron carrying a tray. The matron stared at the bulge in Ida's figure and paused long enough to say curtly, "What are you doing here, missus?"

"My husband," said Ida patiently. "I'd like to see if he's here."

"His name," snapped the matron, hurrying away. "Give his name to Mr. Bannery."

Ida stopped at the second alcove on the south side, where a man with a notebook stood over one of the beds. The patient in the bed wore a bandage around his head, covering one eye.

Ida waited for Mr. Bannery to notice her. Behind the shining glass of the tall case beside him, there were shelves of mechanical devices with cutting edges and wheels and gears. Ida glanced at them with interest, but the patients in the beds had more serious concerns and showed no curiosity.

"Your name?" said Mr. Bannery to the man with the bandaged eye.

"Irwin J. Skedaddle," said the man craftily. He looked at Ida with his one mad eye and grinned. "That's S-K-E sump'n else."

The man with the notebook grimaced and turned away.

Ida spoke up quickly. "Mr. Bannery?"

"Yes, ma'am?"

"I'm looking for my husband, First Lieutenant Seth Morgan."

"Morgan." Mr. Bannery flipped the pages of his notebook. "No Morgan here now. A month ago"—he turned another page—"there was a Lysander Morgan, but he was in Twenty-ninth Pennsylvania, and anyhow he passed away."

Ida plucked up her courage and said, "My husband might be using another name. Please, may I look around for him?"

Mr. Bannery looked at her sharply, and she knew he understood what "another name" meant. So did the man in the bed. He gave a loud laugh and began jabbering. His wound seemed to have excited his brain. "Oh, dearie me, another skulker. Skedaddle W. Skulker. That's S-K-U, right, ma'am? Listen, missus, I hope your blessed event turns out female. You don't want no poor little boy got to go in the army."

Mr. Bannery shook his head and moved into the aisle. His bureaucratic manner softened, and he said, "Some men come in without identification. Kinfolk, they're welcome to look. Just try to keep out of the way."

"Oh, I will," promised Ida. "Thank you." Quickly she began moving along the beds in the center aisle, following a woman who was distributing pamphlets, thrusting them into the hands of men who were sitting up, placing them tenderly on the pillows of those who lay still. Ida saw her set down a leaflet on *The Sin of Swearing* beside the staring face of a man who had surely breathed his last.

There were eight beds in each alcove. Ida went in and out, inspecting every face. Some of the men looked back at her, some ignored her. She felt intrusive, but she had to look, she had to see.

Up and down both sides of the enormous room she went, pausing and moving on, then pausing again. At one of the beds in the center aisle two clerks were examining a patient whose left arm was in a sling. One of them said as she walked past, "Disability rated one-fourth," and the other wrote it down.

Many were sadder cases. Ida ached with pity for a rag of a young man whose body under the sheet went only halfway down. An older man spat blood into a cup. In the next bed a gray-faced boy lay still, a tube from his side draining into a bucket.

Some of the patients were young and clean-shaven, some older and gray-bearded. A few were little more than children. One of them resembled her little brother Eben.

Ida moved on, then stopped and went back. The young boy in the last bed, lying beside a model of a patent reaping machine, not only looked like Eben, he was Eben.

CAMPED NEAR

A SLOUGH

6 Sept. '63

My dear Mother,

You will understand why I can't come home now when I tell you that I have found Eben in the hospital in the Patent Office. He is suffering from a fever. He is very ill.

One of the surgeons takes particular notice of Eben. He tells me he has seen cases as severe who recovered, so I have hope, but as I say, he is very sick. His illness was contracted when his regiment encamped near a slough.

I have concluded to stay and help care for him, nothing preventing. The matron here is very strict, so I must try not to be any trouble.

As for me—now, Mother, you are not to worry, because I am first-rate. I have engaged a woman to help with my lying-in and Mrs. Broad has assisted in getting everything ready. You will remember that I helped at the time Alice came into the

*world, so I am familiar with what is needful. As usual I feel
extremely well, only a little breathless now and then.*

Y'r loving daughter Ida

There were seven other men suffering from high fever in the
same alcove with Eben. Fearing contagion, the surgeons had iso-
lated them by the width of the tall glass cases from the patients
with ordinary battle wounds.

Ida was not the only family member in attendance. A mother
from Georgia never left the bedside of her son until the afternoon
he died. Worn and grief-stricken, she nodded a good-bye to Ida
and followed the litter as it was carried down the long aisle. Sorrowfully Ida watched them go. The dead boy and Eben had
belonged to opposing armies, but there was no quarrel between the
mother of the one and the sister of the other.

The surgeon attending the patients in this part of the ward was
the chief surgeon of the hospital. He was attentive to the men in his
care and gentle with Ida, although it was clear that he didn't know
what on earth to do with a woman on the brink of giving birth.

The nurses knew precisely what to do with her. They all said
the same thing. Some said it kindly—"My dear, you really must go
home to your mother"—some angrily—"Don't expect us to care
for you, missus. Go on, get away from here, go home." Ida felt
unwanted, like a hen shooed away by a flapping apron.

But she did not leave the hospital. She stayed, because Eben was
hovering between life and death. He lay unconscious, his fever rising and falling. Ida heard the awful panting and on his forehead her
hand felt the terrible heat. She sat with him day and night, dozing
in her chair, waking up in alarm and dozing off again, her head
drooping on her breast.

Eben's fever was highest in the watches of the night. But in the
morning it abated a little, and Ida could go out to breathe air
untainted by the odors of the sickroom. Even with the prompt care
of the nurses, there were smells that entered with every new batch
of wounded men—the putrid reek of a gangrenous leg, the stink of
urine-soaked trousers, the rank smells of vomit and diarrhea.

Once Ida jumped to the rescue of a man who was writhing so

violently that he nearly threw himself out of bed. Another time she snatched up a urinal to catch a spout in midair. She helped with the washing of filthy bodies, she mopped up puddles of blood. She knew where to find the sink and where to empty chamber pots.

The antagonism of the nurses grew less, although the matron, Mrs. Thrum, never passed Ida without hissing at her, "You should not be here, girl, you should not be here."

In her brief respites out-of-doors under the monumental portico, Ida looked up at the half-finished frame-work of the Capitol dome where work was going on or watched the traffic moving east and west on F Street. Sometimes a cheerful procession of contrabands tramped along the dusty road, colored men and women who had run away from their masters. Or their mistresses, guessed Ida, southern women struggling to carry on a farm. Sometimes a wagon carried an entire black family—grandparents, mother and father, barefoot children, a baby. One woman looked ready to give birth. She looked up and exchanged a dark glance with Ida.

And sometimes Ida nearly feel asleep, leaning against the cool stone. But whenever a long train of ambulances came creaking up the street, heading for one of the other hospitals—Finlay or Douglas or Armory Square—she woke up and wondered if Seth might be lying in one of them.

Perhaps he had rejoined his regiment. Perhaps he had been wounded in another battle!

"OH MY!"

Thus in silence in dreams' projections,
Returning, resuming, I thread my way through the hospitals,
The hurt and wounded I pacify with soothing hand,
I sit by the restless all the dark night, some are so young,
Some suffer so much . . .
(Many a soldier's loving arms about this neck have cross'd and rested,
Many a soldier's kiss dwells on these bearded lips.)

—WALT WHITMAN

There was a cold hand on Eben's forehead. He shook his head, and the hand went away.

Eben opened his eyes and saw the owner of the hand, sharply as if with a magnifying glass, or maybe he was on a ridge looking across a valley because he'd borrowed the captain's binoculars, so he could see one figure jump out bright and clear but not in any kind of uniform.

Through the glasses Eben could see the man's open collar, his light-colored eyes and gray beard. From across the valley the man reached out and touched Eben's shoulder. Eben closed his eyes and the valley faded, but somebody kissed him.

An hour later he woke up just long enough to see something surprising. He was staring at a toy. It was in a glass case with other toys. The toys had tiny wheels and gears and belts to carry the whiz of one wheel to another wheel, and some of the belts were twisted so the second wheel could whiz in another direction. There was another toy on a higher shelf, and Eben recognized it.

As he closed his eyes he could see Mr. Hosmer on the seat of his reaping machine, clattering across his field of barley. He could even hear the squeaking of the cutter bar.

"You got to grease them shoes," said one of the stewards carrying a litter down the aisle, heading for the stairs and the long descent to the morgue. The man on the litter had lingered a long time after Chancellorsville, but his feeble strength had finally wasted away.

"Dangfool shoes, they're brand-new," grumbled the other steward.

When Eben woke up again, there was another amazing sight. His sister Ida was sitting beside him, beaming at him. "Eben dear," she said.

But then her face changed. "Oh," said Ida. "Oh my."

The chief surgeon was there. He looked at her in consternation and called Mrs. Thrum.

"Great God above," said Mrs. Thrum. "I knew it, I knew it. I told her and I told her, but she wouldn't listen, and now, pshaw! just look what's happened." Mrs. Thrum ran away to arrange for a cot.

The doctor sat down on the edge of Eben's bed and took Ida's hand. It was all he knew how to do.

THE SEWING MACHINE

Ida's bed was the only one in the last alcove at the far end of the room of glass cases. Even so, her pangs made the patients in the rest of the ward uneasy. She tried not to scream, but she couldn't help moaning when the spasms gripped her.

Her muffled cries gave Mrs. Thrum an excuse to scold. Peevishly she informed Ida that she was in the way, that she had no right whatever to that bed, that she was denying it to a brave soldier wounded in the service of his country. "If you think a single soul here is going to assist you," said Mrs. Thrum, glowering down at Ida's suffering face, "you are very much mistaken."

"I'm sorry," whispered Ida. "I'm very sorry."

But it wasn't true that she was denying a bed to a wounded soldier. The heavy influx after First and Second Bull Run and Ball's Bluff and Antietam had mostly been cleared out, and most of the Gettysburg cases had long since been transferred, or else they had recovered or died. A few had been rushed out of the Patent Office to the Kalorama Hospital for smallpox cases.

Ida's brother Eben was one of half a dozen men stricken with typhoid in a swampy camp only a few miles from Culpepper.

So now only a couple of hundred were left, including the long-term cases—gunshot wounds in the lungs, gangrenous compound fractures, resections after amputations, chronic diarrhea or simple debility.

There were many empty beds. The chief surgeon now had time to write up his more interesting cases.

CASE STUDY OF PATIENT 276

Gunshot wound of tibia and fibula, un-united comminuted fracture, leg swollen, offensive, filled with pus. Flap amputation at upper third of leg, stump closed with three stitches and wet strips of muslin . . . hemorrhage . . . tourniquet . . . hemorrhage . . . quinine and iron prescribed, cod-liver oil, egg-nog . . . hemorrhage, tightening of tourniquet, diarrhoea, administration of rhubarb powder, ipecacuanha and opium. Patient rallying, ten ounces of pus removed from thigh, injection of hydrochloric acid and laudanum . . . patient going about on crutches, discharged, paroled, sent south.

CASE STUDY OF PATIENT 1057

Gunshot wound of abdomen. Patient reports that much of the liquid food and drink he took after the injury continued to appear at the orifice of the wound. . . . An incision was made perpendicular to the walls of the belly, the bullet secured and removed. . . . Convalescent patient discharged and sent South, his wound improving, though still fistulous.

CASE STUDY OF PATIENT 1185

Diffuse Traumatic Aneurism; Wound of the Spinal Cord . . . Ligation of the Carotid . . . Death . . . Autopsy.

CASE STUDY OF PATIENT 2070

Sixteen-year-old with typhoid fever. Delousing called for on
admission. Symptoms developed rapidly, chills and fever,
abdominal rash, delirium. . . .

The surgeon had treated Patient
2070 since his admission to the hospital. When the boy's sister
appeared, he had given her the task
of sponging her brother with cool
water to reduce the fever.

Happily the boy now seemed to
have passed the crisis, but his sister
was in extremis. The surgeon felt
utterly helpless. He was used to the
groans and screams of wounded
men, but Ida's whimpering un-
manned him. He knew all there was
to know about battle wounds and
the dangerous diseases contracted in
crowded campgrounds and airless
prisons, but he was unacquainted with female problems. About
childbirth he knew nothing at all.

Of course Ida herself knew a good deal more than the surgeon, having assisted the midwife when her mother had been
brought to bed with Alice. But now she was too humble and in
too much anguish to make suggestions to Chief Surgeon Alexander Clock.

Gritting her teeth, she stared at the object in the glass case beside
her bed, trying to understand how it worked. The little contraption
was a model of Elias Howe's sewing machine. As her pangs grew
worse she forced herself to concentrate on the in-and-out trajec-
tory of the thread. Gasping, she asked the doctor, "Oh, sir, how
does it make a loop?"

But willy-nilly, babies always manage to be born. Shortly after
five o'clock that afternoon, Mary Morgan Kelly's great-grandfather

emerged, howling, into the
world.

But not before a tall
woman wearing a rusty
black bonnet and carrying a
large canvas umbrella came
storming up the aisle. It was
Ida's mother.

PART XIX

THE LAST
SKEDADDLE OF
OTIS PIKE

THE NEEDLE'S EYE

It was Gwen on the phone. "You'll never guess what's happened. Ebenezer's back."

"Who?" It took Homer a minute to remember. "You mean that crazy cousin of yours? He's back? Whatever for?"

"I can't explain. You'll have to see for yourself. And hurry up, because he's about to set out."

"Set out? What do you mean, set out?"

"You'll see."

They went at once. The family homestead, occupied now by Tom Hand and Mary's sister Gwen, was only three miles away as the crow flies, but Mary and Homer were not crows. For their two-thousand-pound Toyota there was no airy flight from Fair Haven Bay over Adams Woods—sacred to wood thrushes, red-tailed hawks and Henry Thoreau—and over the six lanes of Route 2 and the Concord prison and the Assabet River, and no gentle descent to the grass in front of the old house on Barrett's Mill Road.

No, instead of flying they had to bump along the dirt road from Fair Haven Bay to Route 2 and then go *right* instead of left on the highway in order to make a U-turn at the intersection with Route 126 and head back all the way to the traffic circle where they could at last make the turn onto Barrett's Mill Road and pull up beside the old family farm.

Gwen was there on the lawn, and so was Ebenezer. He was, indeed, setting out.

"Ebenezer, wait," cried Gwen, running after him, dodging around the U-Haul truck parked in the driveway.

Homer and Mary leaped out of their car and ran too.

Ebenezer was a hundred yards ahead of them, striding along the road with a staff in his hand, a bewhiskered pilgrim in shorts and Birkenstocks. When they caught up with him he continued to march steadfastly, staring straight ahead. They had to hurry along beside him like fellow wayfarers to a distant shrine.

"But listen, Ebenezer," panted Gwen, "how are you going to live? You can't abandon everything, not absolutely everything. No, no, wait, I know what you're going to say about the lilies, how they toil not, neither do they spin, but really, Ebenezer, you're not a lily."

Ebenezer bowled along, his face radiant, his eyes glittering with a saintly light. The jab of his staff in the weedy shoulder of the road was the proclamation of a new life. "Verily I say unto you," he began, beaming at Homer.

"Oh no you don't," interrupted Homer. 'You don't verily say anything to me. For God's sake, Ebenezer, what are you up to?"

Ebenezer wasn't listening. He had been programmed by the little old lady in Gettysburg to obey the parable of the rich young man (Matthew XIX:16–30), and everything else had vanished from his mind. "Oh, my friend," he babbled to Homer, "why wouldest thou not be perfect?"

"Because I'm perfect already," gasped Homer, but he was falling behind.

"He's penniless," said Gwen to Mary as they galloped along together. "They'll arrest him as a vagrant." She called back, "Homer, have you got any money?"

Homer pawed in his pocket and produced a ten-dollar bill. Mary grabbed it and tried to thrust it into Ebenezer's hand, but he tossed it in the air, bawling something about the needle's eye and the elephant.

The ten-dollar bill rose like a butterfly and fluttered back into Homer's hand. "Elephant?" he said to Mary. "Did he say elephant?"

"Oh, you know about the elephant, Homer," said Mary. "It's easier for an elephant to go through the eye of a needle than for a rich man to enter the kingdom of Heaven."

Gwen dropped back too. "Everybody knows that, Homer. Elephants are even bigger than camels. They simply will not get through that skinny little hole in the needle, no matter how hard they try."

The three of them slowed to a stop and watched Ebenezer's white legs twinkle away in the direction of the traffic circle.

"They'll pick him up," prophesied Gwen. "And then they'll call us and we'll have to bring him home and it will be a colossal pain. But first"—Gwen turned briskly and began jogging back along the road—"quick, quick, before he zigzags in some other crazy direction. When he drove up just now, he had all our stuff packed in his U-Haul truck. If we hurry we can get it all back in the attic before he turns up."

THE QUESTION MARKS

Nothing more was heard from Ebenezer. Perhaps on his strange pilgrimage, he had actually stumbled upon the kingdom of Heaven.

In any case, he did not come back to claim the trash in the back of his U-Haul truck. So that same afternoon the four of them—Gwen and Tom, Mary and Homer—carried every one of Ebenezer's plastic bags up the two flights of stairs to the attic.

Here they were soon organized into a threefold system of containers. Mary taped labels on all of them. The first was a set of plastic trash barrels labeled OUT, and the second, SORT. The cardboard boxes for the third category were labeled simply **?**

Gwen devoted herself to the SORT trash cans, trying to put back in order the memorabilia of two centuries of family life. Before the original appearance of Cousin Ebenezer everything had been neatly arranged in separate boxes. Now it was a jumble.

Tom dumped out the contents of Ebenezer's first bag on the

floor. It was a wild miscellany from ages past—an album of scratchy 78s, including Beethoven's Fifth, a packet of letters from Great-Uncle Bob and Great-Aunt Bea on their trip to Alaska in 1887, a photograph of Grandmother and Grandfather Morgan on camels in front of the Pyramids, ninety-five color slides of Old Faithful and Yellowstone Park, a crumbling wad of newsprint from November 1918—GREAT WAR ENDS—a moldy collection of science fiction paperbacks, a tangle of failed Christmas lights and a plastic Santa.

While Gwen began her sorting, Tom contributed to the organizational procedure by carrying all the cans marked OUT down to the road to be picked up by the town collection service. When that was done, he was smitten by an unhappy thought about Ebenezer's U-Haul truck. The cost of its rental must be increasing every day. Since the fool had so devoutly rejected all treasure upon earth, perhaps he had also rejected the bill for the truck.

Grumpily, Tom drove it to the nearest U-Haul place and learned to his horror that there was no record of any original payment by Ebenezer Flint to the outlet in Washington. He had to pay the whole thing himself with a large check.

In the meantime, Mary and Homer winnowed and sifted, selected and rejected.

"All we care about," said Mary, "is stuff from the 1850s and '60s." She held up a shiny pink shell inscribed *Saint Louis Exposition, 1895,* and handed it to Gwen.

In the end they brought all the question marks downstairs in a couple of cardboard boxes. Compared with the amount of stuff going out and all the miscellaneous things to be sorted, the question-mark collection was small.

But it was crucial.

THREE STITCHES OF
DOUBLE CROCHET

Homer had given his all. He helped Mary bring the question-mark boxes into the house, and then he left for a faculty meeting in Cambridge, complaining as he ran down the porch steps, "I approve of genealogical research on the whole, but ye gods."

Mary was happy to carry on by herself. She took out the bundles of papers and letters and spread them on the table. As she noted them down she told herself firmly, *These came from the attic. They have nothing to do with Bart and his bloodstained coat and all the rest of his so-called Otis Pike collection.*

She loved making lists. She began with the letters. Some of them looked more interesting than others:

1. Two letters in lavender envelopes addressed to *Mrs. Seth Morgan.*

2. An official-looking letter also addressed to *Mrs. Seth Morgan.*

3. Another letter without an envelope—a tender missive beginning *My dearest husband* and ending *Your loving Ida.*

4. A bundle of letters postmarked Washington, D.C., from *A. Clock, USA, Asst. Surgeon,* addressed to *Mrs. Seth Morgan.*

5. Miscellaneous letters from *Mrs. Seth Morgan* to *Mrs. Eudocia Flint* and from *Mrs. Eudocia Flint* to *Mrs. Seth Morgan.*

6. Other letters to and from various Flints and Morgans.

So much for the letters. But there were other papers, as well. Mary began another list:

1. A printed sheet:

Order of Exercises for Commencement
August 30, 1860

(NOTE Item 8! *Literary Disquisition* by Seth Morgan)

2. Farm records for the year 1855—*Reckoned with James Luce accts balanc'd to date hereof, sick Cow slaught'd, rec'vd of Samuel Nation 3000 Shingle Nails.*

3. A book, *Odes of Horace,* Seth Morgan's name on flyleaf.

4. A bundle of marriage, birth and death documents, NOT including a death certificate for Seth Morgan.

5. Five vandalized playbills from theaters in Washington, D.C. (*Why do they all have pieces cut out of the middle?*)

6. Pamphlet from the American Tract Society:

> Lost—until by thee restored,
> Comforter Divine!

There was one other piece of printed matter, but it seemed to belong in the other cardboard box. Mary started a third list, after putting the first item on her head.

1. Straw Shaker bonnet in terrible condition.

2. Child's nightdress (*small gown with embroidered neckline*).

3. Scottish-looking cap.

4. Tattered silk envelope containing six white handkerchiefs— *one with a bloodstained hem!*—all of them embroidered in the corner with the initial *S*.

The extra piece of printed matter was an 1861 ladies' magazine called *Peterson's*. The word *Ida's* had been written on the front, as though the magazine had been handed around among the women of a sewing circle.

Mary was entranced. *Peterson's* was full of elegant fashions for men, women and children, with accompanying pages of patterns. One of the pattern pages had been crisscrossed with penciled squares.

Mary decided at once that the squares were a means for enlarging the pattern, so that Ida could make the "Knickerbocker Suit for a Boy."

Abandoning her lists, she sat down with the magazine, spellbound. There were designs for pillows, bonnets, knitted shoes, pincushions and beaded mats. The dresses had names: "The Clothilde," "The Etruscan," "The Polonaise." There were directions for crocheted edgings: "3 chain," "3 stitches of double crochet."

When Homer walked in, he laughed at the Shaker bonnet and said, "How demure."

"It was Ida's, I'll bet. Isn't it sweet?" Mary stood up and showed him the old copy of *Peterson's*. "Look at this. She must have made this little suit."

"Charming, but I don't see how it helps. What else have you

got?" Homer leaned over the table. "My God, there's so much. Where do we start?"

"With these." Mary picked up the lavender letters. "One for you, one for me."

They were the right place to begin.

DARLING IDA

Both envelopes were addressed in the same looping hand to "Mrs. Seth Morgan, Concord, Maschu'ts," but their postmarks were different. One had been mailed from Washington, D.C., the other from Oshawa, Ontario. The postmarked date on the envelope from Washington was sharp and clear: "3 Dec. 1863." The other was smudged. It was either "12 Feb., 1866," or "12 Feb., 1868." The envelope from Ontario had been crudely blackened around the edges as though it contained bad news.

"Perfume," said Homer, holding it to his nose.

"This one, too," said Mary. "Just a whiff."

"You first."

Mary struggled with the curlicues of the handwriting in the letter from Washington. "It begins, 'Darling Ida,' and it's signed 'Lily.' You don't suppose it's Lily LeBeau, the gorgeous creature in the tasseled panties?"

"Could be," said Homer. "Mine's from Lily, too. Carry on, what does she say?"

Mary read her letter aloud, struggling to distinguish the swooping *p*'s from the *g*'s, and the *h*'s from the *b*'s.

Darling Ida,

> *Well dear girl I have yr adres from Mizzus Broad who tells me you are safe at home with baby. She says the blessed event ocured in the patent Orfis of all playces because it was one of the hosp'ls you vizited in your ridicolos search for your husband I never was so ashamed in my life it was all because of my Fib when I said he was wounded in battle. Now Ida this is the truth on a stak of Bibles he was ashamed to face you altho I tell him it is no shame because these days the Capt'l is jamful of these sort of Peeple (skeedadlers). You will be Amazed the pres and Wife witnissed the marble Heart the other night. O Ida you shud see y'r bwewtious old friend, I have got me a Zouav jkt all over braid. But there! My little epissel is too long!*

> *Love, dearest Ida,*
> *y'r Affec Lily*

Mary looked up, eager to make flabbergasting deductions, but Homer said, "Wait." He was staring at a newspaper clipping from the other envelope, the one that had been mailed from Oshawa, Ontario. Silently he handed it to her.

"Oh, dear," said Mary, reading through it quickly.

DEATH OF A HERO

Oshawa, Feb. 1, 1866. Mr. Seth Morgan, 25, unemployed resident of this city, yesterday plunged into the freezing waters of Lake Ontario to rescue 4-year-old Thomasina McFarland, trapped beneath the ice. After lifting the child to safety, Mr. Morgan was unable to extricate himself. This morning his body was pulled from the lake by Engine Company #1 of the Oshawa Municipal Steam Fire Department.

Though he was a newcomer to Oshawa, we are informed that Mr. Morgan was celebrated in theatrical circles as a dramatist and composer of amusing ditties. Familiar to our readers will be the ballad "Lilybelle."

In gratitude for his heroic sacrifice, Mr. Lysander McFarland has contributed to the Fund for Indigent Thespians the sum of 15 dollars.

"There's a letter too," said Homer. Grimly he read it aloud.

> *Darling Ida,*
>
> *As you can see by the inclosd our dear boy died a hero! I am convolsed with tears and greeve for you as well. I leave Oshawa tonight bownd for city of San Francisco having been ingaged as a dancer by a famous impesario. I don't think dear Ida you ever saw me in preformance on my toes but I asure you I am now a Star having been hired by the great impisario Theodore DeSanto. Alas to my profond distress I cannot stay for the funeral as mr DiSanto desires me to accompany him at once in his diluxe RR sweet. I will write again from the Wild West!*
>
> *Yr loving Lily*
>
> *P. S Seth's pitcher was in the paper I know you will forgive me for keeping it as a tender momentoe.*

"Bitch," said Homer.

The official letter from the War Department was brutal too.

> *Dear Madam,*
>
> *I regret to notify you of the death in Oshawa, Ontario, of your husband, 1st Lt. Seth Morgan. Since his departure from*

the service on 3 July, 1863, took place at a time when his regiment was critically engaged, there will be no widow's pension.

Brig. General James B. Fry,
Provost Marshal General
U. S. War Department,
Washington, D. C.

The letters from Assistant Surgeon Clock were more pleasing. The first was a polite inquiry into the well-being of mother and child. The rest were progressively warmer, the last a proposal of marriage.

FLABBERGASTING
DEDUCTIONS

The unraveling of inferences from all of the letters and documents and the making of flabbergasting deductions was instantaneous.

From the correspondence between Ida and her mother it was clear that Great-Great-Grandmother Ida Morgan, probably seven months pregnant at the time, had rushed to Gettysburg to look for her husband Seth, missing in action.

Failing to find him, she had traveled to Baltimore and then to Washington.

Somehow she had tracked her husband down in the theatrical circle of the actress Lily LeBeau, but she had not been permitted to see him—*Now Ida this is the truth on a stak of Bibles he was ashamed to face you altho I tell him it is no shame because these days the Capt'l is jamful of these sort of Peeple (skeedadlers).*

It was also a fact that Mother Flint had sent Ida's brother Eben to find her and bring her home. *I know you are a grown woman,* wrote Eudocia Flint, *but I request nay order you to come home at once.*

Then, failing to find his sister, Eben had joined the army instead. In the Patent Office hospital Ida had found him at death's door. She had stayed to nurse him and then she had at last given birth to her baby in the same hospital—*the blessed event ocured in the patent Orfis of all playces.*

"I wonder what happened to Eben?" said Mary. "Did he die? The poor kid must have been very young."

"He didn't die," said Homer, plucking out a death certificate for Ebenezer Flint. "At least not until the year 1920."

"Well, I'm glad," said Mary.

But a horrid thought occurred to Homer. "My God, I'll bet he's the ancestor of your cousin Ebenezer."

Mary gasped, then gave a rueful laugh. "Oh well, somebody had to be his ancestor."

"The hell with Cousin Ebenezer. Look here, how does all this information help? There's nothing in this stuff about Otis Pike. And there's nothing to suggest that Seth Morgan was anything but a deserter. The War Department says so because they refused to give his widow a pension. That silly woman Lily LeBeau says so, and the death notice in the Ontario newspaper is not about Otis Pike, it's a sort of left-handed tribute to Seth Morgan."

"But remember how contradictory we thought it all was," protested Mary. "It seemed so fishy that Otis was the one who neglected his studies and got in trouble afterward and kept leaving the ranks—in other words deserting—while Seth's record was fine from the beginning. It was just fine."

Homer held up a triumphant finger. "And don't forget that note from Seth, warning Otis not to do it again."

"Meaning not to desert again. Oh, Homer, I'm beginning to believe in your crazy theory."

"Well, it's about time, because I'm convinced it's what really happened. During the battle Otis came upon the body of Seth and exchanged coats and identities with him, so then it looked as though Otis had died a hero and Seth was the deserter. And then Otis lived the rest of his life pretending to be Seth. His girlfriend

didn't know he was an imposter, and neither did the Ontario newspaper. And neither did poor dear Ida. She never had a clue."

It was growing dark. Mary turned on a lamp. In the glare over
the table the shuffle of letters and papers looked old and pitiful.

Their confidence collapsed. "Who will believe it?" said Mary.

PART XX

THE AGREEMENT

Word over all, beautiful as the sky,
Beautiful that war and all its deeds of carnage must in time be
utterly lost,
That the hands of the sisters Death and Night incessantly softly
wash again, and ever again, this soil'd world. . . .

—WALT WHITMAN

THE SMOKING CAP

It was the turn of Ida's little boy Horace to bounce up and down on Eudocia's lap as she pounded on the keyboard and sang lustily. This time, the song was a jolly one by Stephen Foster, "Camptown Races"—

> Gwine to run all night!
> Gwine to run all day!
> I'll bet my money on de bob-tail nag—
> Somebody bet on de bay.

The four sharps were almost beyond Eudocia's powers, but the words were harmless. These days, she had to be careful what she chose from the songbook, because Seth's mother so often reclined on the settee in the same room.

"Home, Sweet Home" would not do, because Augusta's dear son would never come home. He was not only dead but disgraced.

Nor could Eudocia sing "Kathleen Mavourneen," because of the mournful refrain, "It may be for years, and it may be forever." And of course all the dear old soldier songs were banished for good—"Tenting Tonight on the Old Camp Ground," and "Tramp! Tramp! Tramp, the Boys Are Marching." They were out of the question.

The mind of poor Mother Morgan had been failing before, but now the sorrow and shame of her loss had addled what little was left. Ida's mother-in-law lay on the sofa or sat idly at the table in the kitchen condemning the imbecility of all things. Even God was a blockhead.

But that was just her way. Eudocia attended cheerfully to Augusta's physical needs and ignored her dire pronouncements. Sally and Josh and Alice were polite to Mother Morgan, Eben was mostly away at school and of course, Ida's boy—Augusta's and Eudocia's grandchild—was too young to have any opinion about the mental capacity of the Creator.

Eudocia's singing voice was strong, and it echoed to all corners of the house. Even in her bedroom upstairs Ida could hear it above the whine and buzz of her sewing machine.

It was new, the gift of Dr. Clock, but she had mastered its complexities. Now she hunched over it, guiding the needle down a seam, pedaling vigorously. *Bzzzz, bzzzz, slow down, lift the lever, whirl the sleeve around, lower the lever, give the wheel a push and start again, bzzzz, bzzzz. It was so quick!*

Peterson's Magazine was full of enticing patterns. As soon as she finished the French sacque for little Horace, she'd try the knickerbocker suit, *the favorite style of dress for boys too young to be breeched.*

By midafternoon she had finished the French sacque and begun to copy the pattern for the little suit, when her mother called up the stairs, "Ida?"

Josh had driven the spring wagon to the post office. He had brought home a magazine for his sister and a letter.

Ida ran downstairs and paused in the parlor to kiss her mother-in-law. "Oh, the stupidity," groaned Mother Morgan, "Oh, the shame."

"Now, Augusta," said Eudocia, "remember our agreement. We agreed to say nothing more about that."

Ida's letter was another one from Alexander. She ran upstairs, opened the envelope, and slipped out the closely written sheets. Folded among them was something else, his photograph. Ida gazed at it, pleased that he had done as he had promised.

At once she went to her chest of drawers and found the little hooked case that enclosed the likenesses of herself and Seth. The glass rectangle over Seth's face was smudged where Ida had so often kissed it. Sorrowfully now she kissed it for the last time and wiped the glass clean. Working slowly and carefully, she edged out the gilded frame and with gentle fingers slid Alexander's picture in place over Seth's and pressed the glass down over both of them. Then she straightened the crocheted edging of the dresser scarf and positioned the open case next to the daguerreotype of her father.

Perhaps it was time now to take care of other things. Ida pulled open the drawer in which she had stored away a sacred collection of handkerchiefs among the gloves and winter stockings. She had been making them for Seth—so long ago! Most of them had never been embroidered with the letter *S,* and therefore they had never been sent. But there was a single exception, the handkerchief with the terrifying crimson hem, the one given back to her by Lieutenant Gobright on that fearful night on the battlefield.

Also in Ida's dresser drawer was Seth's last letter, written from an encampment in Maryland, and two more sad things—her own last letter to him and the pamphlet from the American Tract Society. Also in the drawer were the three perfumed letters from Lily LeBeau that had caused her so much anguish.

Under Lily's letters lay other dreadful things, the playbills that had been given out in handfuls by shouting boys on the Avenue when Ida had been living at Mrs. Broad's. She had always taken them eagerly, hoping to find Seth's name printed boldly on the swaggering lists of actors. It was never there, but another name had appeared on every one of them, large and black and abominable. She wanted to throw all the playbills in the fire, but they were heart-wrenching memorials of a bitter kind, and she couldn't let them go.

At least she could make them less hateful. Ida picked up her sewing scissors, remembering an innocent conversation in the cars on the way back from Washington—her mother and Eben, Ida and her baby.

Her mother had wanted to hear about the exciting life of the nation's capital. Had there been public exhibitions with transparencies and fireworks? Had she seen the president and his wife? Famous generals and fashionable ladies in beautiful gowns?

The baby had been fretful. Ida's mother had taken him and asked another question. "Did you see any famous plays, Ida dear?"

"Or famous actors?" said Eben. Ida's brother was thin and pale from lying so long in a hospital bed, but he, too, was eager to hear about the thrilling life of the city.

"Maggie Mitchell?" said Ida's mother. "Charlotte Cushman?"

"Edwin Forrest?" said Eben.

"What about that other one," said Eudocia, trying to remember, "that famous young Shakespearean actor? Wasn't he another Edwin?"

"No, not Edwin." Ida held out her arms for the baby. "His brother, I think. I feel sure it was his brother."

Now Ida snipped and snipped, cutting out pieces from the play-bills. Finished, she put them back in the bottom of the drawer and covered them with cotton stockings. Then she undid the ribbon around Alexander's letters, added the new one, tied up the bundle again, laid it down on her Sunday gloves, and softly closed the drawer.

Something else had come in the mail, the new copy of *Peterson's Magazine*. For a moment Ida leafed through it, and then, smiling, she took it downstairs, deciding to make a present for Alexander— perhaps the handsome smoking cap on page one. "We give here a design, full size, printed in colors, for this very stylish Smoking Cap, so that any subscriber can make it for herself, a very pretty gift for a gentleman."

PART XXI

UNBOUND REGIMENTAL PAPERS

GOD BLESS THE ARCHIVISTS AND ALL THE LIBRARIANS

From the window a moist breeze from the river lifted and ruffled the papers. Letters scudded across the table and fluttered to the floor. Homer stooped to gather them up. "The trouble is, these things aren't good enough. It's got to be more official. You know, regimental. We'll never convince the lords of creation to change that tablet in Memorial Hall with this kind of flimsy evidence."

Mary ran to the window and slammed it down. "I'll bet there's a military archive somewhere. There must be some sort of official record of who died in that regiment at Gettysburg."

"Of course, but where?"

"In Washington, I'll bet." She looked at him brightly. "The National Archives. I'll bet they're open to visitors."

"Washington!" Lightning flashed over the river and in its unearthly light, Homer saw the nature of his coming sacrifice. Hollowly he said, "Look, my darling, do we really care this much about your dear old great-great-grandfather?"

"Oh, Homer, we can't give up now, not when we've come so far. I can't possibly go anywhere right now, you know that. You're the one with time on your hands."

Time on his hands! Homer groaned at this jab below the belt. The reason he had time on his hands was the near approach of his retirement, his sense of being politely edged aside. Whereas Mary . . .

Well, there was no help for it. Homer put his arm around Seth Morgan's great-great-granddaughter and drew her away to bed.

True to his expectation, the journey was a nightmare. When Mary picked him up at the airport, Homer was a physical wreck. His shoulders sagged, his whiskers were wild, his ancient seersucker jacket was sweat-stained and shapeless, and the clammy garment beneath it was clearly an undershirt.

In the car he snoozed in the back seat. At home he collapsed on the sofa, whimpering, "Give me a drink."

It took two whiskeys before Homer could do anything but complain about the horror of his travels, the humiliating disagreement over cab fare, the eight-dollar cheeseburger, the effect on the human body of passing from jungle heat into polar chill, the rain that had poured down on the head of a miserable wretch without an umbrella.

"Oh, my poor darling," said Mary. "I'm sorry it was so awful. But come on, Homer, tell me what you found out."

"Oh, that." Homer sat up and drained his glass. "Well, as a matter of fact, I found out a lot. There were really good folks in the National Archives. Oh, of course it took time, Jesus." Homer stretched a limp arm in the direction of his backpack, couldn't reach it and fell back in a swoon.

Mary grasped it and handed it over. "Yes, yes, it took time. First you had to fill out a lot of forms, I'll bet."

"Not just forms." Homer sat up. "I had to pass through a metal detector and be photographed and then I had to find my way to the right room for Civil War records, room 400, that's what it was, and make out a special form, and then—" Homer yawned and dozed off again. Mary poked him. "Oh, well, then of course I had to wait. But the stuff didn't come to room 400,

it came to room 203, but I couldn't go in there with my backpack, so I had to stuff it in a locker, and then room 203 turned
out to be a big important room in the Archives, with a lot of
scholars in little compartments, and the compartments had these
see-through partitions so nobody could mishandle a precious
document without being observed, but of course all those dedicated scholars didn't care because they were all lost in their own
individual fields of research." Homer's eyes closed again on this
vision of paradise.

"Homer!"

"Right you are." Homer opened his eyes and carried on. "Well,
I had to persuade the archivist to let me see the originals of the
muster rolls for one particular regiment at one particular time, and
of course it took a good deal of dancing around artfully on my ver-
bal toes."

"Actually, Homer dear, it's what you do best."

"So at last they brought them out and set them in front of me,
three brown boxes."

"Three brown boxes," murmured Mary greedily, sharing
Homer's affection for all the paraphernalia of historical investiga-
tion—archival envelopes, file cards, flickering images on computer
screens and brown boxes.

"So I opened them up one by one and took out the papers del-
icately, using only the tips of my fingers. The stuff inside was
bewildering at first. There were muster rolls for every company in
the regiment. They were for two-month periods, so the musters for
those three days at Gettysburg were just lumped in with the rest.
You could see who was present on June thirtieth, the day before the
battle began, but the next roll wasn't till the end of August. But it
was better than nothing. I could see that Morgan and Pike were
both in the company that was commanded by Captain Thomas
Robeson on the day before the battle, but of course they were
missing on the later roll in August, and so was Robeson. Well,
Robeson's name is up there on one of the tablets in Memorial Hall
because he was one of the victims in the assault on Culp's Hill."

"And he's in my scrapbook," said Mary.

"Well, so far there wasn't much we didn't know already. Then
the great guy at the desk told me there were some extra papers, not

just the official forms." Homer put his hands together in prayer and rolled his eyes to the ceiling. "God bless the archivists."

"And the librarians," said Mary, laughing. "Don't forget the librarians."

"Oh, of course. God bless all the librarians."

"Homer, go ahead tell me what was in the extra papers?"

"They were in another lovely brown box, box number 1727, and they were a gold mine."

Mary gave a delighted laugh. "We keep finding gold mines."

"That's the great thing about libraries and collections of archives," said Homer joyfully. "Buried deep down in their secret vaults are all these precious deposits of ancient papers, glittering there in the dark, just waiting to be dug up by you and me. And that's what these papers were, 'The Miscellaneous Unbound Regimental Papers of the Second Massachusetts Volunteer Infantry.' They were a mother lode."

MISCELLANEOUS

Anyone who has cleaned out a family attic knows the difficulty of deciding what is worth keeping and what can be discarded. Imagine the task of sifting through the accumulated records of a nation's official life. . . .

—Pamphlet, National Archives of the United States

Miscellaneous papers," chortled Mary. "Oh, of course. Miscellaneous things are such a nuisance. They don't fit any tidy little category."

"Exactly. Whenever you don't know what to do with something, you file it under Miscellaneous and let it rot there for the rest of your life."

"I've got a drawer like that in the kitchen, a whole drawerful of miscellaneous gadgets that don't belong anywhere else—you know, Homer, corn holders, corks, rubber bands, chopsticks, cup hooks, nuts and bolts, wing nuts—"

"Wing nuts? Why on earth have you got a bunch of wing nuts in the kitchen?"

"I haven't the faintest idea. Take my wing nuts, Homer, take them, take them."

There was a blank pause, and then both of them pounced on the notes Homer had copied so laboriously from "The Miscellaneous

Unbound Regimental Papers of the Massachusetts Second Volunteer Infantry," in room 203 of the National Archives in Washington, D.C.

"My friend the archivist explained it," said Homer. "Since this report came from somebody in another regiment after the army had marched away somewhere else, it was slow in reaching the right adjutant. And then it wasn't on one of the report forms the adjutant was accustomed to, so he probably just stamped it and added it to the regimental records, and maybe he didn't even read it, and then when all the Union army records were gathered together after the war, it was the sort of thing nobody else knew what to do with either, so they invented this category of 'Miscellaneous Unbound Regimental Papers' for irrelevant reports, just like your cup hooks and wing nuts."

"Oh, Homer, what was it that was so interesting?"

"It was a letter from an officer in another regiment. He's in your scrapbook too." Homer grinned at his wife. "Lieutenant Noah Gobright."

"Noah Gobright!" Mary jumped up, ran for her scrapbook, plopped it on the coffee table and opened it to the entry for Gobright. "Look, Homer, here he is. And you're right, he wasn't in the Second Massachusetts at Gettysburg, he was in an artillery regiment. And, oh, Homer, all the men in my scrapbook were in Hasty Pudding, and so was he. He must have known Seth Morgan and Otis Pike."

"He sure did. Listen to his letter." Homer cleared his throat. "It's addressed to 'Captain John Beardsley, Tenth Maine, Commander, Provost Guard, Twelfth Army Corps,' and the first part's dated July tenth, 1863."

"A week after the battle ended? Bring it in the kitchen," said Mary. "Read it to me while I do something about supper."

GOBRIGHT'S REPORT

Homer's vanishing brain cells had reversed course. They were charging back, and throngs of eager neurons were rushing here and there to link them all together. And of course the sound of his own voice was always a comfort. While Mary hovered over the stove he began to read aloud Lieutenant Gobright's report.

TO MAJ. CHARLES F. MORSE, COMMANDER OF REGIMENT, SECOND MASSACHUSETTS VOLUNTEER INFANTRY. 17 JULY, 1863

About seven o'clock on the rainy morning of 4 July, I made my way to a church on the Baltimore Pike, the hospital for the First Corps, to visit a gunner from another battery, wounded the day before by a twelve-pound rebel ball.

Finding him recovering, I left the church and returned

along the road, covering my head and shoulders with my blanket. On the way I encountered bands of drunken men, splashing around in the puddled road. Although suspecting them of being skulkers, I felt it was not up to me to return them to duty.

But when I saw an old acquaintaince sheltering from the rain in the doorway of a log barn, I stopped at once and hailed him, because his coat was drenched with blood. I thought he must be badly wounded. Otis Pike was an old acquaintance, a private in the Second Massachusetts, a regiment in which I had many other friends from college days. For a moment Private Pike failed to hear me, so I came closer and uncovered my head. Recognizing me, he staggered back and nearly fell, but when I offered to help him to White Church hospital, he muttered that he was tolerable and needed no assistance. At once he pushed past me into the downpour and headed south.

However when I saw that he had left several articles behind, I picked them up and ran after him, calling his name. Only then did I notice the shoulder boards of an officer on his bloodstained coat. I assumed that Pike had risen in rank and was no longer a private.

To my surprise, he did not turn around. It occurred to me that his hearing might have been affected by the roar of the guns the day before. After handling a twelve-pounder Napoleon with Capt. Bigelow's battery in the peach orchard on 2 July and taking part in the artillery duel on 3 July, I was a little deaf myself.

However when he began to run, I remembered an unfortunate rumor about my old classmate Otis Pike. Some of my friends in his regiment had told me privately that he was perpetually on the brink of desertion.

Once again I told myself that his case was the business of the Twelfth Corps, not of the Artillery Reserve. Putting his papers in my pocket, I forgot about him. The previous three days had called for violent exertion on the part of the Artillery Reserve, as they did of every regiment in every corps. After the artillery duel our brigade had been placed with those of

General Gibbon's Second Corps directly in the path of the charge by the rebel infantry, where we sustained many losses.

Here I am tempted to quote a passage from Macaulay's *Lays of Ancient Rome* about Lars Porsena at the bridge—:

> And how can man die better
> Than facing fearful odds?

But since this is a military report, I will forbear.

There was a pause while Homer took this in.

Mary looked up from her pot of soup and said, "I think it's a joke."

"Oh, right." Homer went on reading.

When it became apparent that the enemy had left the field, I was ordered by Brig. Gen. Henry Hunt to see to the repair of all artillery pieces damaged in the three-day battle. Thus I remained behind while the rest of the Artillery Reserve followed in pursuit of the rebel army.

In fulfilling my duties I was assisted by members of other batteries. On 15 July, I was in the company of a gunner from the Artillery Brigade of the Twelfth Corps. To my dismay, he told me of the deaths of Lt. Col. Charles Mudge and Capt. Tom Robeson, two of my friends in the Second Massachusetts.

He also passed along the sad news that my old friend 1st. Lt. Seth Morgan had apparently deserted. And then to my astonishment, he informed me that Prvt. Otis Pike had been killed in the very forefront of the battle on the morning of 3 July. His face, said the gunner, was too battered for recognition, but his identification tag was certainly Otis Pike's.

Since I had seen Private Pike alive on the morning of 4 July, far from the place where the others had been killed the day before, I knew that the body on the field could not have been his, no matter how it was identified. I decided to inform you at once of the discrepancy and ask the following important question:

Could it be possible that Private Pike, who, I am told, had deserted three times before, was again abandoning the field, and in so doing, had stumbled upon the body of Lieutenant Morgan? Might he then have stolen his coat and identification and joined the other skulkers on the road to Baltimore?

I must add another piece of evidence. Among the articles left behind in the log barn by Private Pike on 4 July was an envelope addressed to 1st Lt. Seth Morgan, enclosing a letter from his wife.

In this report my intention is not to condemn Private Pike, but to restore the good name of a gallant soldier, my old friend 1st Lt. Seth Morgan.

I have the honor to remain,
Your Obt. Servt.,
N. GOBRIGHT,
First Lieutenant, Artillery Reserve,
Ninth Battery, Massachusetts Light, First Volunteer Brigade
(McGilvery)

"Well, good for Lieutenant Gobright," said Mary, measuring a spoonful of cumin and stirring it into the soup.

"Wait a minute," said Homer. "There's more."

It would perhaps, sir, be of interest to record here my meeting with First Lieutenant Morgan's wife. I came upon Mrs. Ida Morgan one evening a few days later, lying asleep on the battlefield.

"What?" Mary dropped her spoon in the soup.

Homer grinned. "I thought that would electrify you."

"Well, we know from one of her letters that she was in Gettysburg, but, my God, Homer,"—with difficulty, Mary fished up the spoon—"she must have been pretty damned pregnant. She was sleeping on the ground?"

"I suppose she was looking for Seth all over the place. But she was okay. Listen."

Of course I felt constrained to help a woman in her somewhat delicate condition. When I learned that she was Seth Morgan's wife, and that she had spent the day walking all over the battlefield looking for her husband, I commandeered an empty ambulance at the hospital for the wounded of the Twelfth Corps and drove her back into town.

On the way, she told me that she had read in the Philadelphia newspaper after the battle that her husband was listed as missing. Thinking that he might have been wounded, the poor woman had come to Gettysburg to look for him. She had been directed to the barn that was the hospital for the Twelfth Corps, but failing to find him, had fallen into an exhausted sleep on the ground.

I am now deeply sorry that in an attempt to comfort her I said that Seth might still be alive, that he had perhaps simply deserted, and that she might find him in Baltimore. I have no doubt that she set off for that city the next morning.

Not until later did I learn about the strange confusion of identities on the battlefield and begin to suspect that her husband was not a deserter, but a battle casualty, his identity purloined by a member of his own company.

Thus I am doubly anxious to clear her husband's name. I hope, sir, that this report will be acted upon at once.

1st Lt. N. Gobright

"But it wasn't, I'll bet," said Mary, dishing up the soup.

"It couldn't have been, or that famous shame would never have come down in your family."

"Too bad. Poor Ida. You mean it just sat there, all these years, unread?"

"Filed away forever," said Homer sadly, "under Miscellaneous."

OUTPOSTS OF THE CRANIUM

Next morning the summer storm was over, the air was fresh, the sky was clear. In his nightshirt Homer blundered through the house to the front porch to look out at the great curve of the river.

Thank God, it was still there, flowing north from Lee's Bridge and spreading wide as it turned the corner. Somewhere out there a couple of great blue herons would be lurking along the reedy shore. When a small flock of Canada geese came flapping over the hill, Homer watched them cup their wings and splash down, squawking noisily. Near the island a solitary enthusiast was out early, paddling upstream. Homer envied him his tranquil sojourn on the water. For Mary and Homer the river was a more or less sacred stream, a reminder of their courtship—the word *sacred* depending on one's view of the grasping clutch of holy wedlock.

But at the moment the island and the river and all its denizens were irrelevant. What was needed now was a clarion call to the remotest outposts of the cranium. Sighing, Homer turned away from the river and went indoors.

He found Mary in the front room, wide-awake and fully dressed. She was looking around with a critical eye. "We've got to clear everything out of here, Homer," she said, heaving up a large potted plant and dumping it in his arms.

"Whatever for?" whined Homer, lugging it out to the porch.

"Because we've got to think."

They set to work at once, lowering all their electronic equipment to the floor, half a dozen blocky chunks entangled in wires and cables. "Good Lord, Homer," said Mary, "your keyboard's choked with crumbs."

"Dearie me, so it is." Homer turned the keyboard upside down and batted it. "I'll do something about the jelly later." He set the keyboard down and turned his attention to a heap of file folders. "Hey, what's this?"

Under the folders lay a dried-up piece of buttered toast. "Uh-oh," said Mary, "my fault."

The clearing out took half an hour. It wasn't simply a matter of sweeping all the papers together. They had to be organized and shuffled into orderly bundles. The library books were a fearful threat because so many of them were nearly overdue. Mary stuck due dates on them and piled them on the piano, after removing the bust of Dante Alighieri to the front porch.

When the physical task was done, they still couldn't face the intellectual labor. And anyway, it was high time they had breakfast.

But eventually there was no excuse. After drinking second cups of coffee to stimulate the mental fibers, they made a start by setting down on the bare table all their ill-assorted pieces of evidence. It took the rest of the morning to make sense of them and work out a convincing argument in favor of changing one of the names on the tablets in Memorial Hall.

At two-thirty in the afternoon Homer had a new thought. After a good deal of telephonic confusion, he managed to get through to a reference librarian in the public library of Oshawa, Ontario.

At four-thirty, the librarian called back. "I found it," she said. "It's on the way."

Hastily they reattached their equipment, and soon the image

from the *Durham County Courier* of February 1, 1866, appeared on the screen. It was the picture Lily LeBeau had held back when she wrote to Ida about the death of the man she assumed to be Ida's husband.

The image was only an engraving, but the artist had made an exact copy of a photograph they had seen before. It was the man in the top hat.

"It's him," cried Homer. "It's Otis Pike."

"But the name underneath isn't Otis Pike, it's Seth Morgan."

"So it is, by God." Homer was exultant. "But it isn't Seth, we know it isn't Seth, it's Otis Pike. He didn't die at Gettysburg. He died three years later, under the ice on Lake Ontario."

"Well, hurray," said Mary, "I guess." She was exhausted. "Who do we talk to? Who's the big boss in charge of Memorial Hall?"

"A certain very important person," said Homer. "I know who he is. I'll make an appointment."

THE GREAT ROLL CALL
IN THE SKY

Instead of telephoning for an appointment, Homer walked into University Hall and conned the secretary of the very important person into admitting him into the presence of the great being.

But after hearing Homer's reason for wanting an appointment, the important person drummed his fingers on his desk and frowned. "The removal of a name from one of those tablets would be a very serious matter indeed." *Rub-a-dub-dub.*

He was very old. His voice was sepulchral, rising from some hollow crypt deep within his chest. Homer watched his tapping fingers and wondered if the old man might perhaps be the last surviving drummer boy from the Battle of Gettysburg.

"Of course it's a serious matter," said Homer. "But the omission of a name that should be there is also a serious matter."

"Mmm," said the superannuated drummer boy doubtfully, beating a tattoo on his knees.

.   .   .

Afterward Homer explained it to Mary. "Suppose the old gentleman enlisted as a ten-year-old drummer boy in the Army of the
Potomac in the year 1863. He would now be exactly one hundred
and fifty years old. Admittedly that's pretty ancient, but aren't there
a few very aged men and women in Nepal whose cardiovascular
systems are still in great shape because they climb mountains every
day? Might not the old man be a dedicated mountain climber?"

"Oh, Homer, what piffle."

"Anyway, our appointment is for ten o'clock tomorrow morning. We've got to box up all this stuff."

"All of it? You mean everything? But Homer, all we have to
prove is that Seth died at Gettysburg and Otis Pike was alive afterward."

So in the end all their proofs fitted into a briefcase.

Next day the old drummer boy was not in a receptive mood.
Grumpily he said, "The President and Fellows are meeting in half
an hour." But then he bent his shaggy head dutifully over the table
to examine their evidence—the note warning Otis, "Don't do it
again," the memorial biography of Private Otis Pike with its
apologia for his habit of leaving the ranks, the "Miscellaneous
Unbound Regimental Papers" of Lieutenant Gobright and the
photograph of Seth Morgan unearthed by the proprietor of Vanderhoof's Hardware Store.

Nervously, the mouldering drummer boy tapped the table and
said, "Humph." He seemed to be only half listening to their
descriptions and explanations and arguments.

Then Homer produced the new trump card. "And here, sir," he
said smoothly, laying it on the table and setting the others down
beside it, "are three images of Otis Pike."

"The soldier who died at Gettysburg?" The antediluvian per-
cussionist glared at Homer with a fierce and doubting eye. "The
one whose name you wish me to erase from the roll of honor in
Memorial Hall?"

"Exactly." Homer could not resist going too far. "Well, of
course, as you will see, sir, Otis Pike was present a few years later at
the great roll call in the sky, but no, he did not die in the Battle of
Gettysburg."

Mary jumped in quickly. "This photocopy," she said, handing it to the old gentleman, "is a photograph of Otis Pike in the album for the graduating class of 1860."

"Found in the Harvard Archives," added Homer, feeling sure that this highly respectable source would impress the old fossil.

"And this"—Mary picked up the photograph of the man in the top hat—"is obviously the same man a few years later. In other words, it's another picture of Otis Pike."

The doddering drummer boy's gnarled old hands rattled a double tattoo on the table, and he said, "So what?"

Patiently Mary explained the third image, the 1866 newspaper engraving they had summoned electronically from the library in Oshawa, Ontario.

"Well, all right," said the old man testily, "it's the same man, I can see that."

"But you see, sir," said Homer, "his name is different. Here he's called Seth Morgan."

"Why, mercy me, so he is."

Once again they repeated the information from Gobright's report. They recited Seth Morgan's splendid regimental history of service at Antietam and Chancellorsville, and Homer explained his theory about the behavior of Private Otis Pike on the third day of the Battle of Gettysburg.

But it was the three images of Otis that captured the attention of the old drummer boy. He kept looking at them, turning his shaggy head to peer at one after another.

In the end he agreed that the really serious matter was not the removal of a name from one of the tablets in Memorial Hall but the denial to another of its rightful place. The mistake, he said, must be rectified at once. Sitting down with a thump, the old man drummed a call-to-arms on the table and croaked that he would see what he could do.

"Of course he didn't promise anything," said Mary, as they walked away across the Yard. "He still has to consult the other members of the Corporation."

"And he's so old," worried Homer. "I hope he talks to them soon, before it's his turn to answer the great roll call in the sky."

FRESH AND BLEEDING

Almost everything falls away. Slyly, the entire past falls away. Vanishing is what it does best, leaving little trace—a picture, a letter, a garbled rumor. Children get the story wrong and pass it along. And of course some things are mistaken from the beginning.

Ida Morgan never knew that the beloved husband she had ... on the battlefield of Gettysburg and in the cities of ... Washington was not a deserter.

... ting Homer Kelly never understood that Seth was a honor than a casualty of the battle.

"I may uncovered his innocence. They had per- ... in charge of the historic tablets in ... should replace that of the actual ... mer boy had convinced his dis- ... here was to be a ceremony in

... hing off to teach a class. But

Homer was early. When he pulled open the south door of the corridor, the caterers were just setting up a table. The clattering of dishes and the tinkling of glassware echoed from the marble floor and the wooden vaults. Homer stood in the middle of the lofty hall, gazing up, staring at everything, seeing the building in a new way.

For more than a century it had been just another useful part of the university. But at the time of its construction, the galling sores left by the human losses in all those innumerable battles were still fresh and bleeding, the pious words on the walls still passionate with meaning, and the names on the tablets inseparable from the faces of remembered men.

For Homer, as he rambled around the great spaces of Memorial Hall, the building began to turn into the Civil War. Men were stepping down from the tablets to fight again the battles in which they had been killed. As his imagination took fire, he could almost see Colonel Mudge burst through the south door crying, "It's an order," then fall in a hail of bullets from the phone booth at the other end of the hall. High above the door in the west wall, the small gallery had become a boulder on Little Round Top, and there stood Strong Vincent, colonel of a Pennsylvania regiment, pointing and shouting and toppling over the railing, struck down by a sharp-shooter on the staircase across the corridor.

Boom, boom, where was the gunfire? Homer found his way into the dining hall and looked up at the balcony. Drawn up among the chairs, the twelve-pounder Napoleons were roaring in concert, firing down at the students munching their sloppy joes at the tables on the floor below. He watched in horror as one of the guns misfired and killed poor Henry Ropes of the Twentieth Massachusetts.

And tremendous things were going on downstairs. Lined up in military order against the wall, the white busts of generals taking command, opening their marble mouths to shout, and Homer was astonished to see Major General Fra class of 1855, leap down from his memorial window stained glass.

But, oh God, what to do with the bodies? they were mounded all over the floor arou a problem, they were in the way, becaus first-year men and women, a thousand of them, all hungrily eating lunch and pretending not to notice. Well, it was too bad—Homer shook his head in sorrow—but there was nothing he could do but heave the putrid corpses up on the tables among the chicken fingers and the cans of diet Coke, while the poor kids recoiled in disgust and scraped back their chairs and scuttled away.

Puffed up with importance, Homer strolled back into the corridor, the general of all he surveyed, and headed for Sanders Theatre. Surely Sanders might serve some useful purpose. Standing in the glowing ambience of the wooden chamber, he looked up at the stage and saw at once that it was the perfect place for a field hospital. The surgeons could amputate up there in perfect comfort, piling up the sawed-off arms and legs around the marble gown of President Josiah Quincy.

But people were gathering in the corridor. Homer swept away his imaginary Civil War, with all its detritus of swords and rifles and battle flags and careening Parrott guns and caissons, and joined the celebration. But he couldn't help wishing for a mock skirmish or two, right here in Memorial Hall. One or two reenacted battles might wake up the kids as they sat at the tables among the marble busts and painted soldiers. It might persuade them to stand up and take a look at Charles Russell Lowell, who fell at Cedar Creek, and James Savage, killed at Cedar Mountain, and Wilder Dwight, mortally wounded at Antietam, and Robert Gould Shaw, who died at Fort Wagner among the black enlisted men of his Fifty-fourth Massachusetts Volunteers.

But above all, Homer wanted everyone who entered the building to read the tablets in the corridor and grasp the terrible meaning of their inscriptions—*Shiloh, Chancellorsville, Gettysburg, Wilderness, Spotsylvania, Cold Harbor.*

Surely that would be a good thing?

THE FLOWER OF
THE NATION

They should have been listening as the venerable drummer boy stood beside the gleaming new tablet, explaining the substitution of the name of Seth Morgan for that of Otis Pike, but the old man was maundering on at great length.

Only a few people had been invited to gather around him in the memorial corridor. Hamilton Dow, the president of the university, was there as an old friend of Homer and Mary Kelly. Gwen and Tom had been invited of course, along with their children—John and his wife Virginia, Annie and Joe, Fred and Linda, Amanda and her new boyfriend. Even Benny had condescended to witness the restoration to honorable memory of his great-great-great-grandfather. Benny's hair was emerald green.

Cousin Ebenezer had not been informed.

Mary shifted her weight from leg to leg. She was tired of standing, and she was also suffering from a depression of spirits. The return of Seth Morgan's name to the roll of honor did not make her as glad as she might have expected. In spite of everything, she was saddened by the fact that his classmate, poor old Otis Pike, had been dumped in history's rubbish heap. He had died gallantly after all, out there in Oshawa, Ontario.

"The tablets that rise around us on these walls," droned the old man, "represent the flower of the nation. Just as the playing fields of Eton sent their best and finest to die in the trenches of the First World War, so the cream of an entire generation, students at this university, enlisted eagerly in the Union army. Here are recorded the names of those who died, one hundred and thirty-five young men of shining promise who lost their lives in heroic battle, their destinies as future leaders of the nation tragically unfulfilled."

Homer almost piped up to point out that the life of an Illinois farm boy had also been full of promise, but he refrained.

Afterward there was a polite gathering around the refreshment table. The relatives clustered and gossiped, the superannuated drummer boy beat "Parade Rest" on the pockets of his pants and excused himself to take a nap and Homer wandered off with Ham Dow, walking south along the corridor.

"How many names did he say there were?" said Ham.

"A hundred and thirty-five, I think," said Homer.

The tablets beside the south door recorded the names of Law School graduates who had died in the Civil War. Ham looked up at them dreamily and said, "Suppose a hundred men out of that total of one hundred and thirty-five might have married and had offspring if they hadn't died. How many children would have been born in the next generation?"

Homer caught Ham's drift. "Well, if you make a conservative estimate, say two kids apiece, it would be two hundred. Two hundred unborn and nonexistent citizens, children who failed to be born around the year 1870."

"Good," said Ham. They turned and strolled past the tablets on the other side. "Then suppose," Ham went on, "that four hundred more children were born to those two hundred—or rather, not born."

"Right," said Homer. "Roughly speaking, they would have failed to appear around 1895."

"And the third generation? Children who would never have seen the light around the year 1920?"

"Eight hundred more?" Homer was enjoying the game. "And sixteen hundred in 1945?"

"That means thirty-two hundred in 1970."

"And sixty-four hundred in 1995."

"So if we stop there, how many have we got?"

They paused beside the north door, mumbling and counting on their fingers, then said it together, "Twelve thousand six hundred."

With the same impulse, they turned to gaze back along the corridor at the dim white panels recording the names of men who had attended the college in the middle of the nineteenth century, who had paid a bond of four hundred dollars to the President and Fellows to have the privilege of shivering in cold rooms or buying coal from the registrar, who had attended morning prayers and lectures by the likes of Lowell and Longfellow, Sparks and Channing, who had clowned in Hasty Pudding and delivered earnest orations at commencement. Or perhaps for some of them, it had not been like that at all. Perhaps they had merely endured four friendless college years before going off to die on a hundred distant battlegrounds.

Homer was more fantastical by nature than Hamilton Dow. He grinned at Ham. "Why don't we invite all those unborn guys and gals to a celebration?" Flinging himself at the doors opening on Kirkland Street, he shouted into the empty air, "Come on in, y'all! The party's on us."

As usual, he was making himself conspicuous. The clusters of friends and relatives stopped talking and stared. Ham laughed and said he had a meeting. The others shook hands, hugged each other and said good-bye.

But later on, as Mary took the wheel and drove home along Route 2, Homer closed his eyes and expanded the vision in his head.

There they would be outside, nearly thirteen thousand unborn descendants, waiting in a great throng, and they would pour into the building and crowd into the dining hall and sit down at the tables, and there would be wine and song and a six-course banquet, followed by toasts and speeches of thanksgiving. And then all the proud achievers among them—including one or two saviors of the human race—would be asked to stand up, and there would be thunderous applause.

But that was impossible, of course, because if their ancestors had not died in the Civil War, the building itself would not be there at all. That colossal building, that massive displacer of air and sky, would never have occupied the triangle of land bounded by Kirkland Street, Cambridge and Quincy.

And therefore the banquet for all the unborn descendants would have to take place somewhere else. They would have to hire a hall.

THE HORRID BANG

So it was all over, except for one small detail.

Mary came upon it while clearing up everything, inserting new folders in her file cabinet, packing a box with the child's nightdress, the Shaker bonnet, the bloodstained coat and the two little cases of photographs.

Only the handkerchiefs remained to be put away. And it was while she was tucking them back in their silken envelope that the delicate fabric of the lining gave way, releasing a wrinkled sheet of lavender paper. It was another letter from Lily LeBeau.

Mary unfolded it, expecting another piece of foolish silliness.

Lily's letter was silly all right, and foolish in the extreme, but it delivered a blow.

21 April '65

Darling Ida,

    *Tho not in touch these 2 yrs this is to inform you unfettred
by any restraynt that we are safe and sownd. Such ecsitment!
We were backstage at the time but when we heard the HOR-
RID BANG we were AGAST as you can immagin but we
wayted not a moment. We galoped awy on our trustie steed well
acshully a hack with an old nag!*
    *S. wore a grey wig and my black mantua and bonnet you
remember the one with yellow posys and fethers and by good
luck his whiskers was all shaved off beforehand so as to look like
ancient Grease so we were 2 RISPETABLE LADEYS!
Because he was always talking about the old days in that club
when they dressed up like girls! How I laffed! We were so quik
we got across the Chayn bridge altho I heard they baricaded it
soon therafter to prevent excape of You Know Who, but one of
the gards was a gentelman friend of mine so I really had to laff!!
We gave the hack man $50 !!!*
    *The theatre here is more of a tavern not ezactly what we are
accostomed to. For yr sake I hope the baby was a boy, tho prefer-
ing girls myself.*

Yr loving Lily

    Mary pushed open the door to the porch and shouted at Homer.
He was banging out a dent in the aluminum canoe, making such a
din that he didn't hear. But when she screamed at the top of her
lungs, he put down his hammer and followed her indoors.
    "Look at this, Homer," she said, thrusting the letter at him. "It's
a bombshell."
    "Another letter?" Homer's attention had drifted far away from
the problems of his wife's remote ancestor. He glanced at Lily's letter. "What on earth is she talking about?"
    "Oh, Homer, don't you know? Can't you see?" Mary ran to her
file cabinet, wrenched open a drawer, and jerked out the folder for
Ida Morgan. "Look at the playbills," she said, rattling them under
his nose.

"Well, of course I remember the playbills. They're all cut up with scissors."

"Exactly. Ida did it. She cut out a name from all of them. The same name, one of the actors."

"One of the actors?" Homer gaped at her stupidly. "You mean Seth Morgan? Otis Pike?"

"No, no, of course not. Homer, just look at her letter. There was *a horrid bang*, and then Lily and Otis escaped from the theater and ran away. It was April 1865, and only a week later they were safely across the border in Canada."

Homer understood at last. He said, "My God."

"So that's what the family was so ashamed of. Oh, poor Ida, if only she could have known that it wasn't Seth who was mixed up with all those people, it was Otis Pike. No wonder they kept it hushed up, all my ancestors, generation after generation."

"Of course," agreed Homer. "What could have been worse? The truth at last."

Coffin that passes through lanes and streets,
Through day and night with the great cloud darkening the land,
With the pomp of the inloop'd flags with the cities draped in black,
With the show of the States themselves as of crape-veil'd women standing,
With processions long and winding and the flambeaus of the night,
With the countless torches lit, with the silent sea of faces and the unbared
*   heads,*
With the waiting depot, the arriving coffin, and the somber faces,
With dirges through the night, with the thousand voices rising strong and
*   solemn,*
With all the mournful voices of the dirges pour'd around the coffin,
The dim-lit churches and the shuddering organs.
                                        —Walt Whitman

VARIOUS PATRIOTIC
REMARKS

I tremble for my country when I reflect that God is just.
— **THOMAS JEFFERSON,**
Notes on the State of Virginia, 1781

"The good Lord have pity on us!" said
Aunt Chloe. "O! it don't seem as it was
true! What has he done, that Mas'r
should sell him!" . . .

He leaned over the back of the chair,
and covered his face with his large
hands. Sobs, heavy, hoarse, and loud,
shook the chair, and great tears fell
through the fingers on the floor: just
such tears, sir, as you dropped into the
coffin where lay your first-born son; such
tears, woman, as you shed when you
heard the cries of your dying babe. For, sir,
he was a man, and you are but another man.
And, woman, though dressed in silk and jewels,
you are but a woman, and, in life's great straits and
mighty griefs, ye feel but one sorrow!

— **HARRIET BEECHER STOWE,**
Uncle Tom's Cabin, 1852

I hear another ask, Yankee-like, "What will he gain by it?" . . . *Well, no, I don't suppose he could get four-and-sixpence a day for being hung, take the year round; but then he stands a chance to save a considerable part of his soul* . . . *No doubt you can get more in your market for a quart of milk than for a quart of blood, but that is not the market that heroes carry their blood to.*

—HENRY THOREAU,
"A Plea for Captain John Brown," 1859

Those of us whose fortunate lot it was to enlist in the army, during that magic epoch of adventure which has just passed by, will never again find in life a day of such strange excitement as that when they first put on uniform and went into camp . . . the transformation seemed as perfect as if, by some suddenly revealed process, one had learned to swim in air, and were striking out for some new planet. . . . Now . . . already its memories grow dim . . . The aureole is vanished from their lives.

—THOMAS WENTWORTH HIGGINSON
Captain, 51st Mass. V. M., 25 September, 1862: Colonel, 1st S. C. Vols. (33rd U. S. Colored Troops), 10 Nov., 1862; discharged, for disability, 27 Oct., 1864.

. . . if you have been in the picket-line at night in a black and unknown wood, have heard the splat of bullets upon the trees, and . . . felt your foot slip upon a dead man's body, if you have had a blind fierce gallop against the enemy, with your blood up and a pace that left no time for fear . . . you know that man has in him that unspeakable somewhat which makes him . . . able to lift himself by the might of his own soul . . .

As for us, our days of combat are over. Our swords are rust . . . I do not repine. We have shared the incommunicable experience of war; we have felt . . . the passion of life at its top.

—OLIVER WENDELL HOLMES, JR.
Private, 4th Battery Mass. V. M., April, 1861: First Lieutenant, 20th Mass. Vols., 10 July, 1861: Captain, 23 March, 1862: Lt. Colonel 5 July, 1863 . . . mustered out, 17 July, 1864.

The men were brought down from the field and laid on the ground beside the train and so back up the hill 'till they covered acres. . . . By midnight there must have been three thousand helpless men lying in that hay. . . . All night we made compresses and slings—and bound up and wet wounds, when we could get water, fed what we could, travelled miles in that dark over these poor helpless wretches, in terror lest some one's candle fall into the hay and consume them all.

—CLARA BARTON
Second Bull Run,
4 September, 1862

We heard all through the war that the army "was eager to be led against the enemy." It must have been so, for truthful correspondents said so, and editors confirmed it. But when you came to hunt for this particular itch, it was always the next regiment that had it. The truth is, when bullets are whacking against tree-trunks and solid shot are cracking skulls like egg-shells, the consuming passion in the breast of the average man is to get out of the way.

—DAVID THOMPSON
9th New York Volunteers, at Antietam

I asked if any one would like to have his wounds dressed? Some one replied, "There is a man on the floor who cannot help himself, you had better see to him." Stooping over him, I asked for his wound, and he pointed to his leg. Such a horrible sight I had never seen and hope never to see again. His leg was all covered with worms. . . . I am being more used to sights of misery. We do not know until tried what we are capable of.

—SARAH BROADHEAD
Gettysburg, 7 July, 1863

. . . There in the room as I wake
from sleep this vision presses
upon me;
. . . All the scenes at the batteries
rise in detail before me again,
The crashing and smoking, the pride
of the men in their pieces,
The chief-gunner ranges and sights
his piece and selects a fuse of the
right time,
After firing I see him lean aside and
look eagerly off to note the
effect . . .
And ever the sound of the cannon far

or near, (rousing even in dreams a devilish exultation and all the old mad
joy in the depths of my soul.)

— **WALT WHITMAN**

I told him of the woman in the cracker bonnet at the depot at Charlotte who
signaled to her husband as they dragged him off, "Take it easy, Jake—you
desert agin, quick as you kin—come back to your wife and children." And she
continued to yell, "Desert, Jake! desert again, Jake!"

— **MARY CHESNUT,**
South Carolina diarist

Regiment marched at ten about two miles toward new Baltimore where Jewett, 5th Maine, was shot for desertion. . . . The division formed three sides of a square. . . . The prisoner was finally brought out sitting on his coffin in an open army wagon drawn by four horses. . . . He was then taken out and shot in the open side of the square. . . . The body was lying on its face, the balls had come through the back of his head. . . . I came back with a terrible headache.

—**EDMUND HALSEY**
Lieutenant, 15th New Jersey, Sixth Corps, Army of the Potomac

If at any one time of my life, more than another, I was made to drink the bitterest dregs of slavery, that time was during the first six months of my stay with Mr. Covey. . . . It was never too hot or too cold; it could never rain, blow, snow, or hail too hard for us to work in the field. Work, work, work, was scarcely more than the order of the day than of the night. The longest days were too short for him, and the shortest nights were too long for him. I was somewhat unmanageable when I first went there: but a few months of this discipline tamed me. Mr. Covey succeeded in breaking me. I was broken in body, soul and spirit . . . the dark night of slavery closed in upon me; and behold a man transformed into a brute!

—**FREDERICK DOUGLASS**

Stupidity, that's all it was, four years of stupidity.
   —Mrs. Augusta Morgan

The battle of Franklin, Tennessee, November 30, 1864—
Hood's whole army was routed and in full retreat. Nearly every man in the entire army had thrown away his guns and accoutrements. More than ten thousand had stopped and allowed themselves to be captured, while many, dreading the horrors of a Northern prison, kept on, and I saw many . . . even thousands, broken down from sheer exhaustion, with despair and pity written on their features. . . . Broken down and jaded horses and mules refused to pull. . . . Wagon wheels, interlocking each other, soon clogged the road. . . . My boot was full of blood, and my clothing saturated with it. I was at General Hood's headquarters. He was as much agitated and affected, pulling his hair with his one hand (he had but one) and crying like his heart would break. . . .
   —Sam Watkins, "Company Aytch," First Tennessee

Fondly do we hope—fervently do we pray—that this mighty scourge of war may speedily pass away. Yet if God wills that it continue until all the wealth piled by the bondman's two hundred and fifty years of unrequited toil shall be sunk, and until every drop of blood drawn with the lash shall be paid by another drawn with the sword, as was said three thousand years ago, so still it must be said, "The judgments of the Lord are true and righteous altogether."

—ABRAHAM LINCOLN
Second Inaugural, March 4, 1865

AFTERWORD

An afterword is a clumsy appendage to a work of fiction, but once again truth must be sorted out from invention.

Which soldiers are which? Seven are real. Guided by archivist Brian Sullivan, I found their faces in the picture collection of the Harvard University Archives—Charles Redington Mudge, Thomas Rodman Robeson, Henry Ropes, Henry Weld Farrar, Henry Lawrence Eustis, Thomas Wentworth Higginson and Oliver Wendell Holmes, Jr. The regimental histories of all seven are listed in Francis Brown's *Roll of Harvard Students Who Served in the Army or Navy of the United States During the War of the Rebellion*. Memoirs of the three who died at Gettysburg appear in the two volumes of *Harvard Memorial Biographies*.

The fictional characters—soldiers, family members, a surgeon, a nurse, an unhappy farmer and a landlady—turned up among the *cartes de visite* bought from collector Henry Deeks in his antiquarian bookshop in Maynard, Massachusetts. Roaming among hundreds of faces, I bought a small population of unidentified men, women and children.

The photographs of Ida Morgan, Augusta Morgan and top-hatted Otis Pike were found in histories of nineteenth-century fashion. Eben Flint's hospital picture is one of many photographic studies of wounded soldiers in *The Civil War, an Illustrated History,* by Geoffrey C. Ward, with Ric Burns and Ken Burns. The likeness of chubby charmer Lily LeBeau is really a photograph of dancer Laura Le Claire found in *Mr. Lincoln's Cameraman,* a collection of Mathew Brady photographs edited by Roy Meredith.

The three stereographs are from several sources. The one of dead men on the field at Gettysburg is attributed to Alexander Gardner. A copy of the Patent Office stereograph comes from the Patent Office Historical Collection of Judy, Diane and Jim Davis. (It has been slightly doctored.) A famous photograph of a doctor performing an amputation was shamelessly scissored to look like a stereograph.

The "Reference Service Slip" is a real one from the National Archives and Records Administration in Washington, supplied by archivist Michael Musick.

Annette Fern of the Harvard Theatre Collection unearthed several prompt books for *The Marble Heart,* as well as the Hasty Pudding playbill, to which a few fictional names have been added. In Mary Kelly's scrapbook all but two of the listed names are of real men, with the actual parts they played in Hasty Pudding and their later regimental histories.

The melancholy photograph of the armless soldier was found in Bell I. Wiley's *Common Soldier of the Civil War,* identified only as a private in the 147th New York. He might have been at Gettysburg, since his regiment was there. But there was another private who did indeed lose both arms in that battle. In the fighting for Culp's Hill by the Twelfth Corps on the morning of July 3, 1863, a shell from a Union battery *exploded prematurely above the 20th Connecticut, its shards mangling both arms of Private George W. Warner. Carried to the rear, Warner did not learn until he was treated at a hospital that he had lost both limbs—not just the right arm, as he had thought when wounded.* (Jeffry D. Wert, *Gettysburg, Day Three.*)

Although Mr. Tossit is fictional, his grievance is like that of farmer William Bliss, whose barn was destroyed on the Gettysburg battlefield, and whose request for financial restitution was at last denied.

Although several episodes involving actual soldiers Mudge, Robeson, Fox, Ropes, Farrar and Eustis are fictional, the words of Colonel Mudge, "It's murder, but it's an order," have gone down in the history books.

There are undoubtedly many unconscious historical mistakes in this narrative, but I confess to one of which I am fully aware. By the time I learned that the hospital in the Patent Office had been closed before the battle of Gettysburg, I was too infatuated to give it up.

The tablets in Harvard's Memorial Hall are of course real, although I have added two fictional names to one of them. I can't help lamenting the fact that after so many years there are still no memorials to the many Harvard men who died for the Confederacy.

Ida's experiences in the town of Gettysburg borrow graphic detail from a remarkable history of the three-day battle as it appeared to the citizens of the town—*Firestorm at Gettysburg, Civilian Voices,* by Jim Slade and John Alexander, and from *A Vast Sea of Misery,* an exhaustive study by Gregory A. Coco of the nearly 160 hospitals that were hastily set up in tents, houses and public buildings to care for the 21,000 men from both armies who were wounded in the battle of Gettysburg.

Another source book provided three of the case studies composed by my fictional Patent Office surgeon. Actually they are authentic studies reported in 1870 by Surgeon General Joseph K. Barnes. They appear in *One Vast Hospital: The Civil War Hospital Sites in Frederick, Maryland, after Antietam,* by Terry Reimer. (The complete list of wounded patients fills nearly two hundred pages of small print, fifty names to a page.)

Many knowledgeable people informed and corrected this rash venture into history. Professor David Donald recommended the most essential reading. Christopher Morss and Paul Travers loaned dozens of books. Isabelle Plaster loaned old family volumes, Malcolm Ferguson found a rare memoir and reference librarian Jeanne Bracken was tireless in finding faraway titles.

In Gettysburg Jared Peatman twice conducted my son Andy and

me around the several battlefields and on both occasions Professor Jean Potuchek offered the key to her house. By E-mail from Washington Michael Musick explained in detail how Homer Kelly would make his way into the military records of the National Archives, and Patent Office historian Kenneth Dobyns (whose name should appear in letters of gold) began by answering a few questions and went on to provide massive amounts of information, answering endless questions. *Could the guns of Gettysburg be heard in Philadelphia? Where was the B&O station in Washington?* His knowledgeable friend Louis Allahut kindly read the manuscript. A great many more questions were answered by Laurence Golding, a veteran reenactor who gallops across one field of battle after another.

Here at home Tom Blanding supplied helpful history about Concord during the Civil War, Diane and Herbert Haessler explained nineteenth-century medical practices and astronomer Alan Hirshfeld reported on the state of weather and moonlight in Gettysburg during the first week of July in 1863. Norman Levey kept the electronic connections working, Betty Levin and Ellen Raja knew about farming and Katherine Hall Page loaned an album of haunting nineteenth-century faces.

Much of this story is concerned with real and fictional Harvard soldiers. But I agree wholeheartedly with Homer Kelly's disgruntled opinion that the unfulfilled life of an Illinois farmboy was as promising as those of the men whose names are inscribed on the tablets in Harvard's Memorial Hall.